BARBARIAN'S PRIZE

Berkley Titles by Ruby Dixon

Ice Planet Barbarians

ICE PLANET BARBARIANS

BARBARIAN ALIEN

BARBARIAN LOVER

BARBARIAN MINE

BARBARIAN'S PRIZE

BARBARIAN'S PRIZE

PRIZE

RUBY DIXON

BERKLEY ROMANCE
New York

BERKLEY ROMANCE
Published by Berkley
An imprint of Penguin Random House LLC
penguinrandomhouse.com

Library of Congress Cataloging-in-Publication Data

Names: Dixon, Ruby, 1976– author.
Title: Barbarian's prize / Ruby Dixon.
Description: First Berkley Romance Edition. |
New York: Berkley Romance, 2023. | Series: Ice Planet Barbarians
Identifiers: LCCN 2022047566 | ISBN 9780593639450 (trade paperback)
Classification: LCC PS3604.I965 B377 2023 | DDC 813/.6—dc23
LC record available at https://lccn.loc.gov/2022047566

Barbarian's Prize was originally self-published in 2016.

First Berkley Romance Edition: February 2023

Printed in the United States of America
4th Printing

Book design by Kristin del Rosario

BARBARIAN'S
PRIZE

What Has Gone Before

Aliens are real, and they're aware of Earth. Fifteen human women have been abducted by aliens referred to as "Little Green Men." Some are kept in stasis tubes, and some are kept in a pen inside a spaceship, all waiting for sale on an extra-terrestrial black market. While the captive humans staged a breakout, the aliens had ship trouble and dumped their living cargo on the nearest inhabitable planet. It is a wintry, desolate place, dubbed Not-Hoth by the survivors.

On Not-Hoth, the human women discover that they are not the only species to be abandoned. The sa-khui, a tribe of massive, horned blue aliens, live in the icy caves. They hunt and forage and live as barbarians, descendants of a long-ago people who have learned to adapt to the harsh world. The most crucial of adaptations? That of the *khui*, a symbiotic life-form that lives inside the host and ensures its well-being. Every creature of Not-Hoth has a khui, and those without will die within a week, sickened by the air itself. Rescued by the sa-khui, the human women take on a khui symbiont, forever leaving behind any hopes of returning to Earth.

The khui has an unusual side effect on its host: if a compatible pairing is found, the khui will begin to vibrate a song in each host's chest. This is called resonance and is greatly prized by the sa-khui. Only with resonance are the sa-khui able to propagate their species. The sa-khui, whose numbers are dwindling due to a lack of females in their tribe, are overjoyed when several males begin to resonate to human females, thus ensuring the bonding of both peoples and the life of the newly integrated tribe. A male sa-khui is fiercely devoted to his mate, and most humans are now claimed by the males, and pregnant.

The humans have been on the ice planet for over a year and a half, and most have adapted to tribal life. Almost all have taken mates; new babies are being born of human and sa-khui pairings, and the tribe stirs with life once more. Only two human women remain single.

This is where our story picks up.

CHAPTER ONE
Tiffany

It's cramped and dark. Arms and legs are piled onto me and there's an overwhelming stink of unwashed flesh in my nose. Sleep's hard to get, but I try, because sleep's the only escape I have.

Not today, though. A light shines on the cage and goes right to my eyes. I instinctively whimper at the flash of pain that shoots through my head.

One of the orange aliens with the rough skin points at me. He says something in his garbled language and I hear Kira suck in a breath. Oh no.

Not me. It was just a whimper. A small sound of distress. Nothing more.

Bodies peel back from me as the guard enters the cage. He grabs a handful of my hair—wild and sticking out in every direction since I haven't brushed it in over a week—and hauls me forward. Pain shoots through my head again, and even though I want to be silent, a small cry breaks from my lips.

"Don't scream," someone whispers.

It's too late for warnings, though. They're just looking for someone to pick on, and they picked me. The guards haul me forward and out of the storage bay where the captives are kept. I'm dragged down a hallway and then shoved through a door. I land on my hands and knees, and when I look up, there's another guard standing there. He smiles and shows needle-sharp teeth. His smile chills me, and when he grabs a handful of my hair and yanks me to my feet, I go.

Not me. Not me. Not me. The litany repeats in my mind as he touches his collar to loosen his clothing.

"Tiffany," he says, and points at the nearby cot, indicating I should lie down.

Not me. Not me. Please, not me.

"Hey, Tiffany?"

Josie's voice jerks me from my sleep. I sit up, my heart pounding. There's a cold sweat on my skin and my hair is sticking to my face. I push it back and try to act normal. "Mm?"

"You were having a dream," she says softly. "Didn't sound like a good one."

Just a dream. I'm no longer on the alien ship. I'm safe here on the ice planet. There's a cave full of big warriors who won't let anyone grab me and haul me down a hallway to rape me. They'd die before they let anyone try it. The little green men and their bodyguards are dead. I'm safe.

But . . . I don't feel safe. Haven't felt safe since the night I woke up and found out I was abducted by aliens.

I rub my eyes and lie back in my furs. "Thanks, Jo."

"Sure." She yawns loudly and I hear her roll over.

I stare up at the ceiling of my cave and the nubs of stalactites that decorate it. I can't sleep now. If I do, the aliens will be back in my dreams. I need to think about something else for a while. Maybe tanning. Or my plants. Work's good. Work keeps me too tired most nights to dream, so I throw myself into whatever task I'm working on 150 percent. I've been growing a row of the not-potatoes and they seem to be doing okay. I want to try and grow some hraku, too, but I need the seeds and everyone eats those as fast as the plant is harvested. Maybe I can hide some.

"Tiff?"

Josie's not asleep. This must mean it's time to talk. Normally I barely tolerate Josie's late-night musings, but tonight I welcome them. It means I don't have to be alone with my own head anymore. "What's up?"

"You think we're ever going to resonate?" Her voice is small.

It's a question Josie's asked before, and I'm not surprised. As the last two human women to not resonate to a barbarian, we feel a little left out of things. Or at least, Josie does. Me, I'm glad. I don't want to resonate. Resonance means babies and a mate. I don't mind the babies, but the thought of a mate utterly terrifies me.

"What do you think?" I ask her, pitching my voice low. Sound carries in the caves and I don't want anyone hearing our words.

"I think it can happen." Her voice is soft and sweet. She sighs and then I see her turn over in the darkness, putting her hand to her face and cupping it as she looks over at me. "Claire didn't resonate to Ereven until the holiday. And it took Megan a while to resonate to Cashol, remember? Not everyone resonates right away, so I think there's a chance for us."

And that's the difference between Josie and me. Josie's motivated by hope. She hopes someone's going to light up her khui one day and then she'll have a happy ever after. Me, I'm motivated by fear. I live in terror that it's going to happen to me and I'll be dragged to someone's bed once again, kicking and screaming.

Resonance is my biggest fear.

It's the way the sa-khui barbarians have children. Everyone on the planet has a khui—the symbiont that rewrites our systems to ensure we can survive on the harsh planet surface. I've noticed a few changes in my body—I'm stronger and less tired, the weather doesn't affect me as much, and I can't smell a lot of things anymore. My eyes glow blue like Josie's do, a sign that the khui is healthy inside.

The problem with the khui (or cootie, as we humans like to call it) is that it likes to match people up. It decides who's a perfect "baby match" for who, and makes them resonate. Resonance means the khui in your chest starts purring and it makes you crazy horny for your newfound mate until he impregnates you. According to everyone, there's no getting around it. You can't just will resonance to go away. It happens, and boom, end of story.

"Well, we know why you haven't resonated," I tell her. "Did your IUD fall out?"

"Not yet."

Not yet. It might never fall out, because there's no doctor to remove it. But Josie, again, is a creature of hope. I shake my head. "I just don't get why you find it romantic," I tell her, adjusting my blankets. "I don't want to resonate. I want choices."

She sighs again. "I guess because . . . it means family. You know? I never had a family of my own growing up. I went through eight foster homes by the time I was eighteen. No one ever wanted me . . . except for the wrong reasons." Her voice grows a little hard.

I wince, imagining those "wrong" reasons. Josie's got a round face and not much of a chest, but there's a sweet innocence to her that I can imagine attracts the wrong kind of attention. Poor Josie. "Well, you're a woman on a planet full of men. I'm sure someone will want you now."

"Nope, they all want you," she says with amusement. "And that's all right, because when the cootie picks, it won't matter. It'll take one look at someone in the tribe and bam. Instalove. And then we can be happy together and I'll have the family I always wanted."

"And you won't care that he never noticed you before then?" I ask, amused. Josie's painting such a rosy picture.

"Won't matter," she says with a yawn. "Past is past. Future's all that matters."

Another difference between Josie and me. I can't get over my past. I can't move on past the ship and the awful captivity. I can't move past rough hands touching me and forcing me down. I know Josie's optimism is hard-won. She's hinted at her awful, awful childhood and she was also raped on the ship. Josie cried for one night and then tucked the bad memories away. She didn't lose her sunshine.

I really wish I could be more like her. I want to move on, but I can't.

"Well, I'd trade places with you in a heartbeat," I tell her. "I wouldn't mind having an IUD." It'd mean no resonance, because even a cootie can't get past birth control.

"There has to be a reason why you haven't resonated!"

"Nope." I smooth my blankets. "No reason other than my

body doesn't feel like having babies. Or maybe one of these guys isn't my perfect match. Don't know, don't care."

"You really don't care for one of the guys more than any of the others?"

"Nope."

"What about Hassen? He seems nice."

"Eh." They're all nice. They go out of their way to be nice.

"Taushen?"

"He's very . . . attentive." Too much so. Like in a smothering way.

She giggles. "Vaza?"

I snort. "Vaza would hit on anything with tits."

"Maybe that's why he hasn't hit on me," she muses.

We both break into giggles. Josie's biggest lament is that she doesn't have boobs. I don't think she needs them, because she's the sweetest, most giving person I've ever met, and the most cheerful. But I'm not a guy. I can't deny that the guys have been flocking to me a lot more than poor Josie.

Ironic, because I don't want any of the attention.

"What about Bek?" she asks with a yawn. "Didn't he try to give you the necklace he made for Claire?"

"Yeah." I don't like to think about Bek adding himself to my list of suitors. Guy clearly has no idea how to treat a lady. Bek's also a lot more hot-tempered than the others, and that worries me. We've been dropped on a planet full of big, brawny, seven-foot-tall men who are sex deprived. I'm always nice to the guys that leave me presents and I never try to show anyone preferential treatment. I keep them all at arm's length and never encourage anyone.

But I worry there will be a day when one of them snaps. When someone stops asking and starts taking.

"Imagine what would happen if you resonated to Bek!" she says in a scandalous whisper.

"I'd leave," I say flatly.

She gasps and sits up in her furs. "You'd what?"

"Shhh," I tell her, because Josie gets loud when she gets startled. "Seriously, Jo, be quiet!"

She lies back down and all is silent for a moment. I hear the endless drip from the interior of the cavern and the sound of someone shuffling around in the main cave, beyond the privacy screen that covers the entrance to our shared nook.

"You would really leave?" Josie asks again after a moment. "Seriously, Tiff?"

"Seriously." I hug my leather-stuffed pillow close to my body, imagining it. It's a scenario I've planned out in my mind for a while. I have to have a backup plan. I have to be able to take care of myself. Georgie and the others have commented on how I'm such a hard worker and I'm picking up on all the skills we've been taught so quickly. I can make a fire faster than anyone else. I can skin a carcass in no time flat. I can dig a pit trap. I can tan my own hides. I'm doing everything I can, because I don't want to be dependent on staying here.

Living on my own would be hard. Living with someone I don't like and letting them touch me? Ten times harder.

"I can't believe you'd just leave," Josie whispers, and she sounds heartbroken.

I feel guilty. She's taking it badly. I shouldn't have said anything. It's been a secret I've been harboring ever since we landed, and even being here almost a year and a half hasn't made me change my mind. I've accepted that we'll never go home, that I'm going to live on a planet full of ice for the rest of my life, and I'll never wear a bikini or shop at a mall or even have real shampoo ever again. I've made my peace with life here.

But I won't become someone's property to use and abuse ever again.

The sa-khui are wonderful to their mates, of course. Liz and Raahosh fight, but I think it's because they enjoy picking at each other. Aehako dotes on Kira, Vektal worships the ground Georgie walks on, and even Ariana's mate adores her. No one has an abusive mate.

But no one had a choice, either. And the others weren't raped by the aliens. Just me and Josie. Krissy was, but she died in the crash. Dominique was and it broke her mind. She ran out into the snow and froze to death because she was so terrified of it happening again. The others couldn't understand it.

I could.

I'm no good to anyone as a mate. I lock up in terror at the thought of someone touching me. I tried to be like Josie when we first got here. One night Rokan was flirting with me, inviting me to his furs. He's good-looking and easy on the eyes, and I was feeling vulnerable, so I went with him. The moment he touched me? I freaked out. I told everyone it was because of his spur and that I didn't know how to handle it. That I'd thought the spur was a joke. But we never even made it that far. The moment he caressed my shoulder, I lost my shit and ran away screaming.

Poor Rokan. He's never looked at me twice since. I can't blame the guy. I'm a head case.

I hear Josie sniff.

"Are you crying?" I demand.

"I just . . . I don't know what I'll do if you leave," she says sadly. "I can stand being alone because you're here with me and we're in this together. But if you leave, what do I do? I don't want to be the only one left behind."

I know what she means. To Josie, being the only one utterly rejected by her khui's attempts at matchmaking would be devastating. She so desperately wants love and family. Poor Josie. My heart squeezes in sympathy. "It won't matter," I tell her lightly. "You'll be too busy popping out babies for Tall, Dark, and Horny."

She giggles and then there's no more sniffling.

I feel better that she's no longer sad, and relax in my furs. We talk a little longer—though not about resonance—and eventually Josie drifts back off to sleep. I lie awake for a bit longer, because I know the moment I close my eyes, the dreams are going to return. They always do, and I'm not ready to face them. I'm never ready to face any of it.

I'll have to at some point, but for now, I'm putting things off as long as possible.

When the guard takes me back to the holding cell, the others are watching me with wide, solemn eyes. I can feel my lip puffing up from where he hit me, and I feel raw all over. I'm especially raw between my legs but I feel the most raw in my head, like something is broken and can't be fixed no matter how I arrange my clothing so it looks like nothing happened.

They put me back in the holding cell and I squeeze in between Krissy and Megan. Kira's watching me with knowing eyes, and Liz has an arm around Josie, whose shoulders shake with silent sobs.

"Did they hurt you?" Liz whispers when the guards walk away. "You've been gone a while."

"Is she okay?" I ask instead, looking at Josie.

Liz shakes her head, her mouth tightening into a grim line, and I know the worst has happened. Josie was raped, probably in front of the others.

"You?" Megan asks, touching my hand.

"I'm fine. No one touched me." The lie feels awful on my lips. "They just examined me on one of the tables and put me under."

Kira looks relieved. She reaches over and squeezes my shoulder. We all fall silent again, the only sound Josie's muffled sniffs as she tries desperately to keep quiet. Liz rubs her arm and comforts her.

No one touches me, and that's how I like it.

CHAPTER TWO
Salukh

I rub a twig on my teeth as I lean against the cave wall and watch the dark-skinned human woman emerge from her cave. Watching Tee-fah-nee has become one of my favorite pastimes since we moved to the South Cave, and I know I'm not the only one. I'm just the only one that is subtle about it. Nearby, Taushen jumps to his feet at the sight of her. She smiles at him but it doesn't reach her eyes. I want to tell him that's not the way to get her attention, but I don't want to help him out.

Tee-fah-nee is mine. She just doesn't know it yet.

My khui is silent in my breast, but it doesn't matter. It will come around. I rub the stick and continue to watch as Taushen—ever so eager—tries to take the basket from her hands. She shakes her head and says something polite to him, and he wilts. When he returns to the central firepit, he looks as if he's been chastised.

Tee-fah-nee hurries outside. I'll follow her, but in a moment. She needs time to think she is alone. She's skittish, my woman, but that's all right. I am a patient male. Tracking my woman is like tracking any prey—it requires patience and persistence in the hunter. It means watching the movements of the hunted, learning their patterns. In the case of the human, it means befriending her and giving her space when others will not. It means keeping my distance.

For now. When my khui resonates to her, I will no longer have to keep myself at arm's length.

I let a few minutes pass, scraping idly at my teeth and watching my tribe move about the South Cave. Aehako's mate, Kira, is standing nearby with her kit cradled in her arms. The loud one known as Jo-see holds her arms out for the child and her yearning is written all over her round human face. That one does not hide her emotions like Tee-fah-nee. She wears them plainly for all to see. My mother and one of the elders are smoking meat and making travel rations, and nearby several hunters are sharpening their blades, preparing to go out hunting. With the twelve new mouths to feed—plus the young the caves now seem to be full of—there is more of a need than ever to hunt.

But I have no one to hunt for. Not yet. I am a solo hunter with no cave to feed. My furs are yet in the cave with the other unattached hunters. I will hunt soon . . . but first I will visit my female and make her feel needed. I push myself off the cave wall and saunter over to Kemli's side and snatch a square of travel rations. "Ho, mother. I see you are making me food."

She slaps at my hand like I'm a naughty child. "Put that back. You should go hunt."

"Ah, but I am on the hunt." I grin at her and take another bite out of the food. "Just not for meat."

She rolls her eyes and waves me away. My mother would like to see me mated, I think. Other than my young sister,

Farli, I am the last to leave the cave. Both of my brothers, Pashov and Dagesh, mated humans and now have young kits at their hearth. "You cannot have more of the rations, my son. We need them for the upcoming trip."

I swallow my bite and look to the cave entrance where Tee-fah-nee disappeared a short time ago. If I wait too long, someone's going to come by and bother her. I need to go soon, but my mother's words have me curious. "What trip?"

"The human called Har-loh opened three new family caves with her stonecutter, Aehako says. That means there is room for three families to go back to the main tribal caves. Farli, your father, and I are going back. I want to be near my other sons and their mates while their kits are young." She tilts her head, gazing up at me. "You are welcome to come back with us."

"Not yet." I'll go where Tee-fah-nee goes. If she is not moving back yet, then I will stay.

"Because of the human females?" My mother arches one gray eyebrow. She knows me far too well.

I just grin at her. She knows I stalk Tee-fah-nee, though I have yet to resonate to her. I have staked her out as the one that will be mine. The only thing that remains is to convince my khui that she is mine.

It will happen. I am confident it shall be so.

I lean in and grab one more bite of food and race away before my mother can pull on my ear like I'm a naughty kit. She will protest much, but when I leave I hear her chuckle of amusement. I head out of the main cave and step into the snows, my boots sinking into the fresh powder deposited overnight. It is a light snow for the bitter season, but I know the humans despair of the endless cold. To hear them talk, snow is something that only comes for a few short moons. I snort at the thought. Madness.

Tee-fah-nee's tracks are deep in the snow, as the small human feet sink deep and most avoid snowshoes unless necessary. She has not gone far, and I follow her trail around to the far side of the cliff walls, where she has been moving plants and lining them up in a row. She says she is *fahr-meeng* and it will be useful later. I do not know if it is true, but the humans have odd notions, such as eating roots. She is a hard worker, and clever, so there must be a benefit to her strange ways.

I see her kneeling in the snow a short distance away, digging with a stick. From here, I can see the beautiful color of her skin, like the richest of animal hides. Her mane is unusual in that it sprays out in tight spirals like the sweet-weed bushes that grow in rocky niches and make a pleasant tea. I like it, though. She is different but pleasing to look upon, and I like the flash of her blue eyes in her small human face.

I call out as I approach. "Ho, Tee-fah-nee. It is I, Salukh." I raise a hand in the air in greeting as she looks up and shields her eyes. I am always careful to call out a greeting. Once I surprised her and her violent reaction was alarming. I do not wish to scare her again.

She waves a hand at me.

I head toward her, and as I do, I mentally encourage my khui. *There is our mate*, I tell it. *See how lovely she is? How fragile? I need to resonate for her. I need to claim her, to protect her.*

Tee-fah-nee is mine.

Resonate.

Resonate.

Resonate so I may claim her.

But my khui is silent, the traitor, as I walk up to her. Today is not the day, then. No matter. It will be tomorrow or the next. "Enjoying the snow?"

She makes a face at me and shakes her digging stick. "A *fuht* of it fell overnight and covered my plants. I don't know how anyone gets anything done around here!"

"Mmm." I crouch in the snow next to her, studying her setup. She has a leather satchel full of what looks like dung and seeds at her side, and digs her stick into the snow. "What is it you do?"

"I'm trying to plant *crawps*," she says in the strange human language. I learned the human language at the elders' cave, so I can speak to her. The mental picture that springs to mind at the word is of plants grown in specific places for food.

Interesting. I have never paid attention to plants other than to occasionally gather them for one of my mother's teas. I pick up one of the seeds and study it as she goes back to work. "What is it you do when you plant?"

She sits back and brushes her springy hair off her face. The small move is graceful and makes my cock ache with the need to claim her. *Resonate*, I demand of my silent khui. "Well," she says. "Back on *Urth*, we had *fahrms*. They grew food for people who didn't have the space to grow their own. We can make our own plants and store their harvest for the brutal season. I just need to figure out how to make stuff grow in all this snow. I mean, stuff grows in Norway and Siberia and stuff, right? And they grow here. So clearly plants can survive in harsh conditions. But I keep planting seeds and they're not growing. So I don't know what I'm doing wrong." Her mouth presses into a firm line.

I pick up one of the dvisti-dung cakes in her bag and examine it. We use them for fuel because wood is scarce farther down the mountains. "So you wish to throw dung at them like a metlak?"

She chuckles, the sound sweet and throaty, and it ripples over my skin like a caress. "No. I'm trying to nourish the soil."

"With dung?"

"With dung," she agrees. She pulls out her digging stick again and begins to dig a hole. "Animal dung has a lot of *noo-tree-ents* for the soil. At least it did back home. You plant this with the seed and it gives it a boost." She drops the dung cake into the hole, adds a few seeds, and then covers it with the mixture of snow and dirt.

"I see." It's a strange idea, but the humans have many strange ideas. "Do you wish help? I am a strong male and can dig the holes for you."

"So modest," she murmurs, her mouth crooking in a half smile as she looks over at me.

I am not modest in the slightest. I am strong and capable. My body is young and healthy. She should look at me with admiration. I pull my leather tunic off and rub a hand over my chest to see if she notices my fine form.

But she does not. She digs.

Humans are frustrating. I will get her attention yet. She can see what a capable, fit hunter I am and then her khui will decide I am the one for her. I toss my tunic aside and kneel down in the snow, ignoring how it soaks my leather leggings. "How many holes do you wish for this strong male to dig for you, Tee-fah-nee?"

She chuckles again. "Let's start with twenty, about an arm's length apart."

I start to dig for my female. I don't mind the task. It's an odd one, but I'm pleased to do it for her. Creating each hole means I must dig down below the layers of snow to the soil underneath and a little farther. I'm faster than she was with her digging stick. We pass the time in silence. When I pause to wipe my brows of sweat, I notice she's watching me. I make sure to flex my arms as I dig the next one. I am like a scythe-beak preening for its mate, but I do not care. I want her to notice me.

When the holes are dug, I grab a handful of snow and rub it over my face and chest, washing away the sweat. She averts her gaze and concentrates on her seeds. "Thank you, Salukh. This went a lot faster with your help."

Her words are pleased but she looks dejected. Is she sad—as I am—that our khuis are silent? "You do not seem happy."

She looks up, startled. "What do you mean?"

"I mean your words are nice, but your body says something else. You smile here." I lean in and dare greatly as I brush a fingertip to a corner of her full mouth. "But you do not smile here." I tap at her temple, indicating her eyes.

Her smile returns, but it seems more forced. "Busted."

"Are we not friends? Tell me what troubles you." I want to take care of it for her. I want to bring the light back to her shining eyes and the smile—a real smile—to her face.

She bites down on her lip and plays with the leather ties to her satchel, then glances up at me. "I'm just upset about the thought of the caves merging back together. I'll lose my crops."

"Lies," I say immediately. She is an expert at fooling others, but not me. "You have no crops. You have dung and seeds. Something else troubles you."

Tee-fah-nee makes a face at me and throws the bag in my direction. "You're pushy, you know that, Salukh?"

She does not even begin to imagine how much I want to push her. Or that I want to push her into the snow and cover her body with mine. But we are not mated. We do not resonate. Again, I must learn to be patient.

It is difficult to be patient when the woman I want is so close I can touch her soft skin. When her scent fills my nostrils and makes my body crave her touch. I have not felt so out of control since I was a young kit with my first cock-stand. "I am pushy, as you say, but I do so because I am your friend. Your worries trouble me."

She relaxes a little and gives a small nod, as if deciding something. "It's just . . . okay." She blows out a breath. "You . . . have you noticed how things are in the cave?"

"Do you mean, have I noticed that the other males try to get your attention?" Oh, I have noticed. It makes my belly clench with frustration, but I remind myself it does not matter. She will resonate to me and their vying for her favor will be forgotten. "It is hard to miss."

Tee-fah-nee seems embarrassed. "Yeah, I guess it is. Anyhow, that's what's got me all flustered. It bothers me."

"Bothers you? Are you not flattered? You are the most desirable female amongst both caves. It is natural for males to wish to seek your attention and try to influence your khui."

They are welcome to try, but they will have no luck. You are mine.

Instead of seeming pleased at such flattery, her eyes well up and she gets a stricken look on her face. She sniffs and then wipes at her cheeks . . . and grimaces when she brushes away ice.

My heart clenches in my chest. My entire body tenses with fear. This is truly bothering her. There is something that goes deeper than courting games, and she weeps over it? I immediately wish to fix it. I want nothing but her smiles and her happiness. My entire body fills with fury that something has upset her.

"What is it?" My voice is a near growl. I clench one hand around my lashing tail to still it. I don't want her to know how upset her tears make me.

"It's just . . ." She pauses and rubs at her cheeks, brushing away remnants of the tears. "When I was taken captive by the others . . . things happened." Her voice turns to a whisper.

Things? What things? "I do not follow."

She swallows hard and gives me an uneasy look. "I don't want to say it."

"If you do not voice it, how can I help?" If she does not voice it, I will go mad with frustration. I'm selfish, prodding her, but I must know. What things? What *things*? The words race through my mind.

"On the alien ship." She says the words very slowly, as if trying to dredge up her courage. "There was no courting. If males wanted a female's attention, they . . . took without asking." She looks away. "I'm afraid it will happen again."

My head nearly bursts with this knowledge. Fury and outrage wash over me. Males touched her? Males touched my mate? My female? They touched her without her consent? Even Bek, who is the most hardheaded and stubborn of males, never touched Claire without her permission. It is not done.

It is not *right*.

I stare. For the first time in my life, I have no answers. I have no solutions. I have no words. I am filled with helpless rage and anger.

Someone touched my female and made her cry. Someone *took* from her.

The urge to destroy with my bare hands has never been so strong. Bile creeps in my throat and I'm filled with the need to hurt those that touched her. To make them suffer. "No one here would do such a thing," I rasp out. My hand is clenching my tail so hard I am surprised the bones do not snap. I do not care. I am a hair's breadth away from losing control.

"I know," she says softly. "But I cannot get over the fear that it will." She gazes down at her hands in her lap.

I lean down and clasp her hands in mine—and I hate that she flinches. Now I understand, but it does not make it easier. I know why she fears when she is surprised. I know why she holds all at arm's length. "You must conquer your fear, Tee-fah-nee. You cannot live afraid." I hold her soft, cold hands. "Shall I chase the others off?"

"What? No. It's me, it's not them. They're just trying to be nice." She gives me a pained look. "I don't want to be rude or hurt them. I know they want a mate badly. It's just . . . I don't think it's going to be me."

Because you are mine, I want to say, but I cannot. Not now. Not after what she has confessed. She would fear me like the others if I told her of my true feelings. And she cannot be mine until we resonate. That is how things are done. "You will resonate someday," I tell her. "It will fix things."

Instead of seeming relieved, she looks terrified at the thought. "And if I do?"

"Then your mate will claim you."

Her face pales. "I don't want that." She pulls her hands from mine. "That scares me, too."

Helpless, I sit back on my haunches and study her. I understand her fear, but it is not good. Resonance will happen whether she wishes it or not, and the thought of Tee-fah-nee panicking as I try to touch her—because she *will* resonate to me—is a bad one. "You must be strong and push your fear aside."

She nods slowly, a thoughtful look on her face. Her eyes fix on me, and she licks her lips. "You don't scare me, Salukh. It's because we're friends. You don't come after me and shove yourself in my way all the time."

"I do not," I agree, though I feel uneasy at the direction this is heading. Just because I have been subtle does not mean I want her to mistake my intentions. I want Tee-fah-nee as my mate. I want to resonate to her more than anything.

"Will you . . . practice with me?" Her eyes are wide. "So I'm no longer afraid?"

I fall backward onto my rump in the snow, utterly staggered.

What she is offering me . . . there are no words to describe how conflicted I am. It is what I want more than anything else—to touch her. To caress her and claim her as mine. But she is terrified of a man's touch. What if she hates mine? The thought guts me.

Then another, darker thought creeps in. She has not resonated to me. What if I take her to my furs and teach her pleasure and then she goes to another? What if she resonates to Hassen, or Bek, or any one of the hunters paying attention to her?

I would have the greatest gift in my arms . . . and then cruelly yanked away forever.

It would destroy me to have her and then lose her.

Yet how can I refuse her? She stares at me with sad, worried eyes. She does not want my touch, but she does not see any other options.

I have never taken another to my furs. What if . . . what if I do something wrong? What if I do not please her and make it worse? Resonance ensures that both male and female enjoy joining, but there is no resonance between us. I have no skill in the furs.

I cannot think. There is too much to ponder. I get to my feet. "I must consider this."

And because I do not trust myself, I turn and walk away.

CHAPTER THREE
Tiffany

Well . . . that went over like a lead balloon.

I watch as Salukh stalks away, heading back to the tribal cave. I'm a little surprised at his reaction, because I thought we were friends. I trust Salukh more than anyone else in the tribe, because he's been so darn nice to me. He's easy to be around, undemanding, and always ready to help with one of my craft projects, no matter how weird. He doesn't pressure like Vaza, or cling like Taushen. He doesn't insist that I choose a mate, like Hassen.

I like Salukh.

Maybe that's why his reaction being something other than "whee, yes, let's go make out" hurts my feelings. Asking him felt safe. Unburdening my worries to him felt . . . good. Now I just feel like a jerk. I made him uncomfortable, and I worry I've lost our friendship. Now how am I going to live in the same cave as the guy and see him every day and know what happened between us?

Way to go, Tiff. You just made a bad situation even worse.

I put my digging tools back in the bag and clean my hands with snow. I kind of thought Salukh might take me up on things. The guy stripped down to dig holes for me and I have to admit, even though I try not to think about the sa-khui in a sexual way, I was certainly noticing the way his shoulders moved and the way the sweat trickled down his slate-blue abdomen. The way his hair moved like a black curtain when he bent over. I noticed the sweep of his large horns and the way his leggings hugged thick, muscular thighs. I sure noticed his eyes and the elegant strength of his heavy brow. He's damn good-looking—all of the sa-khui are—but there's an intensity to Salukh that calls to me. He looks like the type that doesn't do anything halfway.

Oh well. I guess I can't dwell on the fact that he's rejected me. It stings, but maybe it's for the best. Maybe "conquering" my fears isn't the right answer at the moment. I'll let them sit for a while longer and hopefully, with more time, the nightmares will slow and I can entertain the thought of someone touching me without losing my cool.

Time heals all wounds and all that. Come on, time. I'm ready for you.

I clean up around the little area I've designated as my "field" and then head back into the caves. There's so much to be done. I have furs soaking in my tanning cave like Kashrem showed me. There's food to be prepped and clothing to be sewn and I want to try my wool-carding again if there's enough light left at the end of the day. Work is good. Work keeps my brain busy and I don't stop to think about other things.

The moment I get inside, though, my temper starts to fray. There on the doorstep of my cave is a fresh kill. Two hoppers. Someone's gone hunting on my behalf. Probably Hassen. I mentioned once that I liked the way the little hoppers had such tender meat, and now I seem to get them daily. Ugh. And because it's meat, I feel like I can't waste it. I pick up the small, ratlike creatures by their tufted tails and bring them in to prepare. Maybe Josie will want some stew. She's not in the cave, which means she's probably helping Kira and her new baby. I sit down and pull up my favorite skinning rock and start to prepare the critters for eating.

"Ti-fa-ni?" a voice calls from the front of the cave.

I cringe mentally. "Yes?"

"I dug some of the roots that you like." Taushen hovers in the doorway, and I mentally curse myself for not putting up the privacy screen. He holds them out to me like trophies. "Shall I clean and cook them for you?"

I give him a polite smile. He's young and hasn't been around a lot of single girls. I keep reminding myself of that. "Thank you, Taushen, but I'm good on roots."

His expression sinks, and then brightens a moment later. "Shall I help you clean those?"

"I'm good, truly." I gesture out at the central cave with my small bone knife. "Maybe see if Kira wants them? She has a new kit and would probably love for someone to bring her some food." Come to think of it, I'll probably just bring the stew I'm going to make to her cave. I still have leftover food from yesterday's meals.

Taushen looks disappointed. "You do not want them?"

If I take them, he'll be encouraged. Then again, I have Hassen's kills here, so what's a few more roots? "Sure, go ahead and give them to me."

He surges forward and hands me the roots. Instead of leaving after I thank him, he sits down next to me and hovers, watching me skin the tiny hoppers. I grit my teeth.

"Tafnee?" Vaza's voice bellows through the cavern, alerting me and everyone in the area of his intentions. "Come and see the fine dvisti Bek and I have hunted for you."

Dear God. I have got to get away from here.

That night as I lie in my furs, I contemplate my escape route.

I need to get away for a while. The men are utterly smothering me with their attentions. What started out as thoughtful has turned into an endurance test. I can't take it any longer. All day long, the men hovered. All day long, they drove me utterly crazy with their attentions until I was ready to scream. Or cry. One or the other. And no matter how many times I gently suggest that they turn their attentions elsewhere, it's ignored. I don't know if they want me as much as they just don't want one of the other hunters to win me.

I feel like a carnival prize.

The urge to leave is strong, even though I know it's a cowardly thing to do. It's a bad time to leave, too. Kira's got her new baby and needs help, my leathers need to soak for a few more days, and I just planted my crops. But I can't take another day like today. I'll go stark raving mad.

"Josie," I whisper, and turn over in my furs, facing her side of the cave. It feels weirdly lonely with just the two of us in here. Once upon a time, there were a bunch of human girls piled together in the cave and it felt more like a slumber party than anything. Now it's just us two and it feels sad. "Jo. Wake up."

She snorts and rolls over in her bed. "Mmm, what is it?"

"I think . . ." I lick my dry lips. "I think I want to leave."

Josie bolts upright in her bed. "No, Tiff, you *can't*. Don't leave me here by myself!"

"You're not by yourself," I say, sitting up. "There's a whole cave full of people—"

"And one human reject!" In the sparse light given off by the fire's coals, I can see the distressed look on her round face. "What happened that makes you want to leave? Why now?"

"You saw how they were acting today! The whole cave did." I rub my forehead in frustration. "I can't take much more of their attention, Josie. They're driving me crazy."

"So tell them all to go fuck themselves!"

My mouth feels glued shut. That's the easiest answer, and yet . . . I feel like I can't. Because if I do and one gets upset? I worry someone will try to "convince" me with force. Just the other day Vaza joked that he needed to spirit me away until I resonated to him. He thought it was funny.

I thought it was terrifying.

"I can't tell them that, Josie. It'll just be better if I leave. They'll get over me and focus their attention somewhere else."

"And what will you do?" She sounds heartbroken.

"Set up camp in another cave somewhere, I guess. Hunt for myself and make my own clothes and everything. I'll be fine."

"You'll be alone." She sniffles. "And what are you going to do when they come after you? You know they will."

I freeze, because someone coming after me never crossed my mind. The moment she says it, I know she's right. I'm the most eligible female in their eyes. They won't just let me leave. Someone will come after me.

And I'll be all alone. The thought is abhorrent. I imagine Vaza and his laughing comment about getting me alone. I feel trapped all over again. "I don't know what to do, Josie."

"Let me fix it. Don't leave, okay? Give me a chance to fix everything."

"How?" I ask wearily.

"I'll think of something to keep them occupied. Just give me a chance, okay?"

What choices do I have left? I nod and lie back down in my furs, utterly depressed.

When I wake up, the cave is silent. Josie's not in her furs. I dress and peek out the privacy screen. No suitors hovering at the doorstep. No fresh kills waiting for me. No presents left on my doorstep in the hopes of currying favor. This is . . . a welcome change. I feel like I can breathe. I don't know what Josie did, but she's a stinking genius.

I emerge from the cave and there are people out and about, but my suitors are nowhere to be seen. Salukh is nearby, sharpening the point of a spear. He nods in greeting and watches me as I move toward the central fire. Josie's seated there with Kira. I sit down next to Josie and grab her hand, startling her. "What did you do and how can I thank you?"

She laughs. "I don't know if you're going to be too happy once you hear what I told them."

The baby fusses and Josie hands her back to Kira. The new mother tugs a cord at the neck of her tunic and opens it, deftly sliding the baby against her breast. Kira looks so utterly peaceful and content, and it's easy to see the wistfulness on Josie's face.

I nudge Josie with my knee. "What did you tell them?" I ask.

"Well, I tried to think of a way to get them out of your hair without hurting their feelings. And so when I woke up . . . I told them about the Miss America pageant."

Huh?

My confusion must show on my face. Josie grins. "A competition," she says. "They're going to compete against each other to show you who is the strongest and most clever of the lot. Right now, they're competing to see who can down the snow-cat with the nicest pelt since we're low on those."

Snow-cats are soft and good for baby blankets. I look at Kira's little Kae and realize that must be what inspired this particular contest. "And tomorrow?"

"Tomorrow, it will be all about who can refill the dung chip baskets the fastest." She nods solemnly and pulls something out of her pocket. It's a bright red seed, painted and dried out, probably from the holidays. "I kept a bunch of these because they were so pretty, and now each day that someone wins, they're going to receive one. And each task is going to keep them very busy, keep the cave replenished, and keep them out of your hair."

I grip Josie's hand. "I think you're a genius . . . except I want to know what they win at the end of this." Because my terrified mind can't focus on anything else.

"Oh. Didn't I say? You and I are going to the elders' cave in a few weeks for the language dump, and they're fighting for the honor of escorting us. It'll mean lots of alone time together." She grimaces slightly. "It was the only thing I could think to offer them, short of marrying you off to the victor. It had to be a prize worth the struggle."

A few days with one ardent suitor instead of all of them? I'm game for that. I squeeze her hand tightly. "Thank you so much, Josie." I feel like I can breathe. It's wonderful. They're going to be gone all day and I can just relax.

"I'm surprised you got them to agree to this, Josie," Kira murmurs.

She wiggles her eyebrows. "I went to each one and played it up as an Earth custom . . . which it is. Sort of. And I told them each that the others were doing it, and if it was good enough for them . . ." She spreads her hands.

"I didn't hear any of that," Kira murmurs. "Aehako won't like deceiving them. He understands their point of view a little too much, I think."

I'm a little less eager to hear her quiet rebuke. Her mate, Aehako, is the nicest guy, but he's also the interim leader of the South Cave and takes his job very seriously. Plus, I think of the months that he chased after Kira. Yeah, he would not be a fan of a bogus competition.

"Then you most definitely did not hear any of that," Josie says brightly. "Besides, what's it going to hurt? They volunteered of their own free will. It helps the cave out—and don't tell me that they weren't spending too much time lazing about looking for Tiff when they could have been hunting."

Kira just shakes her head.

"And it's not like they won't win a prize. Tiff and I do need to go get the language dump. We'll need an escort. The way I see it, it's a win-win situation." Her gaze flicks back to me and Josie looks for my approval.

She's done all this for me. How can I not be appreciative? I lean in and hug my friend. "You have saved my sanity, Josie."

She pats my back as she hugs me. "You just leave it all up to me. I'm going to keep them so busy you won't see their faces much for the next few weeks. After all, it's part of the competition that they interact with your go-between instead of you." She winks as she pulls back.

Goodness, Josie's thought of everything. She's awesome. This is either the craziest thing I've ever heard of, or the smartest.

CHAPTER FOUR
Salukh

I was not invited to compete for Tee-fah-nee's attentions. I'm annoyed by this, especially when Tee-fah-nee looks so very delighted to hear that the others are out hunting to show their worth. Is this what some human women want? Jealousy curls in my stomach but I remind myself that all of the games do not matter when resonance happens.

And Tee-fah-nee is going to resonate to *me*.

I remind my khui of this fact over and over as the object of my attentions moves about the cavern, a faint smile on her face. She looks so very happy. I am glad that the misery lurking behind her eyes is gone for a few short hours, but I'm less pleased that her suitors are fighting to win her and I'm not included. She's mine, and my jealousy is hard to reason away.

I think of her invitation from yesterday—to mate with her with no khui involved. To "practice." It goes against everything I have ever wanted for myself . . . but what do I want more than Tee-fah-nee in my furs, yielding to me? I contemplate this, and with the gnawing envy in my belly, I watch her possessively as she gets a basket and heads out of the cave.

I follow after her. We shall discuss her suggestion more in private.

She walks a short way, following the cliff walls, and then stops in front of the tanning cave to light a tallow candle resting on a plate of bone. When she ducks into the small tanning cave, I move forward.

"Ho, Tee-fah-nee," I call out a moment before I enter the cave.

She looks surprised to see me. Her eyes are wide in the flickering candlelight, and then she sets the candle down on one of the rocky ledges. "How are you today?" She picks up a big bone—probably from a sa-kohtsk—and begins to stir the vat of stagnant water, urine, and leathers in the center of the cave.

I squat on my heels as I usually do when relaxing, but that puts me that much closer to the cesspool of water in the center of the cave, and I quickly stand again, my eyes burning. She has taken up the same hobby as Kashrem, and the stink of urine and herbs in the water is overpowering. I take a step backward for fresh air, coughing.

"That good?" she teases, and I hear her throaty laugh echo in the small cave. "Don't stick your face so close next time."

"The smell is unbearable."

"It'll make the leather so soft, though," she says, and her voice is cheerful. There's a happy note in it I have not heard in many days.

"There's leather in there?" It looks like a sludge that I saw once when a dead scythe-beak fell into a pool of water and rotted there.

"Dvisti leather," she tells me. "I scraped the fur off and now I'm treating it. If this works, there's gonna be a run on dvisti."

I do not grasp her words. "We eat many dvisti. Why would we run them?"

"It's a saying. And I wish we didn't eat dvisti." The look on her face grows far away. "I had a pony growing up and he was real shaggy. Reminds me of him a little. Makes the meat hard to choke down."

A poh-nee. I mentally store this information away. "I shall do my best to hunt more snow-cats, then."

She smiles. "What brings you over here? Not hunting?"

"I came to talk to you," I tell her, wiping my still-watering eyes. "About your suggestion."

All the smiles in her fade away. "Oh?" She tries to look casual but I can see the worry on her face. "Did you decide?"

"I am still thinking."

"I see."

"I wish to tell you why I need to think about it."

She stirs the watery mess in the cave pit with the bone. "We're friends, Salukh. You don't have to explain yourself to me."

"I want to take you up on your offer," I tell her bluntly. When she looks up in surprise, I go on. "But there are things that make me hesitate."

She pauses and studies me. "That's fair. What kinds of things?"

"I was waiting for resonance. I wanted to share my first time with my mate."

"Oh." Her face softens. "Oh, that's sweet, Salukh. I understand."

She is beautiful in the candlelight, her eyes glowing bright, her hair like a cloud around her face. I do not tell her that it is her I wish to resonate to. Tee-fah-nee is skittish. "Your suggestion has merit, though. I do not wish to go to my mate clueless."

"You don't have to explain yourself, really. It was just a suggestion."

"I am still considering." I study her, imagining her body beneath mine. My hand in her curly hair, my fingers touching that oddly smooth human skin. And then I imagine her cringing away from my touch. The thought is an unpleasant one. "I wish to know more. What is it we would practice?"

"Oh." Her mouth forms a small, plump circle. "I . . . don't suppose I thought it through. Well, we could practice kissing."

The mouth matings that humans are so fond of? My cock grows hard immediately, and it takes everything I have not to spill there on the floor in front of my future mate at the thought of my mouth on hers, my tongue fucking her. "Sa-khui do not kiss."

"But you might want to learn," she points out, and averts her face, stirring her mess once more. "What if you mate a human?"

Does she like the thought? There are only Jo-see and Tee-fah-nee left amongst the humans. Does she speak of herself, then? "Then I would wish to please her."

"There's more than kissing, of course. There's touching. And caressing." She bites her lip and shudders. "I . . . need practice with all of that."

Her face is averted but I can tell from the hunch of her shoulders that she has gone to a bad place. My entire body tenses with the need to comfort her, but I know my touch is not welcome. This here, with her cringing, is my greatest concern—what if Tee-fah-nee loathes my touch because others have taken from her? The idea destroys me.

"I am still deciding," I bark at her and storm out of the cave. I must leave before she becomes more frightened, or my need to hold her and comfort her becomes overwhelming.

I do not know what to do. I need advice. Aehako is off on a hunting trail, and many of the other males have never had a mate. There is Hemalo, but he does not make his mate, Asha, happy. He is not the one to ask for advice.

There is one that springs to mind, though.

When I wake up the next morning, Taushen is bragging to Haeden. "I have won two of the red seeds so far and no one else has won a single one." He shoves them proudly under the surly hunter's face. "I will have my time alone with Ti-fa-ni and then she will resonate to me!"

I roll out of my furs, irritated. I'm still irritated after I relieve my bladder outside and grab a bite of yesterday's smoked meat for a meal. I should go out hunting. Get some game. Clear my head of my worries about Tee-fah-nee and the men who endlessly chase her. It does not matter if they chase her. She will resonate to me. She will be my mate and all of their silly seeds will matter not at all.

I return to the cave to retrieve my spear and see Taushen is grabbing his nets. He grins at me. "I am off to catch the biggest kes-fish in the river! Wish me luck so I might bring home a third seed."

I narrow my eyes. I do not want him to have luck. But he is in high spirits and ignores my silence, heading off to meet the others for their day's competition.

Haeden looks over at me and his lip curls. "You do not join their game to win favor from the females?"

I shake my head. "I am busy."

"Your hands are idle," he says, tightening a spearhead with a bit of leather and then getting to his feet. "There are many to feed and more every day. We have no time for the entire cave to sit about and mope over whether or not the females like them."

Is that what I am doing? I eye Haeden as he straps on his boots. He and I think alike: courting is nothing, because resonance is all that matters. But I have been offered an incredible temptation, and I do not know if I am strong enough to hold out for my khui to catch up to my heart. "What do you hunt today?" I ask him. I will join Haeden and discuss my problem with him. Haeden has felt the pull of resonance. He has had a female in the past. He has much knowledge. "Snow-cat? Quilled beast?"

"Dvisti."

I grimace. "So many dvisti." I think of Tee-fah-nee's words. She likes the animals and would not be pleased to hear of me hunting them.

"Much meat. Little effort." He straightens. "Are you coming?"

I nod and get my own spears. He's right. There are many mouths to feed, and with so many pregnant females, all of the hunters feel the urgency to fill the stores and ready for the next brutal season. This last one wiped out all of the stored food. The weather will turn, and there will be more young than ever. No one must go hungry. Dvisti must be hunted, no matter how beautiful Tee-fah-nee feels about it. She is practical. She will understand.

Haeden and I set out from the caves and cross into the next valley before we catch sight of a trail. Dvisti leave a distinctive hoof print in the snow, and they are easy to follow. Haeden is silent, communicating with a nod and a pointed finger where we should go. I let him lead, my head still full of thoughts of Tee-fah-nee and the men who wish to claim her. If I join their challenges, what then? What if another wins over me through luck? I am more skilled in the hunt than Taushen, but Hassen is a very capable tracker, and strong. Vaza has much knowledge because he is elder. And Bek? Bek is so stubborn he is like a fang-face that will latch onto something with his teeth and never give up.

The thought of competing with my tribe for Tee-fah-nee irritates me. I am full of irritation this day. The hunt will be good.

We find a nearby herd and close in. The wind changes as we circle wide, and the dvisti get nervous at our scent. Haeden gives me a frustrated look, as if this is somehow my fault. When we close in, they scatter and my spear lands wide of its mark. Haeden's brings down a fat dvisti and the rest of the herd flees over the next hill.

"Piss-poor hunting," Haeden comments as we trudge through the snows to retrieve our weapons. "Your aim was worse than a metlak's."

So it was. I'm distracted still, thinking about Tee-fah-nee. I snatch my spear from the ground. "I have a problem, Haeden."

"I agree. Your aim needs work." He jerks his spear out of the dvisti and then bends over to slice the throat open and drain the blood.

I laugh. "If only that were the problem that troubles me."

"It should trouble you," he says sourly.

"I am worried about my mate."

"Eh?" He looks up from his cutting and squints at me. "Did you resonate?"

"Not yet. But I shall."

He snorts and turns back to the kill. "Foolishness."

I clench a fist and hold it over my heart. "I know Tee-fah-nee is mine. I feel it in my spirit. It is just a matter of waiting for my khui to respond."

"So you say." Haeden's voice is thick with disbelief as he slits the belly of the creature open and begins to remove the offal. Once he has finished dressing the kill, he will tie it to his spear and bring it back to the cave for the others to use, and then he will return to check his traps. Haeden hunts tirelessly, out longer than anyone else in the tribe. I think some of it is so he can escape his own thoughts.

"I do say."

"Then what is the problem? I do not know how to make a khui sing."

I lean on my spear. "Tee-fah-nee has been . . . hurt. She does not want a male's touch." He looks up at me, puzzled, and I explain the situation as best I understand it. That the ones that brought her here took mating from her without her permission, and that the others frighten her. That she wants to practice in the furs with me. All the while, Haeden's brows draw together until he's frowning fiercely at me.

"The female you want invites you to her furs and you spend the day yipping at me?"

He doesn't grasp what I am worried about. "I was saving myself for resonance. I wanted her to know she is mine forever before I touched her. But now I worry that if I touch her and she reacts badly, it will not go well. I worry that resonance will overpower me and I will hurt her."

Haeden shakes his head. "So take her and make her scream. Lick her long and hard and she will forget everything else."

"But . . . there is no resonance. Not yet." I rub my chest, encouraging my khui. I firmly believe that I will resonate to none but Tee-fah-nee, but there is a small part of me that is filled with doubt. "What if I give her pleasure and then she resonates to another?"

"Then she resonates to another," he says flatly. "I thought you were certain she was to be your mate?"

"I am. But I do not know if my khui is listening. I . . . do not want to have her just to lose her." The thought makes me ill. I would wish her happiness if she resonated to another, but for me, it would be unending misery. "What do you think I should do?"

"I think you should stop yipping and start acting." He stands up, wiping his hands. "Do you want to touch her?"

"More than anything."

His gaze is hard. "And she is offering herself to you? Despite her fears?"

I nod.

Haeden's face is hard, unyielding. His jaw clenches and he casts his gaze around before finally fixing on me with hard, blazing eyes. "Then why do you hesitate, Salukh? Take what you want and do not question. Enjoy each time you touch her. Treat it as a gift. If you do not take this and you lose her, you will forever regret each wasted moment." His voice catches on the last word, and then he turns away, kneeling next to his kill again. His hands move quickly, as if he's determined to somehow outrace his thoughts. "Do not leave yourself with nothing."

He's in pain. I can tell that from his posture, the stiffness of his movements. It's clear to me that he's thinking of before, when he resonated and lost his mate before he could touch her. Does he regret it every day? Is he filled with loneliness? He's a friend, and I hate that he's so miserable. I reach out and touch his shoulder. "You know, there is a human female that has no mate—"

He flings my hand off his shoulder and glares up at me with furious eyes. His voice is deadly. "There is *nothing* for me."

I stare at him, shocked at his vehemence.

Haeden closes his eyes and gives a small shake of his head. "Leave me be, Salukh. Go and chase your female." He returns to gutting his kill.

I watch him for a moment, then turn to leave. It's obvious he does not want my company. He wants to be alone with his miserable memories and his self-hate. But I'm not ready to go back to the caves yet. The thought of returning empty-handed when the other males are being praised for their efforts in the competition? It will not do. So I track the dvisti herd, following it over the rise and down into the next valley. There is still time before the twin suns go down, and I am in no rush. When I find the herd again, I skirt wide, careful of the wind and paying attention to the creatures. If I throw my spear again and miss, someone will go hungry. I must be careful. I crouch low in the snow and wait for the dvisti to forget my presence.

My mind is full of Tee-fah-nee and her warm skin and her small human body. The graceful way she moves. If I close my eyes, I can imagine her scent enveloping me. How fine would it be to be able to touch her? To lick her sweet body and bring her pleasure? I can hear mating pairs in the caves late at night, and I know it's important to bring your female pleasure, preferably more than once. I want nothing more than to please her with my touch. My cock grows hard at the thought and I want to free it from my leggings and stroke myself to pleasure at the simple thought of her. I won't, though. I'm going to save everything I am for her.

I am going to take her up on her offer, I realize. It does not matter that we do not resonate, or that four others vie for her attention.

She is mine and it is time I claimed her.

Renewed, I slowly get to my feet and move toward the herd. They have wandered away a short distance, their movements easy and unafraid. I eye the herd, looking for a weaker one, an easy mark. I do not want sickly, because diseased meat is no good. Nor do I want a healthy buck or a nursing mother, because the dvisti tribe must stay full of young for next year's meals. My gaze falls upon a shaggy mare at the back of the herd. She has a kit at her side, small and bleating. One of the mare's hooves is raised up out of the snow, and when the herd moves forward again, she limps behind, slower than the others.

She and her kit will be easy prey for the next predator in the area. She will fall behind the safety of the herd and the snow-cats will be on them, tearing them to pieces. This will be my hunt for the day, then. I ready my spear, and then hesitate. My gaze falls on the kit. It's very small and young, and I think of Tee-fah-nee's words. She likes the dvisti. They remind her of animals she owned back at her home.

I think of Sessah and the small two-teeth he feeds back at the main cave. It's practically tame, scurrying up to any of the tribe in hopes of a handout. The thing is ugly and fat but Sessah adores it.

The kit bleats at its mother, searching for her udders. The female limps and shifts on her feet, nosing the baby away. She will not feed it while her leg hurts her, and it scurries around her, making hungry noises.

I creep up on mother and kit, keeping low to the ground. My movements are slow and patient, and it takes many long breaths before I make it close enough to launch my spear. The others in the herd are wandering farther away, and still the female limps behind, her kit bawling its hunger.

I strike, racing forward. The dvisti herd panics and flees in a storm of hooves and angry braying, heading out of the valley. The female tries to limp after them, but she does not move fast. I'm able to move up on her quickly and throw my spear at short range, right into her neck. It gushes blood and she collapses to the ground, dead. As I walk up to my kill, the baby bleats and circles in the snow nearby, confused by the smell of blood. When it doesn't leave and the herd does not return to round it up, my mind is decided. I dress my kill quickly, and when it's ready, I look around for the kit.

It stands nearby on thin, twiggy legs, blinking bright blue eyes at me. It bleats again and races away a few feet, then begins to circle back toward its dead mother. I slowly remove my cloak and hold it out from my body, creeping up on the dvisti kit. "Come, little one," I croon. "You will be a fine gift for my Tee-fah-nee."

It whines at me and prances away, skittish.

I continue to move slowly, and when the kit does not flee, I fling my cloak over it and then pounce, neatly trapping it under the fur. It screams then, and bites at my hands when I wrap it in the cloak and tuck it under my arm. It's a biter, and it's in a panic. The breath hisses from me when its tiny teeth clamp down on bare skin.

I swear under my breath and hold it tighter as I get to my feet. The little creature kicks and bites me again, but I don't release it. "You are for my mate," I tell it. "Best you behave, because it is a long walk home."

It bleats plaintively in response.

Juggling my dual burdens is not the easiest task, because the dead mother is unwieldy and heavy, and the child is wriggling and angry. I eventually manage to tie the mother's legs to my spear with one hand—my other arm holding the kit captive—and sling it over one arm. The child I keep tucked against my chest, and I ignore when it starts to chew on my hair.

If it must bite something, then it can bite my mane.

CHAPTER FIVE
Tiffany

I study my rows of planted seeds, hoping for a sprig here or there. Right now, there is nothing, just an upraised row in the snow where the dirt was piled back onto them. Frustrated, I move down the row I've marked with a few sticks, but there's nothing to be seen. Surely plants here can't be that different from plants on Earth, can they? The snow is throwing me off, but it's still water, and plants need water to grow. I shove my fingers into my glove and then kneel near one of the small mounds, digging. There has to be something. If there's even a hint of a sprout on one of my seeds, I'll have hope.

I dig down maybe a foot into the snow and stop when I see a hint of pink threading through the white. Sure enough, one of my seeds has sprouted and is pushing its way through the snow. It's working! Excited, I pile the snow back on top with a pat and get to my feet. Wait until I tell Salukh!

As if my thoughts have summoned him, a familiar male silhouette appears on the ridge, burdened by a kill. He seems to be walking strangely, and I dust the snow off my hands and surge forward. Is he hurt? He's moving slow. For a moment I almost think it's one of the elders, but there's no mistaking the way Salukh's horns curve up at the ends, or his long fluttering hair. He drags a dead dvisti behind him and cradles one arm against his chest, and my heart hammers. Does he need the healer? Maylak's at the other cave, though, and it's at least a half a day's journey to get to her. "Salukh, are you all right?" I call as I push through the snow to get to his side. "Can I help?"

"You can help," he agrees, and as I get to his side, he thrusts a cloak-covered bundle into my arms. "Cursed thing bit me all the way here."

I blink in surprise as the bundle tries to leap from my arms and bleats angrily. I tighten my grip on it and stare at the hunter. "What is this?"

"A dvisti kit. The mother was lame and so she became fodder for my spear. But I could not kill the young one. I brought it for you."

"Me?"

"Yes, you." He drops the spear on the ground, letting his kill tumble into the snow, and then rotates one big arm, rubbing sore muscles. "Ah, that feels good."

I try not to watch as he rubs one big blue bicep, but . . . mercy. Those are *big* biceps. Hard, too. The creature in my hands wriggles, and my attention turns back to it. "I . . . Do you guys even do pets?"

"Sessah has a two-teeth he feeds back at the main cave."

"And no one tries to eat it for dinner?" I don't want to get attached to something only to come home and find someone roasting my pet.

"I will not allow them to touch it." His words are so sure, so bold.

I feel a weird surge of warmth and smile at him.

He reaches forward to uncover the creature's head, and then two big, blue, khui-lit eyes are gazing at me. The head is tiny, a bit like a fawn, but covered in long, crazy fur like a sheepdog. It bleats angrily at me.

And I laugh because it's so ridiculous looking and cute at the same time. It's all nose and googly eyes and shaggy hair. "I love it."

He gives a masculine grunt. "I am glad it pleases you."

"It's sweet of you to think of me," I admit. I'm endlessly showered with useful things by the other guys, but this is the first time someone's thought to give me something completely . . . frivolous. And a pet truly is frivolous in a setting like this, but I really love it, and I love that Salukh was so thoughtful. "Thank you."

His gaze burns into mine. "I have been thinking upon your words, Tee-fah-nee."

I shiver. The way he says my name always makes me think he's mentally caressing each syllable, and it makes me feel things that I thought were long gone.

He steps forward and he doesn't touch me, though he is close enough that our faces could practically press together if we were the same height. As it is, I'm staring at a lot of broad, velvety-blue pectorals. The baby dvisti in my arms snaps at a bit of fringe on his vest and begins to chew on it.

I suddenly feel flushed and overheated despite the ever-present ice. "My words?"

"You wish to practice in the furs." His intense look pins me in place. "I wish to be the male you practice with."

My eyes widen. He . . . he wants to go for what I suggested? "I thought you were waiting for resonance?"

"I have changed my mind. I wish to pleasure you."

I feel my cheeks heat at those bold words. "Um, wow. That's very nice of you. But you really don't have to—"

"Make no mistake, Tee-fah-nee. This is my decision. I have thought many hours about how fine it would be to touch you, and I am eager to make you scream with pleasure instead of fear."

Did all the guys here talk so forward to the women they took to their furs? No wonder all of the human women walk around with dreamy expressions. I resist the urge to fan myself and juggle the wriggling baby dvisti in my arms. "So like . . . now?"

His brows draw together. "Now?"

"Um, did you want to practice now?" I feel stupid for even having to ask.

Realization dawns on his face and a slow, devastating grin crosses his handsome features. "You are eager."

"I— What? No! I just meant—" I break off, flustered. "You know what? Never mind. I was just bringing it up because you're here and I'm here and—"

"And you are eager," he interrupts again, looking pleased. "This is good. We shall come very hard together, Tee-fah-nee."

Oh *lord*, the mouth on this man. "If you say so," I reply faintly.

"Today is not good," he says.

"It's not?" Why do I feel weirdly disappointed by that?

"You have a kit to care for," he says, and pulls a piece of leather fringe out of the biting little dvisti's mouth. "He is hungry. And I must take this to my mother's cave so she may prepare it." He gestures at the carcass lying at his feet.

"Oh. Of course." *Duh, Tiffany. Where's your brain?* I

know where my brain is, though. It's all wrapped up in the thought of *YOU'RE GOING TO HAVE SEX WITH THIS BIG GUY*. And I'm utterly terrified and kind of curiously aroused at the same time.

"When shall we meet so I may give you pleasure?"

I blink. He's leaving it up to me? That makes things . . . trickier. Because I have to basically say, *I can squeeze in an orgasm by noon if that's good for you*. Provided I orgasm, of course. Provided I don't run away screaming. Provided I don't chicken out of things entirely.

Putting it on me kind of scares me. It makes things entirely my choice. It means I'm asking for everything that happens. Which is a good thing, of course, but also terrifying. What if it's awful and I freak out? What if I just can't get aroused at all? I tense, and peek up at Salukh. He's watching me with heavy-lidded eyes, that fierce, consuming look on his face.

Somehow I doubt boredom would be a problem with this guy.

"Tomorrow, I guess? Somewhere private." I don't want to have our make-out parties in the main cave. That would be weird. "Is there somewhere we can go that isn't out in the open?" The only place I know of that's close by and not frequented by many people is the leather curing cave, and the stench in there isn't exactly conducive to sexytimes.

"I know of a cave about an hour's hike from here. It's small but it will suit our needs. I will bring furs." He nods solemnly. "You must be kept warm."

Well, there's no way to back out now, is there? Not with this big male looking down at me so intently and making all these plans to please *me*. "I don't want to tell anyone what we're doing, all right?"

His brows draw down. "You do not wish for them to know I am pleasuring you?"

I shake my head. "Amongst my people, taking someone to your furs for fun is . . . private." I've heard that the sa-khui aren't the same as us, that fur-hopping amongst single un-mated women is no big deal, but the single women are few and far between and I'm not built that way. Plus, I have four other guys watching my every move and I don't want one of them flipping out or getting super possessive. That would be bad. "If anyone asks, we're going herb gathering, all right? That can be our code word for it."

"Coad-werd," he repeats. "I do not know what this is."

"It's a secret term you use. So when I say I want to go herb gathering with you . . ."

Realization dawns. "You wish to be pleasured."

All this "pleasure" talk is making me super flustered. "Sure. We'll go with that."

"Are there other human customs I should know? Other coad-werds?"

Well, there are condoms, but he can't make me pregnant if we're not resonating, so that doesn't matter. And there's nothing on this planet that I know of that would pass for lube—and nothing I'd be comfortable sticking up in unmentionable places anyhow. "I can't think of anything."

He nods solemnly, still devouring me with his eyes. "I will bring the furs tonight, so none will question why we bring them for a plant-gathering trip."

"Good idea." I wipe a stray bit of blood off his arm and then feel weird for reaching out and touching the guy. "You should probably bathe as well."

He nods in recognition. "It will be part of my herb-gathering preparation."

"Great." I gesture at the cave. "I should, um, probably go back." The thing in my arms wiggles, trying to escape.

"I shall, too." He nods at me again. "Then, tomorrow?"

"Tomorrow." I feel myself blushing again.

Tomorrow, everything changes.

It's a good thing I have the baby dvisti to distract me from tomorrow's upcoming make-out session. I'm a nervous wreck, but the tribe's reaction to my new pet means I don't have a lot of time to spend thinking about Salukh. Farli is utterly enchanted. It only takes about five minutes before she declares she wants one, much to her mother's dismay. The other sakhui are just puzzled as to why I'd want to keep one.

My suitors? They're not pleased that I have such a big gift from someone not even competing. They sit by the fire and murmur all night, casting unhappy looks in my direction, and Salukh's, too. For his part, Salukh is utterly oblivious to the bitter whispers, and so I ignore them as well. Haeden takes one look at my baby dvisti, shoots Salukh a disgusted look, and then heads off to his own cave. It's all very strange.

"He's so cute," Josie tells me as we fashion a crude gate from whippy tree branches, old privacy screens, and a bit of rope. There's a small cave in the back of the tribal cave that's gone unused, and it's going to serve as the little dvisti's pen. "He's kinda bitey, though."

"That's why I'm calling him Chompy. Or her. I can't tell if it's a boy or a girl." Chompy has too much fur and wiggles too much for me to check the undercarriage, so we're going with a nice gender-neutral name. Chompy has also bitten me three times, Josie twice, and Farli once. He's indeed a chomper.

The little dvisti prances around his stall as we secure the gate, sniffing everything and then testing things out with a few nips of his mouth. He bites the leather blankets I've put down for him, the handfuls of skinny leaves that Farli spent all afternoon harvesting, and anything else he comes into contact with.

"What are you going to do with it?" Josie asks. She extends her fingers over the rickety gate and Chompy trots up, licking her fingers and then making a sad bleating noise. "I think he's hungry."

"Domesticate him, I suppose. A horse might be pretty useful."

"He's more like a deer crossed with a sheepdog, though," Josie says thoughtfully. She glances at me. "Haeden was pissed about it."

"He can be pissed. I don't care. You shouldn't, either."

"I don't," she says quickly. "I just know you don't want to make anyone upset."

She's right, but for some reason, Haeden's anger doesn't bother me. For one, he's always a sourpuss and Chompy's appearance hasn't really changed that. Haeden also hasn't shown the slightest bit of interest in me, so I feel safe around him. I trust Salukh, too. He wouldn't have given me the little dvisti as a present if he thought it would encourage the others to act badly.

I glance over at the fire and Salukh is seated there between his father, Borran, and Elder Vadren. They have spearpoints in their hands and are sharpening them while idly chatting. Salukh's gaze is on me, though, and not his spears. Even now he watches me with intense, glittering eyes. I shiver and turn back to my tiny pet. "I should feed him."

Anything to distract from the fact that Salukh's focused attention is making me feel unsettled.

The dvisti graze on the thin, tough plants that manage to grow on the mostly barren hills and valleys between the mountains that we call home. I grew up on a farm, though, and I know baby grazers—like foals and calves—can be fed a warm mash when the mama isn't available. I mash up one of the not-potatoes and add water until it forms a goopy paste. I pour it into a bladder used for toting water and nip off the end, and Farli holds Chompy for me as I feed him. It takes a while but we get some of the mash in him, and once he's fed, he's a lot calmer when he returns to his stall.

I'm exhausted from a day of watching him, though, and thinking about Salukh. When Farli asks to put her furs in front of the pen so she can watch over the little dvisti, I gladly accept. I'm ready to crawl into my own bed and get some shut-eye.

But even as I do, I keep thinking about Salukh and what tomorrow will bring. I'm terrified I'm going to freak out on him. Just the thought of kissing is making me hyperventilate, and when I close my eyes, I can almost imagine the feel of rough, pebbly orange skin against mine. I shudder, queasy. The memories won't go away and I wish they would.

I'd give anything to be free.

Salukh

When Tee-fah-nee emerges from her cave in the morning, her eyes are hollow and unhappy. Dark smudges speak of a poor night's sleep, and I wonder if she'll change her mind. I also had a poor night's sleep, but it was due to the fact that my cock was hard all night at the thought of being able to touch her this morning. Not even Haeden's snoring could distract me from thoughts of her and her soft skin, her curvy body.

But she does not come to tell me she has changed her mind. She gives me a faint smile, checks on her little dvisti, and moves around the cave as if it were any other day. I watch her out of the corner of my eye, and then when I can stand it no longer, I approach her. She's by the dvisti's cave, talking softly to Farli. Farli does not speak the human language, but they communicate well enough, and it's clear that Farli is fascinated by the little creature.

Tee-fah-nee looks over at me and gives me a faint, tired smile. "Farli's going to watch Chompy for me while we go herb gathering."

"Are you well?" She does not look well.

"Just bad dreams, that's all." Her smile does not reach her eyes. "I'm fine."

"Then I am eager to gather herbs with you," I tell her slowly. The falsehood feels strange on my tongue, but if that is what she wants to call it, so be it.

Farli clasps her hands and looks back and forth at myself and Tee-fah-nee. "Are you going to capture more dvisti kits?"

"No," I tell her gently. "We must see if this one survives before we claim more. Tee-fah-nee and I shall go gather herbs."

Farli's young face is full of confusion. "You will gather herbs? But you are a hunter."

"Today I am an herb gatherer," I tell her. "You will watch the creature for Tee-fah-nee?"

She nods happily. "He no longer bites me. It is a good sign."

"What are you two saying?" Tee-fah-nee asks.

I switch to her language. "Farli wishes us well on our herb gathering and is excited to watch your creature."

She smiles at Farli and moves to her cave. "Let me get my cloak." She returns a moment later and is bundled from head to toe in warm furs. "I'm ready."

"Let us go before the day gets too late." I turn to look at Farli, but she's frowning at us. "What is it?"

"Your herb baskets?" Farli asks. "Do you not need them?"

Ah. I turn to Tee-fah-nee. "Farli wants to know where your herb baskets are."

"Oh!" Her face darkens in one of the charming human flushes and she flees back to her cave. A moment later, she comes out with two baskets and shoves one into my hands. "I'm so embarrassed."

"Do not be embarrassed," I tell her. "Your mind is elsewhere."

"You can say that again," she mutters.

"Your mind is elsewhere," I repeat dutifully.

She just sighs. "Figure of speech."

The words make no sense to me. I give her a curious look and she waves a hand, indicating it was nothing. All right, then. Basket in hand, I head out of the cave with her.

It's a short walk for a sa-khui to get to the cave I have in mind; our strides are long and we handle the snow very well. It takes longer for my human companion, though. Tee-fah-nee's strides are short and she struggles with the deeper snow, sinking with each step. I slow my strides so she can keep up, but as I do, I worry this is a poor choice. Should I have picked someplace closer to the caves? I do not want her to be too exhausted to practice mouth-mating with me. But she does not complain about the walk, and I am pleased; she is stronger than she looks.

The cave mouth appears just ahead, and I gesture at it to Tee-fah-nee. "I brought furs yesterday afternoon so we will be comfortable. Let me go and make sure there are no scavengers waiting."

"Scavengers?" she asks, her tone wary. She pulls her heavy fur cloak tighter around her body.

"Metlaks will sometimes hide in our hunting caves. They are dangerous when cornered." Usually they destroy everything they find when they do, because they do not like the scent of the sa-khui. "Wait here."

She nods and takes my basket from my hands. I unsheathe one of my bone knives and approach the cave. All is well inside, the furs I brought undisturbed, and I gesture her forward. Tee-fah-nee enters the cave, and she is small enough that she does not need to stoop to enter as I did. "It's small," she says, surprise in her voice.

I grunt agreement. "Too small to use as shelter for hunters, and too close to the main caves. But it is perfect for our needs." Light filters in from the entrance, and is enough to see by. I did not bring a candle or fire-making equipment, as we will not be here by night. The cave is not warm enough for such things and it is not safe for Tee-fah-nee.

She sets her baskets down by the entrance and does not move forward. She is nervous, then.

I must make her comfortable. I pull off my own cloak and toss it aside, too warm now that I am out of the wind. Then I spread the furs out to create a nice, cozy nest for her. I gesture at them. "Will you sit?"

Her eyes are wide, but she does. She clasps her small human hands in her lap and looks around, as if she wants to look anywhere but at me. She is nervous. I am, too. I want to do this right. I want to fill her with pleasure and take away her memories of those who hurt her.

"I am not familiar with human mating customs," I tell her. I rub my chest, barely covered by my thin leather vest. "I did wash for you, though."

She gives a small, nervous laugh. "That's a start."

"What next, then?" I am trying not to be too eager . . . and failing, I suspect.

"Well," she says softly. "Probably kissing."

"The mouth matings? How does that work?"

She twists her hands. "Well, we put our mouths together and use tongues and lips to give each other pleasure. There's really not a rulebook."

"Ruhl-bookh?"

"A set of standards," she corrects. "You mostly go by instinct."

I am eager to try it. I want Tee-fah-nee's taste on my mouth, against my tongue. The thought of her smaller tongue darting against mine makes my cock ache. Why did I wait so many days to say yes to this? I can barely restrain myself from grabbing her and holding her down in the furs and claiming her as it is. "Do you wish to put your tongue in my mouth, then?"

She blinks at me. "I . . . guess we should give it a shot." But she doesn't look eager. She looks terrified.

I sit forward and she flinches back. "We do not have to—"

"No," she blurts out. "This was my idea, and we should try it." But she wrings her hands again and looks frightened.

My heart squeezes. This is going all wrong. I knew she would not be eager, but I didn't expect her to look as if I have driven a spear through her chest. I remain still as she shrugs some of her heavy furs off of her body and tosses them over next to mine. She's wearing a simple leather dress that goes to her calves and is edged with white fur, with leggings underneath. Her body is covered from head to toe even after she removes her furs, and I catch no glimpse of soft exposed skin. But even frightened, Tee-fah-nee is lovely. She's graceful with her movements, and my hand itches to sink into her curly mane.

She leans closer to me and puts a hand on my chest. She sits beside me in the furs and it takes all of my power not to grab her and pull her into my lap, to press her against my chest and hold her close. Instead, I put my hands down to my sides so I don't inadvertently touch her. It strikes me that it would be a bad idea, especially right now. I can feel her small form trembling against me, even as she boldly straddles my lap and pushes her hips down against my cock.

"I can tell one of us is excited to be here," she breathes. I think she's trying to be funny but it just comes out breathless and wobbly.

"I will control myself," I tell her. "Do not worry."

"I know you will." But she doesn't look like she believes it herself. Her hands flutter over my vest and she still won't look me in the eye. "I'll, um, start."

I wait quietly. I scarcely dare to breathe, because I'm afraid that if I make a sudden movement, she will be gone, utterly terrified.

She takes a few deep, gulping breaths. Her gaze flicks to my face, and then she grabs the sides of my jaw and pulls my face to hers. Her lips mash against mine. Stunned, I don't move, and I feel her tongue flick against the tight seam of my mouth.

And I'm lost.

CHAPTER SIX
Salukh

I open my mouth to allow her tongue to slide in and it flicks against mine. It's smooth and silky, just like her skin, and I groan. The feel is like nothing I imagined. My eyes close with the wonder of it all. Her weight on my cock combined with the feel of her tongue flicking into my mouth? I will stroke my cock to this moment for the rest of my life.

Her mouth moves against mine and her tongue strokes deep. Her body presses against mine and I can't resist touching her. I grab her arms and hold her so I can mate my mouth with hers. This is what I have dreamed of. *Now*, I demand of my khui. *Resonate now. Claim her as ours.*

She stiffens in my arms and jerks backward. "No!" Her hands claw at my skin frantically, and she's desperate to get away.

I release her, shocked at her violent reaction. That wasn't what I wanted at all. I . . . I thought she was enjoying herself as I was.

Tee-fah-nee flings my hands off of her and curls her arms around herself, hunching over and shuddering.

I want to touch her and reassure her, but I dare not. "I . . . I did not mean—"

"It's not you," she says, and I can hear the tears in her voice, even though I cannot see her face. It is hidden behind her glorious hair. "It's me. It's all me. I'm broken."

"You are perfect," I tell her, my voice husky with disappointment and anguish for her. My mate hurts and I don't know how to fix it. Never have I felt so helpless, so hopeless. To think that just moments ago I was begging my khui to claim her. Now I am relieved it is silent. Giving in to its call now would be nothing short of what the others took from her.

I will never take unless Tee-fah-nee gives.

"You still think I am perfect after all this?" She looks up at me, and tears slide down her lovely cheeks. I long to brush them away, but my hands remain at my sides.

I nod. How could I ever think less of her? How can she think that? "Nothing will ever change my mind. You are strong simply for trying. You are perfect just as you are."

Her face crumples and she flings herself forward into my lap again, her arms going around my neck. Her head burrows against my throat and she sobs bitterly against me.

And I let her.

This has all gone terribly wrong. I was so eager for this, but now I feel nothing but regret. My poor Tee-fah-nee. She is worried she has disappointed me, and all I feel is anger for those that touched her without permission, who gave her these mental wounds that I cannot bring to the healer. So she cries, and I let her cling to me like a baby metlak. I am careful not to touch her, because I don't want to set her off again. Her weeping makes my chest ache. I wish I could fix this for her.

Her hands dig into my hair and she wets my neck with her tears. Her boots dig into my legs but I do not move, because I do not want to scare her. She could pull a knife out and shove it into my gut and I would not flex a single muscle. I am hers to abuse in this moment.

I am hers entirely.

Tee-fah-nee's sobs die down to soft hiccups, and she still burrows against me. I feel her fragile body shiver against mine, and my hands twitch with the need to hold her and comfort her. "May I touch you?" I ask, my voice low and husky. "Just to comfort?"

I feel her nod against my shoulder.

Gently, I slide a hand to the center of her back. She stiffens against me, but when I make no further moves, she relaxes little by little. Her body leans into mine again, and I simply hold her. It is a pleasure just to touch her even like this, to feel her warmth against mine. I did not realize how much I hunger for her until this moment. Not being near her is like starvation to my spirit.

When her shuddering slows, I move my hand up and down her back, stroking it as I would a kit. I held my little sister, Farli, when she was nothing but a tiny, squalling kit. I know how to comfort with a gentle touch, though I would do so much more for Tee-fah-nee if she would let me. My hand glides up and down her back, lightly rubbing. *You are safe*, I tell her without words. *No one shall ever hurt you again.*

Eventually, her tears stop wetting my shoulder. She gives a little sigh and I feel her cheek press against my skin. "I'm sorry, Salukh."

"There is nothing to be sorry for, sweet one." I stroke her back slowly, my movements even and easy to keep her from panicking. For the moment, it is pleasure enough that she lets me touch her. "Your fear will fade with time. I am a patient male and content to wait."

She gives a small, hiccupy laugh. "Most guys wouldn't say something like that."

"Most are fools." I am happy with where I am. She has ceased her heartbreaking weeping, her body is warm against mine, and if I angle my head, I can take in the scent of her hair. Truly, I feel as if I am the luckiest male alive to even have this opportunity.

Tee-fah-nee just sighs again and makes no move to get up. I am content to hold her, and when her breathing evens out, I realize she's fallen into an exhausted slumber on my chest. She has worn herself out with her worry and her tears.

And even though today has not turned out as I wished, I am pleased that my future mate feels comfortable enough in my presence to fall asleep. It is something. Not much, but something.

Tiffany

Warmth surrounds me. The blanket I lie on feels soft against my cheek, but it's lumpy and hard underneath. I don't want to move, though, because I feel protected for the first time since landing on this planet. Strange that a big warm blanket will do that for me. I keep my eyes closed even as I shift, determined to slide back into delicious sleep.

Except I can feel something hard between my spread legs.

Then, I remember where I am. I'm not in my nest of furs in the cave I share with Josie. I'm in a tiny anonymous cave away from the others, and I'm straddling Salukh.

Correction: I'm straddling Salukh *after I cried all over him when he touched me.*

God, I'm such an asshole.

I feel terrible. Well, sort of. I also feel really loose and relaxed, and I don't want to get up. I still feel protected and his big hand is on my back, slowly rubbing. I don't know how long I've been out, but it's the first good sleep I've had in a while. There were no dreams. Zero. I'm so relieved.

I'm *so* sitting right on top of his boner.

"Should I get up?" I ask him. It's hard for me not to notice his hard-on when I'm straddling it.

"If you like." He doesn't stop stroking my back. Nor does he try to do anything else. It's like he's content to simply hold me.

It's . . . nice. Really nice. I'm no longer freaking out, either. It's like all the anxiety that built up overnight exploded in a torrent of tears and all that's left is me, kind of boneless and content. "Are you uncomfortable?"

"No. I like you here."

"I'm really sorry about the kiss." I mentally wince, even as I curl my hands against his vest and snuggle in against his chest. The softness I'm feeling? It's not his clothing but his skin. He feels like velvety suede. I knew the sa-khui have a downy layer of light fur on their bodies from a passing touch or two, but it feels different when you graze someone's hand versus pressing your body against them. I want to touch more of him and explore the texture, but I'm afraid I'll freak out again. I bite my lip. "Just so you know, most kisses don't end up like that."

He chuckles. "I suspected as much." He pats my back with one enormous hand, like he would a child. "You do not have to explain anything to me, Tee-fah-nee. I am happy simply to be the male you chose to spend the day with."

"I . . . cried all over you."

"Mmm. You were emotional. There are many bad memories in your head." His hand resumes stroking my back. "It will take more than one afternoon to make them go silent."

He's so understanding. I'm lucky to be here with him, that we're friends first and foremost. I don't think Taushen or Hassen—or, shudder, Bek—would be quite so understanding. There's no sense of urgency with Salukh. No desperation or worry that if I displease him, he'll retaliate. There's something about him that makes me realize that he never would. He's intense, but protective. It's not his style to attack. Yet another reason why I like him so much.

I sigh. "I wish I wasn't so messed up."

"There is a saying amongst my people," he muses. "'We may wish for many things, but it is easier to wish for snow. The snow is more likely to happen.'"

"Reminds me of an Earth saying: 'Wish in one hand, shit in the other, and see which one fills up faster.'"

A deep laugh rumbles out of his chest, and I bounce against him as he moves. "I like that. Though if the dvisti shit, I would not mind so much. It would save me many hours of dung chip gathering."

I smile against his chest. "You're a good guy, you know that, Salukh?"

He strokes my back again.

I relax against him, not quite ready to move. If he's not dying for me to get up, I'll take advantage of the moment. "I don't know what to do," I confess. "I'm scared to try again."

"Then we do not try again."

"I feel like I need to." If nothing else, so I can conquer my own head. I can't live in fear forever. "Can we try again tomorrow?"

"Of course. We can try again as many times as you like."

CHAPTER SEVEN
Tiffany

We try for the next week. Every day, we meet to "gather herbs" and head off to our cave. Each time, I'm not able to move into kissing. We end up just cuddling for a long time, and honestly . . . I really like it. Salukh never demands anything of me, and our cave time has turned into just "touch and talk" time. He strokes my back as I talk about whatever comes to mind—things I miss back home, my ideas for how to start farming here on the ice planet, or whatever Chompy has bitten into today. In the last week he's eaten three shoes, half of his gate, and whatever else shows up in his pen. Farli has been spending a lot of time watching him, and she's a wonderful help because I seem to be gone for long hours of the day with Salukh.

If my other suitors have noticed we're spending a lot of time together, they haven't said anything. They're too busy winning more of Josie's seeds. Yesterday was a running competition, and the day before, she had them braiding sinew into long cords of rope for the tribe. So far, Taushen is still in the lead but Hassen is close behind him. The men have been giving me more space lately, but I think it's just because Josie's been running them ragged with her endless competitions. At some point they're going to demand that I pay up. Josie's game is a two-edged sword. It's great that it keeps them off my back for now, but at some point, they're going to want answers from me, and I'm not sure I have anything to give.

But I can't focus on that. And I don't share those worries with Salukh. We have enough going on between us.

Like right now. Currently I'm lying on top of him in our cave like we normally do. I still straddle him every time, because I feel like I need to mentally acknowledge the fact that he's aroused. Plus, I kind of like draping myself over him and letting him caress my back and arms. He never reaches farther down, never grabs my butt or tries to push me into anything else. It's just one long cuddle session each day and nothing more.

Weirdly enough, I've come to anticipate them. The stress of meeting with him is gone because I know he won't push me into anything. It's hours away from the endless scrutiny of the caves, Josie's questioning looks, and the bustle of endless preparation for both the upcoming brutal season and the move back to the main cave once Harlow gets her rock cutter working again. Though I'm looking forward to seeing the rest of the humans again, I'm *not* looking forward to returning to the main cave. If I thought the South Cave was full of people, moving us all back to one big boisterous tribe is going to mean even more people are underfoot and privacy will be at a premium.

One big hand idly strokes my back. "What is it you think about, Tee-fah-nee?"

I smile, eyes closed as I lean against his big chest. I can hear his heart beating evenly, and I love listening to it. I could listen for hours, provided he held me close and petted me. "Just about the tribes moving back together." Kemli and her family left this morning, along with Vadren and a few of the elders. Farli stayed behind to help me with Chompy, and Salukh stayed, too, of course. "We're all going to pile back into the one cave and it's going to be crowded."

"It is not a bad thing, though. More hands and friendly faces to make the day's work go by faster."

"Less alone time, though," I point out. "And we're still not anywhere close to my goal." I sit up and look at him, troubled. "Maybe we should try the kissing again." Even as I say it, though, my entire body tenses and I feel a cold sweat coming on.

"I can sense your fear," he says gently, and rubs my arms encouragingly. I've become addicted to his touch in the last week. Why is it that I love the thought of cuddling with him but the moment I think about kissing, I shut down? "What would make you less afraid?"

I give him a faint smile, considering. "I don't know."

"You already make great progress. Think of when we first came to this cave." He brushes a finger over my cheek. "Now I can touch you and you do not weep."

Jeez. Guilt shoots through me. I'm not being very fair to him, am I? "I wish we could skip ahead, but the touching is hard for me."

"Then we do not touch?"

I frown at him. "What do you mean?"

He looks surprised. "Do humans not touch themselves for pleasure?"

Oh. Masturbation. My cheeks feel hot. "You mean . . . in front of each other?" Why does that sound so utterly scandalous? Why am I not just dismissing the idea immediately? I'm kind of mutely horrified at the thought of touching myself in front of him, but an even bigger part of me is rather curious about what he'll do. Is it awful that I want to see him do it?

"Well, I have done it in private many times, but I do not think it will help you much if I do so again."

A horrified chuckle escapes me. This is the most bizarrely frank conversation. "No, I suppose not."

"And we can talk through it if you like."

I bite my lip and think about what he's offering. Dirty talk and masturbation. I'm intrigued and I'm also freaked out. It feels like a big step. And yet, if I never take any steps forward, I'm not going to go anywhere. Strangely enough, it feels less intimate than kissing. "I don't want to go first."

He nods slowly, and the burning, intense look is back in his eyes, making me shiver. "I will go first, then. Are you ready?"

Oh God. *Am* I ready? I want to tell him to wait, that I'm not prepared. That I'm not sure about any of this. But time is running out. I know the moment we all move back to the main cave, we won't be able to get away together like we have been. Someone will be on to us. My suitors will tire of the games that Josie sends them off to play and turn back to bothering me.

Salukh gives me a patient look and gently pulls me off of his lap. "I cannot do this with you seated right there."

Of course. I move into the furs and tuck my legs under me, all casual-like. But I'm staring. I can't help but stare. He reaches for the tie at the waist of his leather leggings and my mouth goes dry. He's going to perform for me . . . because it might help ease me back into things? Or is it because he wants to perform *for* me?

The thought is surprisingly titillating.

As I wait in shocked silence, he finishes untying his pants and down they go. He's . . . not wearing underwear. I'm not surprised, because I'm pretty sure they're a foreign concept to the sa-khui, who dress like it's a nice spring day instead of endless winter. And then, of course, I'm eye level with the biggest blue dong I've ever seen in my life. I tell myself I shouldn't stare, but who am I kidding? I stare. Because damn, there's a lot to see. His thighs are massive, strong and thick and a delicious shade of blue that's just begging for me to run my hands over them. The strange, bony ridges common to the sa-khui creep down the front of each muscular thigh and cap at his knees. As he kicks off his pants I get a glimpse of strong calves and my gaze creeps back up.

Back to his dick, because I'm only human. And I've got to be honest, it's a really great dick for all that it's rather . . . different than human dick. The sa-khui apparently have the same plate-y ridges on their cocks as they do their skin, and he's got an impressive spur sticking out on top. His balls are heavy and dark, and he's hairless on his groin, unlike a human man. But the head of his cock is thick and his skin looks just as velvety here. I've seen a few dicks in my day and this one's probably the best one. It's not circumcised, but that doesn't change how impressively big and meaty it is. My, my.

The little cave suddenly feels awful warm.

I tear my gaze away from his equipment and look up as Salukh tugs his vest off his shoulders in a sensual motion that makes me feel like I should have a few dollars to shove into a G-string or something. The man can move. Damn.

When he's completely naked, he gazes down at me. His long black hair swings over his shoulder and he tosses it back with another graceful move. Then, he considers the furs at his feet. "Do you want me to sit or stand?"

Why's he asking *me*? "Um, whatever makes you the most comfortable."

He considers for a moment, hand on his hips. It draws attention to the fact that, fully erect, his cock is jutting out almost obscenely from his body. I . . . can't stop staring at it. "I normally sit." He folds his big body down and sits in the furs again, and immediately one hand goes to his cock. He curls his fingers around the base and then looks expectantly at me.

"What?" I squirm uncomfortably in my seat. I feel off kilter and curiously exposed in this situation. It's not . . . bad. It's just strange. I've had sex in the past, before my rape. Lord knows I've masturbated. It's not that I don't feel safe. I just feel . . . strangely breathless. I clamp my thighs together because my pulse is starting to thrum between them.

"Tell me what you want me to do."

"M-me?" I stammer. "What do you mean?"

"I want you to tell me what you wish me to do. How I should touch myself to please you." His eyes are gleaming with that wild intensity again, and as my gaze flicks from his face back to his dick, I see even more pre-cum beading on the head of it, as if just talking to me is turning him on like there's no tomorrow.

"Why do you want me to direct you?"

"Because it pleases me," he says, voice blunt. There's a rasp in his tone that wasn't there before, and I watch as his hand tenses around his cock, as if he's having to will himself not to stroke it without permission. "And because I want you to realize that I will only do what gives you pleasure. Nothing else."

Oh boy. I wrap my arms around myself and stare at him. He doesn't move, and when I realize that he's waiting patiently for me, dick in hand, I feel safe. He's letting me have all the control. If touching scares me, then we'll do other naughty things to work up to the touching. He's willing to do whatever it is I want, as long as it helps me.

Not that this is a hardship for him, I'm sure.

I wet my lips with my tongue and start to speak, then pause. I notice his gaze is on my mouth now. I glance down at his cock, and his hand is tight around the base. "Stroke it," I whisper, feeling daring. "Slowly."

It's utterly titillating to me when his fisted hand moves up and down with excruciating slowness. He pumps it once, giving a little twist of his wrist when he gets to the head before sliding back down the shaft. Oh. That's fascinating to me. "Do that again."

"What part?" His voice is thick with lust.

"All of it." I can't stop watching as he does it again, dragging his big hand over his cock. It makes me feel hollow inside, as if I need to be filled up with that big cock. I'm not ready for that, but I'm encouraged by the fact that I'm feeling aroused at the sight of him touching himself. "Squeeze the head," I tell him when he strokes again.

He does, and I watch more pre-cum bead on the crown. It's dripping with his juices now, and I feel the overwhelming urge to lean over and lick it up. I bet he'd taste like he smells— musky and delicious—but I don't move a muscle. I'm not brave enough yet. Instead, I just clasp my hands and stick them between my thighs. I'm feeling twitchy all over, and the cave definitely feels hotter than before. Maybe it's me that's overheating.

Salukh pauses in his motions, and gives me another intense look. He's waiting for more direction. I'm not sure what else guys do when they jerk off. They just stroke their cocks, right? I know men aren't like women and they don't need as much stimulus, but it seems a shame to have all this glorious masculinity in front of me and just have him quickly jerk one out. So I scan his big body, and think about what I'd touch, what I'm longing to run my hands over. His soft, suede-like skin is appealing to me. "Can you . . . Can you slide one of your hands down your chest?"

His brows draw together, but he nods and moves a hand quickly down his front.

"Slowly," I tell him, and I'm surprised at how breathless I sound. I shift on my knees, my thighs clamping tight together again. "Like I was touching you."

His eyes flare with such intense longing that it takes my breath away.

Not yet. But hopefully soon.

He puts a hand to his breastbone and then slowly trails his fingers down his chest, gliding over hard pectorals and down the rippling six-pack that seems to go on for ever and ever, his belly flat and gorgeous.

"Your nipples," I tell him, and I feel my own harden in response.

Salukh hesitates a moment and then grazes his fingers over his nipple without a lot of interest.

"Not doing it for you?" I ask, smiling. He just seems so oddly confused by the touch.

"I do not have much feeling here," he tells me. "The skin is hard, like my knees."

Oh. It is? My fingers itch to touch and find out for myself, but not today. Today there's an unspoken boundary between us. "Then how about your spur?"

This makes his eyes flare again. He slowly glides his hand down his stomach the way I like, and as I watch, he caresses and encircles the small, hornlike protuberance. I remember Georgie telling me it was like a thumb and hit all the right spots on a human woman. It seems like it's interesting for Salukh, too. The way he circles the base of it tells me he's touched this spot before.

"Keep touching it," I tell him. "And use your other hand to work your cock."

He inhales sharply and does as I ask. Instead of slow, languid movements, though, his hand grips his cock hard and he gives it a rough stroke. His fingers drag hard over the ridges, and I watch as his other hand teases his spur. He's really into it now, and I lick my lips watching him.

I'm definitely feeling things. Not fear, either. I'm feeling . . . horny. For the first time in a long time. And it feels really good.

"I think of you," he growls, and my startled gaze goes from his cock back to his face. He's watching me with that focused gaze, his blue eyes hypnotizing in their fierceness. "When I touch myself, I think of you. No others. Just you."

I suck in a breath. "You do?"

He nods slowly, and I watch as his jaw clenches. His head falls back against the rock wall of the cave and he strokes his cock even harder. "I think of your soft skin and your small human body under mine. I think of claiming you as mine and sinking so deep inside you that your cunt clasps around me like a fist."

Oh God, the urge to stick my hand down the front of my leggings and touch myself is getting stronger by the moment. "Because I'm the only one available?"

"Because you are Tee-fah-nee," he says, voice thick around the syllables of my name. Heat flutters through me and I watch him do that tawdry little wrist flick as he strokes over the head of his cock again. "I like your smile, and your skin, and your hair, and the way you smell. I like the look of your ass when you walk away. I like to imagine what your cunt will look like stretched around my cock."

A little gasp escapes me. His words are filthy, but . . . I love it. My nipples feel impossibly hard, begging to be touched. My own breathing has quickened, and as I look over at Salukh working his cock, I see he's breathing hard, too.

"Are you going to come soon?" I ask, and my fascinated gaze moves back down to his cock. He's working it furiously with his hand now, his other teasing and circling against his spur.

"Do you want me to?" he asks, voice thick.

I nod. "I want to see it," I whisper. I want to watch him as he comes and see what he looks like. I want to see his face, because I know he'll be thinking of me as he comes, and for some reason, I find that intensely appealing.

I thought we were just friends. But friends don't picture other friends when they masturbate, do they? Something tells me we've gone over the friendship line at some point and I never even noticed.

Nor do I care. I like being around Salukh. I'm attracted to him. I gaze at all that blue, velvety skin rippling over taut muscles and the thick, coarse black hair that flows down his horned head and over his shoulders. I eye the big, thick cock he's pumping in his hands furiously. How can I not be attracted to all this? He's gorgeous, raw and masculine in ways that most Earth guys aren't.

The breath hisses from between his fangs, and then Salukh comes. His body stiffens and I watch in fascination as his cock spurts clear, pale semen all over his hands and spatters his chest. He groans my name and continues to milk his cock, sending more ropes of come over his skin.

Oh, wow. That was beautiful. I'm utterly fascinated and I can't stop staring, even as he slowly gives his cock a few more strokes and then releases it. There's come all over him, and he's covered by a faint sheen of sweat, but I've never seen him look so satisfied.

Or so utterly possessive as he looks at me.

He nods to something behind me. "There is a cloth over there. Hand it to me so I may clean myself up?"

Oh. Of course. I'm blushing like a schoolgirl for some reason. I hand it to him and try to be all nonchalant as he wipes the gleaming remnants of his spend off his lickable abs. "Your come looks different than human come."

He seems surprised. "Does it?"

"Thinner," I point out, though I'm just babbling. "More liquid. It's not a big deal. I just thought it was curious."

He grunts and finishes cleaning himself off, then tosses the small towel aside and looks at me with those hot, hot eyes. "Shall I stay naked for you?"

I tilt my head, curious. Stay naked? Not that I mind, of course, I'm just wondering . . . naked for what?

The question must be written on my face. A devilish smile curves his mouth. "It is your turn now, Tee-fah-nee."

CHAPTER EIGHT
Salukh

I don't think I've ever felt so good. Tee-fah-nee has been very brave this day, and we are making great strides. Soon I will be able to touch her and pleasure her as my mate, resonance or not. Today, I touched myself, but with her watching, it felt as if we were one. I have never rubbed my cock so hard, and never have I come so much. Her lovely face was fascinated as I came, and I felt like the strongest, most virile man on the planet as she commanded me to touch myself for her pleasure. And now it is time for her to touch herself.

Her pretty mouth opens and gapes like a fish's. "Me?"

"Yes, you." I gesture at myself, still boldly naked, my cock still twitching and semihard from my recent play. "Did my efforts not please you?"

She squirms, but she doesn't look miserable at the thought. Just shy. "Salukh, I don't know . . ."

I desperately want to touch her, but I do not know how she will take it. "There is no shame in this cave, Tee-fah-nee. No shame between us. Are we not friends?"

"I don't do this sort of thing with my friends," she huffs, but she starts to pull off her leather dress, and it's all I can do not to jump to my feet with excitement and help strip the clothing off of her. I long to see her naked. I've seen her bathing in the pool back at the main cave—my people are not shy about bodily functions of any kind—but the humans are quick to cover their bodies up and they act as if naked breasts and thighs are things to be worried over. For her to strip down in front of me feels like a treat just for my eyes, and I am hungry for it.

She slowly removes her tunic, revealing a leather band wrapped tightly around her breasts. Curious. I say nothing, simply watching as she gets to her feet and daintily begins to remove her leggings and boots. She is graceful in her movements, my human, and her smooth skin invites the touch. I long for the day when I will be able to caress her as my own.

Not today, I tell my khui. *But soon.*

She pulls her clothing off and then she is dressed in nothing but the band around her breasts, and she pulls that free a moment later and stands in front of me, body proud. She is so lovely it makes my jaw ache. I drink in the sight of her, of her full hips that flare out, the gentle curve of her belly, the surprising fullness of her breasts. They are tipped with dark nipples and my mouth waters at the thought of sucking them. She also has a dark thatch of fur between her thighs, right over her sex. I find it strange but charming, and soon I will be able to bury my face in those curls and lick her as a mate should.

"Did you get a good look?" she teases, but there's a nervous note in her voice.

"I would look more," I say, voice thick with the ache to claim her as my own.

To my delight, she chuckles and gives a little turn, showing off her tailless bottom to me. It's rounded and full and so beautiful I want to put my hands on her right now. I clench them into fists and force them to my sides. If I grab her now, she will panic.

She finishes her twirl and then sits down in the furs. As I watch, she shivers and fine little bumps raise on her skin.

"Cold?" I ask.

She shrugs. "Always cold."

"Come and sit with me, then. I will keep you warm."

The look she gives me is utterly scandalized. Her gaze darts to my naked body, my cock still somewhat hard (and getting harder by the moment). "You're naked. We're both naked."

"You're cold," I tell her. "And I will not touch you. That is our agreement for today. You commanded me to touch myself, and now I will command you for your pleasure. And you will have more pleasure if you are warm." I gesture at my lap again. It's not entirely an unselfish move—I want her warm body pressing up against mine while she touches herself. If I cannot put my hands on her, it is the next best thing.

She hesitates and then rubs her arms. I notice her nipples have grown tight, the peaks extending, and I want to touch them and feel if they are as soft as the rest of her. *Patience*, I tell myself, even as she settles onto one of my thighs. *Look at how she comes to you so sweetly now. Do not ruin it because you think with your cock.*

Ah, but my cock has all the good ideas.

Tee-fah-nee wiggles a little as she tries to get comfortable on my leg. "This feels strange."

"Put your back on my chest," I tell her. "Lean against me." It will give me the perfect view to watch her touch herself, and I feel my cock growing hard with excitement at the thought.

She does, and I feel her soft skin slide against mine. I stifle the groan rising in my throat, because she feels better than anything I have ever felt in my life. Her skin touching mine? There is no greater pleasure to be found. Her bottom nestles against my hard cock and her thighs slide open. "I feel weird," she confesses.

The word does not register. "I do not know this 'weird,' but you are beautiful to me."

She sighs, pleased by my words, and leans back against me. Her hands go to her breasts, and she begins to play with her nipples. I watch hungrily as she strokes her fingers lightly over her skin.

"You're watching me," she says in a low voice. "I can feel your gaze on me." Her fingertips glide over her nipple and it hardens as she circles it.

"I am watching you," I admit. "There is no shame in that. You are beautiful and I enjoy the sight of you touching yourself."

Her small laugh is sweet, as is the sight of her hand skimming to her belly. I watch with eagerness as her legs part and her fingers slide to the curls between her legs. Suddenly, I catch the faint scent of arousal perfuming the air.

I groan aloud, unable to help myself. "You're wet, aren't you? I can smell your scent."

"You can?" Her legs immediately snap closed. "Oh my God, that's so embarrassing."

"There is nothing to be embarrassed of," I tell her, and have to force myself not to grab her knees and pry them apart again. "Your scent is delicious. I long to bathe my tongue in it."

Her little moan catches me off guard, and as I look down, her knees slowly part again. "You'd . . . you'd tongue me?"

"For hours," I rasp, imagining the joy of it. "I would push my face between your legs and drink from you. I would run my tongue over every last bit of your skin and make sure that all of it has been thoroughly licked. I would fuck your cunt with my tongue. I would mate it with my mouth."

Her breath shudders and, as I watch, her hand slides between her legs. She spreads her folds and the scent of her envelops me. I bite back another groan, because she starts to play with herself. There's a little nipple between her legs, just like Vektal told us of the humans, and she caresses and plays with it as I watch. My cock aches, pressed between her body and mine, but I would not move in this moment for anything. The sight of her touching herself is too lovely to interrupt.

"Tell me more," she whispers.

So I do. I go into great detail of all the things I would do to her, the things I would use my tongue to do. I have never coupled, but I have a great imagination and I let it carry my fantasies from my mind out to her ears. With each bold statement, she shudders and rubs herself a little more. She likes my words. She finds them arousing. I can feel the wetness coating her thighs and sliding onto mine, and the urge to lick it up is strong. I cannot wait to taste her.

Her body begins to tense against mine, and her movements become frantic, uneven. She is close to coming, and I cannot help myself; I lean down and press my nose into her bouncy, curly hair. "All of that will be nothing compared to what I do for you with my cock."

She cries out and her back arches, her nipples pointing at the air. I bite down on the inside of my cheek, my hands gripping at the wall with the effort not to touch her, not to scare her. She moans long and hard, and her entire body shudders.

Her splayed legs tremble, and then I feel another rush of wetness drip onto my thighs. She's come, and come hard.

Tee-fah-nee falls back against my chest and moans. "Oh, good gravy."

These words do not make sense together, but the look on her face is one of bliss, and she turns and cuddles against my chest. Daring, I slowly put my arms around her and am pleased when she doesn't pull away.

"Well, that was . . . something else," she says, breathless.

I agree. I cannot wait to do it again.

CHAPTER NINE
Tiffany

The guards are standing outside of our cell. It's cramped, and someone's legs are tangled with mine. My hip hurts from resting on the same spot for the last few days, but I don't have any other options. There's no room to move around.

An orange, two-fingered hand slides over the bars, almost caressing them. It sends a warning prickle up my spine, but there are people pressing against me on all sides and I can't move.

The door to the cage opens. We all cringe backward as one of the guards steps forward. He points a finger and sweeps it across the people in the cell.

Not me, I think. Not me.

To my horror, I'm saying the words aloud. "Not me. Not me." Oh God. They don't like it when we make noise. The orange, rough-textured hand pauses in its sweep.

The others flee from me to the opposite ends of the cage. It's not that they're cowards. I don't blame them for running. It's that we're in a hole so deep that self-preservation is the only thing that matters anymore. I cringe backward, but there's no one around me anymore. I'm all alone.

The hand points.

Not me. Not me. Please, not me.

No one's listening anymore, though. Rough hands grab my bare arms, tear at my skin. I start to scream. "Not me! Not me!"

"Tiffany—wake up."

I jerk awake, gasping. Fear drums through my body, my heart racing in my chest. I cringe back when a skinny white arm reaches out through the darkness to pat my shoulder.

"Bad dream again," Josie murmurs, voice low. "Didn't want you to have to sleep through it."

I rub my forehead. The panic still feels all too real. "Thanks."

"You okay?"

"I'll live." Sometimes I wonder if I'll ever be "okay" again. I rub my arms under my blankets, positive I can still feel rough hands gripping me, holding me down, pulling my legs apart despite my efforts.

Josie's quiet for a moment, then whispers again. "I was just wondering, you know. You haven't had any dreams in the last while and I thought you were getting better. Are the guys bugging you? I've been trying to keep them busy."

"You're doing an awesome job, really, Jo. I'm so thankful."

I can practically hear her beaming in the dark of the cave. "I'm glad. I've been working on a really big competition for the next round. It's gonna be epic."

"Great." I try to muster enthusiasm, but I don't care about the competition, because I don't want the winner.

A pause. "You sure you're okay?"

"Yeah." I know what's triggered me today. It was the heavy-petting time with Salukh. While I enjoyed it, clearly my brain hasn't unpacked all my baggage about the situation.

"You'd tell me if you weren't, right? Because you haven't had a nightmare in over a week." She emphasizes this again.

She doesn't believe me and I don't blame her. "I'm fine, really. I just . . . the only times I seem to get good sleep are with Salukh around."

I hear her blankets rustle and she sits up. "Salukh?" Her gasp is overloud in the too-quiet caves. "Oh em gee," she whispers after a moment. "Are you two doing it?"

"No! We're just friends."

"Riiiight. Friends that gather herbs together. You can't see it, but in the dark I'm putting air quotes around the words 'gathering herbs.' Because don't think I'm the only one that's noticed that there's not a lot of herbs in those baskets when you guys are gone all day."

I can't even find it in me to be embarrassed. I think of his big, lean blue body and the way his skin felt against mine. Yeah. "I do like him," I admit softly.

"So bring him in and snuggle with him for a good night's sleep," she tells me with a yawn. "I don't care. I just worry about you. It's not good to hold on to the past."

Says Josie. The woman who never thinks of anything but her happy ever after.

She settles back into her blankets and eventually falls back off to sleep. I stay awake a while longer, thinking about Salukh and our interlude at the cave earlier. It's strange, but I'm looking forward to what the next day will bring.

Maybe tomorrow will be the day that we can really, truly kiss.

Bright and early that morning, I wake up and take care of Chompy, switching out the old, dirty leathers that act as puppy pads, feeding him another bottle, and then cuddling him for a bit. When Farli wakes up, she takes over for me, and I'm a little chagrined to see that my own pet acts far more delighted to see her than me. I can't blame the little guy—she spends every waking moment with him and I just show up for feeding times.

I head over to the main fire to eat. Kira's there, cooking. Aehako's back from one of his trips, and he's seated there, baby Kae in his lap. He cuddles and coos at the fat, smiling baby, his own face wreathed in grins. It's clear that Kae got her sunny personality from her father, because Kira is more solemn than anyone I've met. They make a cute family, though, and I ignore the wistful pang of jealousy I feel. I'm happy for Kira and her happiness. I sit next to them and help myself to one of the root-cakes that Kira's cooking on a hot stone plate.

"We're sending two more over to the main caves," Aehako says as I nibble on my hot breakfast. He sticks his nose in the baby's face and laughs when Kae grabs ahold of his nose ridges.

"That's nice."

Aehako glances over at me. "Do you wish to go? I can send you and Josie. I'd like to keep more of the hunters here to support the rest of us since it might be a few more moons before we all migrate over."

I freeze. My appetite dies and I force myself to take another bite of root-cake. Go back to the main cave? I'll be free of my four annoying suitors, but . . . Salukh won't be there. And for the first time in a long, long time, I feel like I'm making a breakthrough. Spending time with him has been cathartic. I've had feelings waking up that I thought were long dead. "I . . . think I'd like to stay."

"Ah. For your games?" He winks at me. "Do you favor any of the suitors in particular?"

Oh God, he thinks it's because I like all the attention? Ugh. "They are all equal in my eyes." Because I don't want any of them.

He nods, and when Kae throws a chubby baby fist toward his face, he pretends to bite it. "I'll send two of the elders, then."

"Any word on when Harlow's going to have the stonecutter fixed?"

"I have heard nothing. If we get more signs that this will be a truly brutal season, then we will go over anyhow. It is better to starve together than separately."

"Jeez." My stomach's in knots but I force myself to eat my root-cake after hearing that. "Think it will be bad?"

"Watch your little dvisti friend," he tells me. "It will grow a darker coat if the snows will be terrible."

I'll have to pay attention.

"Tef-i-nee," a voice booms. "It is good to see your lovely face this morning!" Hassen approaches the fire, spear in hand. He puts one big foot on one of the sitting rocks and thrusts his chest out. He's a good-looking man, but gazing at him, all I can think of is Salukh with his intense eyes and the way he strokes my back.

"Hi, Hassen." I try to keep my tone warm and feign a cheeriness I don't feel.

"I am only two seeds behind Taushen," he tells me boldly. "Do you have a task I can do to gain more of your favor?"

Eep. "I'm leaving it all in Josie's hands." I give him a bright smile to make up for my noncommittal words. "She has no bias so I trust her."

"Bye-hass?" He frowns at the unfamiliar word.

"She does not lean one way or another," I correct.

"Ah." He leans in and there's a gleam in his eyes. "Shall I hunt you something to eat? Even if I cannot persuade you, I can feed you."

I notice Kira stills, her hands freezing over the root-cakes. Then she collects herself and puts another down on the hot rocks.

I feel the tension prickling at the back of my neck. "I'm good, but thank you, Hassen."

"You must let me take care of you," he insists. He gets up and moves toward me. "It is my duty as a strong male of the tribe."

"Really, I'm fine," I protest, mentally willing myself not to flinch away as he approaches. I keep smiling, but it's getting difficult to remain cheerful. He's persistent. All of them are.

As if my thoughts have summoned them, Vaza and Taushen arrive in the main cave. "I thought I heard Ti-fa-ni's sweet voice," Taushen calls. "May I feed you, beautiful human?"

I hear Aehako snort under his breath. I know they're being ridiculous. They're also pushy and I seem to freeze up whenever they start to insist.

"I am the elder," Vaza protests. "It is my job to feed Tafnee."

"I've already eaten, but I'm sure the rest of the cave would be glad for food," I say.

They look at me as if I've grown another head.

"They do not want to mate the rest of the tribe," Aehako murmurs. "A hunter feeds his mate first and foremost."

"Yes, but I don't have a mate," I say tightly. I force myself to stare at one of the root-cakes Kira's grilling as if it's the most fascinating thing on the planet. There are too many eyes on me at the moment.

"I think they noticed that," Aehako teases. He jiggles the baby on his lap and then looks up at the hovering hunters. "There is no hunting today. The elders are moving back to the main cave and we will help them prepare their goods for travel. There is much dried meat to send back, as well, and furs. I will need strong bodies to help. The hunt can wait for tomorrow."

"Then we shall spend the day around Tafnee," Vaza declares. "It will be a good day."

A good day for everyone but "Tafnee," it seems. I swallow back my sigh. So much for sneaking away with Salukh.

The day seems to last forever, and by the time I head for my cave that night, I feel as if I've been pecked to death by a horde of well-meaning suitors. Everywhere I turned, someone was there to offer to carry something, to fetch me something to eat, to get me a fur wrap in case I was cold. It's enough to make a girl crazy. Even Asha, the grumpiest woman ever, is casting me sympathetic looks.

The moment I lie down, though, I can't sleep. My mind is racing and I'm uneasy. The competition Josie has been making the men run around in has a negative side effect; they're getting more proprietary of me. As I ate dinner, I was flanked by both Vaza and Taushen. Bek frowned every time another man talked to me, even Aehako. They've been giving me more room and the last week has been wonderful, but now I'm starting to worry what I've bought into.

I knew the competition was a bad idea all along, but I've been so low on options. My hands clench in my furs and I turn over repeatedly.

Josie mumbles in her furs, then slaps one of her furry pillows over her ear. "You're driving me crazy, Tiff. Just go get your snuggle bunny already. I need to sleep." She pulls the blankets higher over her head until she looks like nothing but a fur caterpillar.

I consider her words. I missed Salukh today, weirdly enough. He was around, but he was busy helping the others move their gear, lashing cords and packing sleds. And of course, my suitors were hanging all over me, so he didn't venture too near. Every time I looked up, though, he was watching me with that intense gaze. As if he was allowing them to fawn over me but he would step in if things got out of hand.

As if I were his.

A delicious shiver moves through me at the thought. I sit up and peek over at Josie's nest of blankets. She's just a small lump in the darkness, her pallet set across the cave from mine. I could sneak Salukh in and he could hold me while I sleep. It's a selfish thought, but . . . somehow I think he'd be fine with it.

I slide out of my blankets and pick up my fur cloak. My long, threadbare cotton sleep shirt is the only thing I have left from before, back on Earth. There are holes along the collar and the sleeves, patches in several places, and my panties are long gone, but I still wear the shirt to sleep in. Maybe it's a bad idea because of old memories, but I can't bring myself to part with it. It's practically indecent now, but feels good against my skin. I wrap the cloak around my body and move to the mouth of the cave, peeking over the leather privacy screen that acts as a door.

The central community fire has burned low, and it's quiet out in the main cavern. It's late and Salukh has probably already gone to sleep. I should turn around and head back to my own furs and try to rest.

Instead, I pad out into the main cavern and move to the firepit, staring down at the glowing orange coals. If I can't sleep, I'll just be out here again anyhow. Kira's left her drinking canteen out by the fire, likely distracted by her new baby. I pick it up and it sloshes, still half-full. I pull off the stopper and lift it to my lips.

As I do, I see a pair of blue eyes shining out in the darkness.

My body freezes, and I drop the water bladder. Dark images immediately flash through my mind. *Not me. Not me.*

A big, horned form steps forward, blue chest without his normal vest, tail twitching against one legging-clad thigh. Salukh. Shocked relief spirals through me and I stagger. My body's trembling, my mind gone back to that terrible place. Did I think I was unsettled before? I'm practically crawling out of my skin now.

Salukh moves to my side and hitches my cloak around my shoulders from where it's fallen. "Careful," he murmurs in a low voice. "You're near to falling into the fire."

Am I? I can't stop shaking. My fingers pluck at the cloak, but I can't seem to grip it. I'm freaking out. I should calm myself, pick up Kira's waterskin, which is leaking its contents all over the cold stone floor, but I can't move.

His big, warm hand caresses my cheek. Suede knuckles trace my jaw. "Tee-fah-nee? Are you well?"

His touch is oddly comforting. I lean into it, and then push forward until I'm pressing my cheek to his bare chest. So warm. So strong. So safe. "Will you come hold me while I sleep?"

Salukh's body tenses, and then he strokes my back. "Of course."

I'm so relieved. I take his hand in mine and pull him back toward my cave. I won't have to face the night alone. I do feel a bit guilty for sneaking a guy back to my bed. Feels a bit like when I was growing up back on my aunt's farm and I'd sneak a boy into my room. Of course, that boy would have expected to get laid. Salukh doesn't expect that of me. He just wants me to be comforted.

I put the privacy screen in place as Salukh walks in after me, and then peer over at Josie's furs. She's moved to the far side of the cave, her face to the wall. She's such an awesome friend. She's giving us as much privacy as she can, and I love her for it. I lead Salukh over to my pallet of furs and sink down. He immediately climbs in next to me and stretches his big body out. He's also taking up most of the bed, but I can't find it in me to care. I just like that he's here.

I pull my cloak off and toss it aside, then snuggle up next to him. My cheek goes to his chest and I give a small sigh of contentment. His big form chases the shadows away.

He presses his mouth to my brow and his arms go around me. One big hand starts to stroke my back, and I slide an arm around his torso. My body is hugged against his, and oh, God, it feels amazing. I'm warm and safe, and all of my anxiety feels as if it's slipping away. If his tail is twitching slightly, I can ignore it. It doesn't spoil the utter perfection of having him here against me.

"Thank you," I whisper.

"You do not need to thank me," he murmurs into my ear, hot breath tickling my skin. "I find great pleasure in holding you."

Yeah, well, he isn't the only one. I find great pleasure in him holding me, too.

"Are you well?" His hand moves to my hair and he brushes my curls back from my face. "You seemed nervous all day."

"Just a lot of unwanted attention," I tell him. I don't want to think about it anymore, though. I just want to relax and forget about it until tomorrow, when I have to face reality again. I nestle in against him and press my body closer to his.

His hand slides up and down my spine, caressing me. He's just touching me and holding me. It feels so good that a small sigh escapes me and I find myself stroking his skin in response. My fingers glide over the raised-up ridges along his arm, and then over the taut muscles. His skin is velvety soft, but the body underneath is so firm and so perfect it's like he's been hewn from stone.

I can't stop touching him . . . and I don't want to. I'm enjoying exploring his body, because he feels safe. I know that Salukh would never hurt me. He would never lose control and attack me. To him, I'm a person and a friend. To the aliens that kidnapped me, I was just spare cargo. My life didn't matter.

To Taushen, Hassen, Vaza, and Bek, I'm not really a person, either. I'm a trophy, a prize to be won. None of them have shown any interest in me as a person. They don't know that I have fun with the leather-making or that I want to grow crops.

No one has ever asked me about my childhood, or what I think about anything. I'm pretty and I'm available, and that's all they need to know.

But Salukh is different. When he looks at me . . . it's like no one else in the world exists. And every time he looks at me that way, it seems to pierce me right to my soul. Even now I shiver, just thinking about his intense gaze resting on me, like he wants to take me back to his furs and devour me in dirty, naughty ways.

And for the first time in what feels like forever, the thought of something like that happening doesn't freak me out. Instead, I'm curious and aroused at the thought of what sex with Salukh might be like.

To be fair, I should probably start with kisses, though. Baby steps.

He rubs my shoulders vigorously and tightens the furs around us. "You are trembling."

"Just thinking." His chest is so close to my lips I could practically brush them against him. The thought is tempting.

"You should stop doing that."

A small laugh escapes me. He made a joke? Cute, cute man. Cute alien. "Less thinking and more doing?"

"If you like."

I can feel arousal strumming through my body, aided by the fact that his big, warm, delicious form is draped over me. That his bare chest is rubbing against my nightgown and causing the most aggravating—and wonderful—friction against my nipples when he moves.

Less thinking and more doing? He's right. I need to get out of my own head and stop worrying about everything and start living again.

His scent is enveloping me and it's intoxicating. The strange, savage planet that is now my home feels very far away at the moment. There's only me, Salukh, and my furs.

Well, and Josie on the other side of the cave. I still, listening for the sound of even breathing. When she gives a soft snore, a wave of relief rushes through me. We're really alone, he and I.

My hand slides over his chest. I feel him stiffen against me, and when I press my palm over the ridged, plated section in the center of his chest, I can feel his heart thumping fast.

Less thinking. More doing.

I slide my hand lower and let my fingers encircle his cock.

He goes utterly still against me. I look up at him and his blue eyes are blazing into mine, the intensity so heated that it makes me want to do even more to him, just to get more of a reaction.

"What is it you do, Tee-fah-nee?"

"I want you to kiss me," I whisper to him. "I want to try again."

"You want my mouth?" He makes a soft, strangled noise. "It is not my mouth you are holding."

Another giggle threatens to escape me. "I know what I'm holding." Boy, do I know. I've been thinking about our mutual masturbation time a lot over the last week. I remember the way his glorious body looked, all muscle and blue suede, and I remember distinctly the rather enormous size of his cock. I remember the vein that traced along the side, the way it was ridged, and the way he reacted when he touched his own spur.

And I want to do all of that for him.

But first, I want to kiss him. I hope I won't freak out. I close my eyes, bracing myself, because a lot of my bad memories on the ship were of . . . things that happened with my mouth. I don't like to think about those. I need new memories, and Salukh's tongue might just be the prescription I need . . .

Unless I start crying again. That would be bad.

But I can't live like this forever. And tonight, I'm feeling good. Desire is humming through my veins, my nipples are hard, and I can feel myself getting wet between my legs. If there's ever a time to get over my fear of kissing, it's tonight. Now.

My hand slides over his cock, the hard, erect outline pressing against the leather of his pants. "I think I want to try kissing again," I tell him.

He nods slowly but doesn't move. He's letting me take the lead. I like that. It's more of me giving than something being taken. Tonight, I want to give him all kinds of enjoyment.

Reluctantly, I pull my hand away from his cock and put it back on his chest. I shimmy up a bit higher, since he's seven feet tall and our faces don't quite match up at this angle. When I'm close enough, I study his face in the darkness. Other than the intense glow of his eyes, I can barely make out a nose and horns. The rest is lost in shadow.

My fingers slide to his face, and I trace his jaw. He's breathing heavily, but his gaze on me is calm. Patient. I let my fingertips move over his mouth, and brush over his lips. His mouth feels softer and more pleasant than it looks in the daylight. I almost hope he'll nip at one of my exploring fingers, but he's utterly still. He's letting me take control.

So I do. I gently press my mouth to his and tense, waiting. Waiting for the onslaught of awful memories to ruin this moment, for the bile to rush up in my throat. The memories creep in, and as I push my mouth against his, it becomes harder to keep them at bay. I want this to work so desperately, but I'm not quite there yet.

Then, his hand gently cups my cheek and he strokes it with his thumb.

Just one small move, but it reminds me that I'm here with him. I'm safe, and I'm with Salukh. It's his mouth under mine. And I'm giving instead of being taken from.

The memories fade, and then it's just Salukh, his warm body hard against mine, his scent in my nose and his thick hair brushing against my arm. His mouth is soft, his lips together. I kiss him gently, just to prove to myself that I can. He's got a pleasant taste to him—a bit smoky like fire, a bit spicy and musky like his scent. And I want more. I kiss his mouth over and over, small, gentle kisses that let me play without asking for more than I'm willing to give.

All the while, his thumb brushes my cheek, caressing me, reminding me that he's here, and this is good.

My kisses slowly grow more urgent, and now, when I kiss his mouth, my tongue strokes against the seam of his lips, encouraging him to open for me. It takes a few brushes of my tongue to let him know what I'm wanting, and then he gives me more. My tongue teases into his mouth, bolder than I feel. This is a big step, the next rung on the ladder back to normalcy.

His tongue rubs against mine in response, and I feel the ridges on it drag against my own tongue.

I pull away, surprised. Why do I always forget that the sakhui seem to be ridged everywhere? I've seen just how *everywhere* those ridges are. Yet the stroke of his tongue against mine felt startling.

"Soft," he murmurs and nuzzles my nose.

"Hmm?"

"You're so soft everywhere," he tells me. "Your little tongue especially. I like it."

It's oddly flattering to hear that. I smile and lean in to kiss him again, letting my "soft little tongue" lead the way. I slick it back into his mouth, and this time, when his tongue caresses mine, I'm not startled. The drag of those ridges against my smooth tongue makes happy little prickles move over my body, and soon I'm kissing him not because I feel like I have to but because I'm into it.

I love kissing Salukh, I decide somewhere between all the lust-hazed kisses. I love his mouth. I love the way he lets me take the lead. I love the taste of him and the teasing flicks of his tongue.

I decide I really, really like the tongue.

We kiss endlessly, our mouths meshing together in gentle, easy caresses. There's no hurry in any of this, no rush to move on to better things. There's only the pure enjoyment of mouth to mouth, our noses occasionally bumping. After a time, I grow dissatisfied with just kissing his lips. I want more of him.

Heck, I want all of him. I'm greedy.

So I lift my mouth and instead of pressing my next kiss to his lips, I change the angle and gently nip at his strong chin. I can feel the tremor that rocks through him in response, and it encourages me to do more. To tease more. To explore more.

My hands slide to the thick mass of his hair. It reminds me a bit of a horse's mane back on Earth—thick and a bit coarse, but still beautiful in its own way. I brush it aside to expose one ear, and give it a cautious lick. No matter how sexy I find him, he's not human, and maybe his ears aren't erogenous zones like they are to us.

His body stiffens and his hands fall away from me.

I back up a little, mindful of his big, powerful horns. "Was . . . was that bad?"

"No," he rasps, and he reaches up to caress my cheek again. "It was too good. I did not trust myself not to grab you and scare you."

Oh. I nod in understanding. "Then, can I do it again?"

"If you like."

"Did *you* like?"

He nods slowly, and his hand glides over my shoulder, then down my arm. Then, it moves around my waist and he pulls me back down against him.

All righty, then. He likes it. I bury my hands in his wonderful hair again and lean in to nibble on his earlobe. His ear, like the rest of him, is bigger than I anticipate, but the lobe feels soft and human enough. My teeth gently scrape over the skin, and then I move my tongue over it.

His face presses up against my shoulder and the muffled moan that escapes him is still loud enough to make me freeze. I sit up, clap a hand over his mouth, and look over at Josie. After a moment, it becomes clear that she's still asleep, and I relax.

"I am sorry," Salukh whispers. "I will control myself better."

I trace my fingers over his mouth again. "I kinda like you out of control . . . but let's not wake her up." If Josie hears us making out, not only will I be mortified, but the spell will be broken.

I want things to keep going.

When I'm assured Josie's still asleep, I lean in and lick his ear again, exploring its shape with the tip of my tongue. To my amusement, it's ridged at the top of the shell. I drag my tongue over it and am pleased when he gives another muffled gasp against my shoulder. He's definitely sensitive here. I do my best to torture him, using my tongue and licking and sucking at the sensitive bit of flesh. His fingers dig into my nightgown and he holds me tight against him, but it doesn't bother me. I like it. I like that he's silently giving me all these messages about how much I'm turning him on.

I'm not content with stopping at his ear, though. I kiss down his neck, loving how warm his skin is. I move down his shoulder and press a hand there, a silent request for him to roll onto his back. He doesn't hesitate, and then that big, beautiful body is spread out for me to touch and lick at my leisure. Sigh. I press kisses down his chest, briefly pausing at his nipples before remembering that they're not sensitive. I continue to his belly button and lick it, and then start to descend lower.

He grabs my arm, his eyes wide. There's a startled look on his face and he tugs me back closer to him to whisper in my ear, "What is it you do, Tee-fah-nee?"

"Oral?"

He tilts his head. "I do not understand this word."

"This," I say, tapping my lip. "Goes down here." And I reach down and brush my fingers over his cock.

I hear him suck in a breath. "Why would you do that?"

"Why wouldn't I? Don't men do that for their mates here?" If not, then get me off this planet ASAP.

"That is different. A male must please his woman."

Er, okay. "What if I want to please my man?"

His eyes take on that intense look again. His thumb traces my lower lip. "Am I yours, then?"

Oh boy. I'm not ready to answer that. "At the moment, you are."

Salukh's gaze narrows imperceptibly and he nods.

The moment's ruined, though. Now I feel like if I put my mouth on him, he'll think we're married. Or he'll try to go down on me. And while I'd normally say yes please, this was just supposed to be light, fun petting. Nothing more. All of that would take things to another level and I'm not sure I'm ready for that level.

I lean in and kiss him again, and fall in love with his wonderful mouth all over again. It is such a pleasure to kiss him. My horrible memories are gone, and all that's in the moment is Salukh's scorchingly hot mouth against mine, his tongue slicking against my own. I slide back into the moment and change my game plan.

Maybe we're not ready for oral yet, but it doesn't mean that the night has to end like this.

My hand goes back to his cock and I stroke him through his leggings again. He feels extremely hard, his girth impossibly thick. It makes me feel achy deep inside just to imagine that big length pushing into me. A small sigh escapes me and I rub him through the leather. "I like this."

"Do you?" His voice is so low it's practically a growl, and it makes my nipples tighten to hear it.

I nod and lean in to kiss him again, my lips playing against his. "I'm going to take it out and play with it."

He sucks in a breath and I feel a tremor pass through his body. Salukh likes that thought more than he's trying to let on. My fingers find the laces that hold the waistband of his leggings up and I pull the knot until it comes loose. There's a flap of decorative fabric over the groin and I push that aside, and then his cock is free.

His skin is scorching hot now that he's free from the leggings, and his body has gone entirely still as my hand explores his length. There's pre-cum all over the tip of his cock and I wet the pads of my fingers on the silky liquid, moving it along the crown.

Salukh closes his eyes, the bright glow going temporarily dim. Interesting. Now it just feels like me and his cock here, having playtime. I stifle my chuckle of amusement and slide my fingers down his length. I rub along the ridges, admiring the textures and imagining how that would feel inside a woman. I move down to his balls, caressing them. It feels strange to feel a sac so hairless and so large at the same time, but it's just another reminder that I'm not in Kansas anymore. His spur is another reminder that Things Are Different, and I spend a little time exploring that aspect of his anatomy with my fingers, too. It's hard and almost bonelike, but I don't see the point of one. Then again, I don't see the point of a lot of anatomy.

When I've teased his skin and explored all of him by touch, I move back to his length and curl my fingers around the root of his cock. He's so big and thick I can't even touch my fingertips on the other side when I encircle him. I've never had sex with someone that big, and while part of me thinks it might not be fun, I haven't heard a single complaint from any of the other mated women. That tells me that there's nothing to be afraid of, size-wise. I grip him tight and lean in to kiss him again.

This time when my lips brush against his, he groans into my mouth and his cock jerks against my hand. It's a sign that he's not as impassive as he's trying to pretend, and I love it. With my hand tight around him, I stroke his cock, and I stroke it hard.

He breaks. A moment later, Salukh shoves his head, horns and all, to my shoulder. He muffles his face against me as he thrusts into my hand. I'm shocked by the sudden movement, but titillated as well, and I stroke him again, and again. His hips buck against my hand and he's thrusting his cock into the circle of my fingers more rapidly than I could ever pump him, and I'm getting aroused at just how wild the touching has made him. His face presses against my breast, as if he can't trust himself to be silent, and his cock pumps against the circle of my fingers. Then his hand grips mine and he's using my hand to work himself over.

And okay, that is sexy as hell. I can feel my pussy getting wetter and wetter as he fucks my fist, his body frantic against mine.

Then it's over—hot, creamy seed spills over my fingers and onto my arm. It splatters my thighs and he clenches against my chest, groaning so loud that I'm positive Josie's going to wake up and see me covered in Salukh's come. With my other hand, I stroke the hair back from his face, pressing kisses to the skin I can reach. I feel buzzy and pleasant, and I'm happy I was able to give him this satisfaction. He came and came hard, all because of my touch.

He nuzzles my neck, breathing hard. "Never have I felt so lucky."

I smile into the darkness. "I wanted to make you feel good."

"I could scale mountains right now," he whispers into my ear. "Except it would mean leaving your bed."

I know the feeling. I don't want him to leave, either, not when I'm feeling good and relaxed. I didn't come, but I'm basking in the fact that he did. No bad memories is enough for me.

"Do you have a cloth to clean up?" he murmurs.

Oh. I don't know that I do. Not close, and leaving bed might mean waking Josie up. I wasn't anticipating spending my bedtime hours this way. After a moment's thought, I pull at my nightgown and tug it over my head, then use it to mop up my hand and his stomach. When he's cleaned off, I slide back into his arms, and I jerk in surprise when my hard nipples brush against his chest, because it feels entirely too good. Maybe I'm not as relaxed as I thought, because my pulse starts pounding again.

He pulls me against him and his hands slide over my bare back, and it feels deliciously close to being petted. I have to stifle a groan of my own, and resist the urge to straddle his leg and rub myself off. Salukh nuzzles me, his nose bumping against mine. "May I touch you?" he whispers. "Like you did me?"

My nails dig into his arms and it's all I can do to keep from whimpering aloud. I nod, and in case he doesn't see that in the dark, I whisper a yes.

The big hands stop sliding over my back. He pulls me against him, until I'm leaning against his chest. Then his hand goes to my breast and he caresses it. His fingers tease my nipples, and they're already so tight and aching that I want to crawl out of my skin.

This time, I'm the one hiding my face to muffle my sounds. I burrow against his neck, and that only makes things worse because his thick, gorgeous hair slides against my skin and the scent of him is stronger here. I can't help but lick at his throat even as he teases my nipples. I hook a leg over his hip and try to drag his thigh against me, but his body is too long. Dammit.

Salukh must sense my need, because his hand leaves my breast and slides down my belly. His movements are slow, cautious, in case I panic and push him away. I'm not about to, though. I'm ready for him to move down, down, down, and I'm practically quivering with tension by the time his fingers brush the curls of my sex. Hell, I'm ready to mount his hand.

But when he finally touches me—and God, it feels like forever—he's so, so gentle that tears spring to my eyes. When was the last time that someone touched me like I'm the finest thing they've ever seen? Like I'm a goddess to be worshipped? It makes me want to weep because I feel so cherished.

His fingers feel huge as he lightly explores my folds. I'm so wet that I can hear the sounds my body is making, and I should want to cringe with embarrassment, but oddly enough, I feel no shame with him. Everything is a wonder. When he lifts his hand to his mouth and sucks on his fingers, I realize he's tasting me. Another bolt of lust sears through my body, and I grab his hand from his lips and push it back toward my pussy, insistent.

"Tee-fah-nee," he breathes, and then his fingers glide over my clit, and I nearly come off the furs with the intensity of that small touch. I want him to push into me with his fingers, but he only circles my clit, dragging my wetness over the sensitive skin. I realize he's mimicking what I did when I touched myself, and I have to bite down on his shoulder to keep from moaning aloud. I'm so wet. I'm so aroused.

I'm about to come so, so hard.

It doesn't take long. I rock my hips, pushing against his

fingers as he caresses my clit and clinging to him like a koala as my body ratchets up into an orgasm. When I explode, it's almost impossible to do it in silence, and I end up making a loud, choking gasp as I cream and more wetness coats his hand. He inhales sharply and then his hand goes to his mouth again.

He can't get enough of me, that sexy beast.

Josie snorts in her sleep and then rolls over. I freeze, holding on to Salukh, but she doesn't wake up. Eventually I relax, and he tucks the blankets around my body and pulls me close against him.

"You have given me a gift this night, Tee-fah-nee," he whispers, barely audible. "I shall never forget."

Me, either. Tonight seems to be imprinted into my brain, and I welcome it. I'd love for Salukh to crowd out all of the bad memories left behind until there's nothing but gorgeous blue alien in my brain.

This time, when I fall asleep, there are no shadows. No bad dreams. Just blue skin and warm bodies.

CHAPTER TEN
Salukh

Now, I tell my khui. *Claim her now. Resonate. We will take her as ours and put my kit inside her.*

But my cursed khui is utterly silent, the traitor. Surely it wants the same thing I do? I feel the need to take Tee-fah-nee as my own like I need the air to breathe, or water to drink. She is mine, and I want the world to know it. I want to see her rounded with my kit. I want her in my furs every night for the rest of our lives, putting her small, cold human feet against my legs like she is right now.

This is all I have ever wanted. Yet my khui denies me. For a brief, shining moment, I hate it. I hate that it will not recognize her as mine and resonate. My arms tighten around her and I force myself to breathe deep. I must be calm. Tee-fah-nee will be mine in time. If not now, then soon. I merely have to wait for her khui to sing to mine, or mine to hers. It will happen.

Reluctantly, I rise from her furs. The morning is coming, and I must slip out of her cave and back into my own before anyone sees. She does not want questions, and I do not wish trouble upon her. There will come a day when I can announce proudly to the tribe that she is mine, and if it clenches in my gut that I must sneak away, I will swallow it down for her sake.

I tie the laces of my leggings again, my cock hardening as I think about last night, and the way Tee-fah-nee moved all over me, her mouth on my skin. Being with her has exceeded all of my expectations. I know what is done in the furs—I have watched others claim their mates. Privacy is impossible with such crowded caves. But the humans seem to have different ideas, and it explains several of the wide grins of the mated men. I look forward to exploring more things with Tee-fah-nee.

I'm still caught up in thoughts of her when I push aside the privacy screen covering their cave and enter the main cavern. Maybe that's why I don't realize that Hassen is by the central firepit until he throws down the spear he's sharpening and lunges for me.

"Betrayer!" he snarls and knocks me to the ground. "She belongs to me!"

A rush of emotions sweeps through me at his words. I briefly understand his anger. To him, I am going behind his back and stealing the female he is pursuing. But my own possessive need sweeps through me, overpowering all other thoughts.

Tee-fah-nee is mine. No one else will touch her but me. No one else will drink the sweet juice from her cunt but me. All of her belongs to me. She is *my* mate.

Hassen's body slams into mine and he reaches for one of my horns, to twist it and make me yield. Never. I am stronger than he is, and I thrust him aside with a straight arm and then roll to my feet. "You have no claim on her."

He snarls at me and lowers his head, pointing his horns in my direction. It's a sign of aggression. "She will be mine and you are trying to steal her from under my nose!"

"*She is not yours.*" I shout the words and fling myself forward, my horns crashing into his. We buck against each other, feet scuffing on the rock floor. Our arms lock together and we grapple, trying to get the upper hand. I will never give up, though. Tee-fah-nee is mine, and losing to him is not an option.

His foot kicks mine out from under me, and I drop to a knee. A moment later he pounces on me again, and then we roll once more, until I have the upper hand. I sit on his chest, my hand gripping a handful of his hair as he snarls up at me.

"Stop!"

I dimly hear Aehako's voice over the blood rushing through my ears. The cave seems to be full of sound now, despite the early hour. There are cries and angry shouts and loud gasps that filter in over the pounding of my heart.

An angry hand grabs one of my horns and wrenches me back. Aehako glares down at me. "Cease this!"

I fling his hand off and slowly get to my feet. The cavern is full of people, most of them newly risen from sleep. Tee-fah-nee is one, and she's looking at me with horror and confusion as I loom over Hassen. Nearby, Taushen and Vaza talk in low voices, anger on their faces. Bek looks as if he's ready to lunge into the fight and join Hassen to bring me down.

This is . . . not right. I did not start it, but I should not continue it.

"What is going on with you?" Aehako shouts, glaring at both myself and Hassen. "You brawl like two ill-behaved kits!"

I look over at Tee-fah-nee. She's now flanked by Aehako's mate, Kira, and Jo-see. All three women look shocked at the display, and I'm not surprised. It's not often that the males of the tribe fight. I refuse to feel ashamed, though. I will fight for my mate.

Hassen gets to his feet slowly, glaring hate at me. He wipes a bit of blood from the corner of his mouth, and I am shocked to see it. I did not even realize I had struck him. "I started the fight."

"Why?" Aehako steps between us, as if we will claw at each other again.

"Because I found him emerging from Tef-i-nee's furs!" Hassen's nostrils flare with anger and his fists clench. "He thinks to steal her while we work on our courting competition!"

Bek growls low in his throat nearby.

Aehako points at him and shakes his head. "Do not even consider it." He looks at me, and there is reproach in his normally laughing eyes. "Is this true?"

I straighten. "She is my mate."

More angry growls.

Aehako's brows rise. "Did you resonate?"

"Not yet."

He gives me an exasperated look. "Then you have both chosen to be pleasure mates and the contest should end?"

I say nothing. I have not declared my thoughts to Tee-fah-nee, and I'm ashamed I did so just now.

"Well?" Aehako looks past me over to the humans. "Do you claim this one as your pleasure mate until one of you resonates to another?"

My body tenses, and I want to hear the words spill forth from her mouth. I want her to claim me as her own. I want to show the others that she cares for me as I do for her. That the bond between us is real.

But Tee-fah-nee is frozen in place. Her entire body is trembling, and she clutches the furs to her shoulders. Her normally dusky face is bleached pale, and her nervous gaze flicks back and forth between all of the angry men.

She doesn't look at me and my heart sinks. She will not claim me this day, then.

Aehako claps me on my shoulder. "That is your answer, my friend. Any claim to her is in your mind. If you want her favor, it is only fair that you join the competition with the others, or we call the entire thing off."

My jaw clenches, but I force myself to nod. "Then I will join the competition."

"Bah," Hassen says. He throws his hands in the air and stalks away to his furs. "This is madness! All of this competition and not an end to be had."

"He speaks truth," Aehako says, and casts a stern glance over at the humans. "We are not familiar with your ways, but surely there must be an end to the game at some point?"

"O-one more round," Jo-see stammers. "One big round and then the winner will be chosen."

"Then that solves it." Aehako nods at me. "No more fighting. Understand?"

I understand. I will need all of my strength and skill to best the others, because they will all now be coming after me.

Tiffany

I hide in my cave all day.

I'm not ashamed of what I did with Salukh. I feel good about it. But I'm ashamed that we got caught. That the others stared at me with such anger and reproach, and I can't blame them. I've been making them run through hoops—courtesy of Josie's competition—to get my "favor" and then I take another guy to bed? Of course they freak out. The sa-khui aren't judgy people, and I suspect if I'd have let Hassen or another into my furs, they wouldn't have batted an eye. It's that Salukh wasn't even competing for me that made the other men upset.

Not that Salukh is safe anymore, either.

I didn't speak up to claim him. How can I, when resonance effectively negates any sort of relationship? And there's no reason why I haven't resonated yet, which means it's just a matter of time. How can I claim him and then abandon him?

There's a more cowardly reason behind my silence, though. I looked at my suitors—Hassen, Bek, Vaza, and Taushen—and saw anger in their faces. It frightened me. I spiraled right back to that awful mental state of fear, and couldn't act. All I could think about was the fight between Hassen and Salukh, and how the spurned males would act toward me after making them do the competition. They'd hate me . . . or worse. And while I haven't seen violence against women so far? I've seen enough "firsts" with the human-sa-khui inbreeding that I don't want to be the first case of a woman taken against her will. These men are hard up as it is. To come this close to "getting" a girl and then someone else swoops in? It could break even a stable mind.

So I hide like a coward and hate myself for doing so. I want to be brave. I want to more than anything. But every time I think about leaving my cave and speaking up, my body freezes in terror and I can't breathe.

In the end, I say nothing.

Josie doesn't offer any sort of recrimination, though. She's a good friend. She goes out to the central fire and gets me breakfast when I'm too afraid to go and get my own. She heads off with Aehako in the afternoon to go over the rest of the "competition" because he wants to see it done—and me selecting a winner—to keep the tribe harmony.

I nap in my furs, but even that makes me sad because they still smell faintly of Salukh's warm, spicy skin and I wonder if I've ruined everything. He says he'll fight for me with the others, but will he be upset if he loses? Will the others freak out if he wins? What am I going to do if he doesn't win? The others have more of the seeds that Josie's been handing out as prizes. The gnawing knot in the pit of my stomach only grows worse.

"Knock knock," calls Kira, interrupting my self-flagellating thoughts. "Can I come in?"

I sit up in my furs and adjust my clothing. "Sure. Come on in."

She ducks into the cave a moment later, baby in her arms. "I see Farli's watching over Chompy."

"Again. Yup." Just another thing I feel guilty about, though I do feel less guilt over that aspect because Farli gets such pleasure from taking care of the small dvisti.

"I hadn't seen you all day and thought I'd stop by and see how you were doing." Her smile is faint.

"I'm doing terrible, thanks for asking." I get up and pull out an overstuffed pillow for her to sit on, and place it across from the firepit. "How about you?"

"Oh, I'm fine. A little sleep deprived, but good overall." She sits down in one fluid motion and crosses her legs on the pillow, all without disturbing the baby cradled in her arms. "But I didn't come here to talk about me."

"Yeah, I figured." I give her a half smile and sit back down in my blankets again. "Aehako mad?"

"Not at you. He's furious the men started a fight, though. He likes to keep the peace." She pulls the furs back from Kae's round little face and glances over at me. "A lot of it has to do with the competition."

I nod glumly. I hate that I'm the problem. I like to fly under the radar, to skate by attention. Lately it seems I can't do that at all. I don't blame Aehako for stepping in and laying down the law, though. He's not the chief—that's Vektal, Georgie's mate—but while we live in the South Cave, he's our leader. And it's hard to piss off easygoing, smiling Aehako, which means that things are worse than I think. Greaaat. "In retrospect, the competition was probably a stupid idea. We just didn't know what to do to get them off my back."

"Well, sleeping with someone else probably wasn't the way to do it."

Ouch. "Thanks."

"Sorry." She sighs. "I'm not judging, I'm really not, Tiff. But I don't understand. Why make everyone compete for your attention if you don't want any of them?"

I pull my blankets over my shoulders and stare at the small fire in our cave. Probably needs another dung chip added to it but I can't bring myself to get up. I shrug my shoulders. I never told Kira that I was raped by the aliens—the basketball heads. I told everyone that they'd just examined me on a medical table. No more. Backtracking now seems like a lot of work and talking about things I don't ever want to think about again. "I didn't know how to say no to them."

The words sound lame even as they leave my mouth.

"So say no now!" Kira exclaims. "Tell them you've picked Salukh and call everything off."

I can't, though. I'm terrified of what their anger might be like. What if I declare that I want Salukh, and then two days later, I resonate to someone like Bek? He won't be kind and understanding, and I'll be stuck with him, having his babies. It'd be a nightmare scenario.

However bad things are, I'm safer at the moment by taking no action.

Kira sighs again. She reaches out and touches my knee. "You can talk to me."

"It's hard to explain." *My head's a mess and I'm living in terror. I want to be like Josie, who only looks ahead, never behind.*

"Then you won't call it off?"

I'm silent.

"Then you have to live with the consequences, Tiff."

Like I don't already know that?

CHAPTER ELEVEN
Tiffany

I sleep in my furs alone that evening, and the nightmares return. Nightmares of being grabbed and held down, nightmares of men pushing me to do things against my will. This time, instead of the aliens, they have familiar faces—Vaza and Taushen. I wake up in a cold sweat, shuddering, and spend the rest of the night staring at the embers of the fire and wishing I wasn't such a coward.

Josie wakes me up the next morning. "You sleeping in?"

"I'm not now." I rub the sleep out of my eyes and I feel as if I've been stomped on. Ugh. "What's up?"

"We're about to start the final round and Aehako wants you there."

Ugh. I'll have to face my actions after all. "All right."

"Dress warm, we're going outside."

I nod and get dressed in my warm layers. Time to face the firing squad. Josie remains at my side, and I'm grateful for her presence. As we pass through the main cavern, I notice it's rather empty, and I get a funny feeling in the pit of my stomach.

The funny feeling continues when we trek out into the snow and I notice it's churned up from many booted feet heading out before us.

I'm not surprised when we follow the cliff wall and I see everyone's waiting for us out in the snow. Kira, Farli, the elders, even grumpy Haeden. The five men are off to one side, Salukh standing proudly at the end of the line. He gives me another devouring gaze and I feel like a jerk for letting him down. I should speak up, call the whole thing off.

Then I look over at the other four men. They're casting me angry, betrayed looks, and my bravado fails. Any protest I want to make dies in my throat. I want to race back to the safety of my cave, but Josie puts an arm around my waist and leads me to stand next to Aehako off to one side.

"This is the final round of the competition," Josie declares. "Let's have a quick seed count update before we start, shall we? Hassen, how many?"

Hassen steps forward and shoots me a burning look. "Three."

Taushen is next. His smile is wide and proud. "Four."

Vaza moves up next. "One."

Then Bek. "One."

I'm not surprised that Hassen is doing well, but I am a little surprised that wiry, excitable Taushen is in the lead. I smile to try and ward off the unhappy looks being cast in my direction, like I'm pleased with the results.

Salukh steps forward. "None."

There's an awkward silence. I glance away, because I can't look over and see the unspoken demand in his eyes. I know what he wants me to do. I'm just so afraid.

Josie speaks again. "Today's contest is split into four parts, and that means there will be four seeds up for grabs. Whoever ends up with the most seeds at the end of the day will be the winner. If there is a tie, we'll hold one final competition between the two as a tiebreaker."

Clever Josie. She's giving Salukh a chance to catch up. I could hug her right about now.

"And then after this," Aehako interrupts, stepping forward to the center of the group. He casts a stern look at the men. "No more fighting over her attention."

"I just want to clarify that this contest is just to escort Tiffany to the elders' cave," Josie protests. "Not to win her hand in marriage."

Off to one side, I hear an irritated snort that sounds as if it's coming from Haeden. He intensely dislikes Josie, and I have no idea why.

She scowls over in his direction and then looks back at the men who are competing. "After this, you will have shown off all your skills. She will know of your prowess as hunters and providers. If Tiffany wants a guy's attention, she'll come to you. Understand?"

Silence.

"It is understood," Aehako answers on their behalf. He crosses his arms over his brawny chest and gazes over at me and Josie. "Let us proceed."

"All right," Josie says, and steps forward. "Like I said, this last competition is split into four parts. There's one for brains." She ticks off a finger, then another. "Brawn. Talent. The last one is for effort, and the tribe itself will vote on who has put in the most effort for the day. And we're going to go ahead and start with brains. That's why we're standing out here next to the cliff." She turns and points up.

I turn to look at what she's pointing at, and so does everyone else. There are five specks of color high on the cliff, a bright red that I didn't notice until now.

"Up there are five bone medallions that have been dyed red so you can see them. All five medallions are the same, and all five are hanging several feet down from the lip of the cliff. Your job is to get one medallion down and bring it back to me. The first one to place a medallion in my hands gets a seed to add to their count."

I eye the sheer cliff with more than a bit of trepidation. Already I can see the men sizing up the climb, and I worry—it's extremely steep and there aren't a lot of handholds. Climbing up will be extremely dangerous, and I don't want anyone to fall and hurt themselves. I cling to Kira's arm, panicking at the thought. The healer's a half a day away in the other caves. What if Salukh gets hurt? What if someone pushes him off the cliff?

"There's only one rule—you cannot climb the cliff wall," Josie adds. "Everything else is fair game."

I'm relieved to hear it. I clutch Kira's arm a little less tightly now, relaxing.

"Everyone ready?" Josie raises a hand in the air, and all five men tense. Then, she brings her arm down. "Begin!"

The men pause, and I can see the wheels turning in their heads. Salukh glances over at me, and our eyes make contact. He's got that intense look on his face that tells me he's going to give it his all, and I want to shout encouragement to him.

Before I can say anything, though, he turns and begins a sprint along the cliff. I'm confused at first, and then as two other men—Vaza and Bek—take off after him, I realize he's going to go the long route and hike up the cliff from behind, then retrieve a medallion and bring it back. He's banking on the fact that the others won't be able to do it faster. I cross my fingers quietly behind my back, hoping he's right. I'm a little worried that Vaza and Bek—not the most easygoing twosome— are hiking along with him.

Taushen and Hassen remain at the base of the cliff. As I watch, Taushen moves around, all nervous energy, and then wads a snowball into one hand, tossing it at the medallions. It doesn't have much impact, and it's clear that's not going to work. Hassen merely rubs his chin, thoughtful, staring up at the medallions and thinking hard.

Next to me, Kira leans in. "What do you think?" She jiggles the baby in her arms, smoothing the blankets around Kae's small face. "Does Salukh stand a chance?"

"I don't know." And I don't. I'm not sure what to think. I'm sure he can win a footrace against the other two if it's fair, but the clincher is the "fair" part. I'm also a little worried that they'll take too long. Taushen's running around like a chicken with his head cut off, but Hassen's cool and just studying the medallions. There's a shrewd look on his face that tells me he's got something in mind but isn't ready to act on it yet.

A moment later, I'm surprised when Hassen breaks through the crowd and begins to run for the main cave. A few people murmur, but no one leaves the competition area, especially since Taushen is now finding rocks to put in his snowballs and lobbing them harder, all to no avail. I hear Farli stifle a giggle behind her hand. Poor Taushen. Brains are clearly not his strong suit.

Hassen returns a few minutes later with a sling in hand, just as a light snow starts to fall. I pull my furs tighter around my body, watching with a worried sort of anticipation as

Hassen fits a stone into the cradle of his sling and then begins to whirl the leather over his head with easy, powerful strokes. Then, he lets the stone fly.

It hits the mark perfectly, of course. He's a skilled hunter and has excellent aim. The medallion shivers in place and sways, but remains put. I suck in a breath, surprised.

"They're hooked onto a rock lip," Josie whispers, moving toward us. "Just smacking it isn't going to do anything."

Nearby, Haeden grunts. "This is foolishness. If anyone needs me, I will be off hunting and providing for the tribe like the rest of these fools should be." He casts a baleful glare at all of us and storms away.

"Grumpy pants," Josie mutters. "I'm freaking brilliant with this competition. He's just in a pissy mood as usual."

I do have to admit that Josie's competitions have been clever and tailored toward useful things. Maybe not so much today, but the men have been hunting a great deal and the supplies in the cave have been steadily growing greater. This competition hasn't been all bad, I suppose. At least not for the tribe.

Taushen, meanwhile, hurries off to the caves to retrieve his own weapon, no doubt, as Hassen rubs his chin again. As Taushen returns with a spear, Hassen leaves once more. To no one's surprise, Taushen's spear appears to be equally ineffective in retrieving a medallion, and he makes a noise of frustration before heading back into the cave again.

"Look up," Kira whispers. "They must have run the entire way."

I shield my eyes and gaze up at the top of the cliff. There's a tall figure squatting down against the edge of the cliff, and as I watch, he goes to his stomach and leans an arm over, neatly plucking one of the medallions from the cliff wall. That sweep of dark, beautiful hair can't be anyone but Salukh, and my heart pitter-pats in my breast.

The moment he disappears from sight again, the two others are right behind him, and I hold my breath. It's going to be close if it comes down to the footrace.

Hassen returns with something new—a twisted, large bone fishhook tied onto a length of leather-braided rope. He kneels in the snow and ties one of his slingstones into the leather near the hook, and then begins to swing it over his head like he did the sling. A moment later, the weighted hook goes flying and smacks against the cliff wall. It doesn't connect, and Hassen pulls the rope back and tries again.

On his second attempt, it's hooked, and I watch with dismay as he pulls the medallion down off the cliff wall and trots over to retrieve it. He brings it to Josie, a triumphant look in his eyes.

"The winner for the brains category is Hassen," Josie declares and hands him one of the brightly painted red seeds. Hassen takes it with a little bow and then nods in my direction as if to say, *See how capable I am?*

I give him a faint smile, even though I'm tempted to run back into the cave and hide. Oh, Salukh. He's not going to win. I should have spoken up, and now it's too late. I'm in this mess hip-deep.

Taushen hides his disappointment well, congratulating Hassen. Then we all wait for the three runners to return. I'm surprised that both Vaza and Bek show up ahead of Salukh. He was in first—what happened between when he'd arrived at the top of the cliff and now?

I get my answer in the exchange of smug looks between

Bek and Vaza. Several minutes later, Salukh shows up with his medallion . . . and a bloody nose. There are several bruises and scratches on his chest and face and I suck in a breath, noting that one of his eyes is blackened and swollen. It's my fault the others are taking out their frustration on him, because I invited him to my furs.

Aehako steps forward, a thunderous frown on his face as he studies Salukh. "What happened?"

"Nothing," Salukh says flatly.

"That is dvisti piss and you know it." Aehako casts a baleful look at Bek and Vaza. "This competition ends now. It is clear to me that you cannot be men and must behave like kits."

The men make noises of protest, clearly pissed that they're not going to get a chance for more seeds. I don't care. Right now all I can see is the blood trickling from Salukh's nostril.

"No," Salukh says. "The contest should continue."

I suck in a breath. Aehako frowns at him.

"It is dangerous if no one can control themselves. I will not allow—"

"It will not happen again," Salukh says flatly. "I will not give up my claim on Tee-fah-nee because of a scuffle."

I look over at Vaza and Bek, and realize for the first time that Vaza's got a fat lip and Bek's got a bruise shadowing one cheek. At least Salukh was able to hit back.

"We are not continuing unless I am assured by all that this will not happen again." Aehako turns and glares at the men.

There are mumbles of assent, and it's agreed that the challenge will continue. I have a sick feeling in my stomach as I watch the men line up again. Escorting me to the elders' cave isn't worth this. It's not worth fighting amongst men that have been friends from childhood.

They are willing to do anything for a chance at a mate. I should be flattered, but it scares me.

The day wears on and it becomes clear to me that Salukh never stood a chance at winning. The "brawn" competition involves the men racing to retrieve boulders from a nearby plain and then carrying them through an obstacle course that Josie has set up. Though I know Salukh is strong and fast, the other men work against him. They leave the largest of boulders for him to carry, and they push and shove at him as they run. They knock over obstacles into Salukh's path that slow him down. It's not a fair fight and both Josie and Aehako are making unhappy noises when a triumphant Bek arrives for the win.

For the "talent" competition, Josie gives the men a list of creatures to hunt: a scythe-beak, a fang-face, and a quilled beast. One is a bird, one is a fish, and one is a land creature. They're to bring them back to the cave, and whoever returns the quickest with all three kills will be the winner. If they have nothing by sunset, they are to head back to the cave, the contest over.

The men set off in different directions with their weapons. As I watch Salukh jog away from the cave, I'm surprised to see Vaza change course and head after him.

"That cheater," Kira murmurs. "He's going to tail him and scare away his game. Vaza knows he's not going to win so he's going to make sure that Salukh fails at all of the challenges."

My guilt chokes me. I head back to the cave with the others, but there's no joy in the afternoon for me. I spend some time with Chompy, brushing him and cleaning out his cave.

Farli hangs around with me, but she's silent company since we don't speak the same language. That suits me fine—I'm not in a talking mood anyhow.

It seems like an eternity before someone returns to the cave with their trophies. It's Taushen, utterly triumphant. Hassen comes back a short time after, and he's less than pleased. He deposits his kills and then stalks to his cave to sulk. Bek arrives at sunset, only two kills out of three in his hands.

Salukh and Vaza show up when it's fully dark, and there is no kill in Salukh's hands. The frustration on his face is evident.

"Congratulations, Taushen," Josie says as the tribe tucks into the fresh meat. I don't eat a thing, because I have no appetite. She awards the hunter his latest seed and then glances around the cavern. "The only contest left is that of 'Effort.' The tribe is supposed to judge it, but it doesn't matter at this point. Taushen is the clear winner. He has more seeds than anyone else."

The young hunter whoops in delight and rushes over to me, looking for encouragement.

I give him a faint smile, even though I feel like throwing up.

"When shall I escort you to the elders' cave, Ti-fa-ni?" He squats on the ground near me, his face puppyish in its adoration. I can't hate him. He's just lonely and has a crush. I wish it wasn't on me, though. "Shall we go tomorrow?"

"Sure, tomorrow," I say. What choice do I have?

CHAPTER TWELVE
Salukh

Anger burns in my belly as I tear a leg off of the fresh-killed quilled beast and then head out of the cavern to eat under the stars. Normally I would welcome company, but tonight my head is full of frustration and I want to see no one. I want to be alone with my angry thoughts.

Tee-fah-nee has slipped through my grasp for the moment. The others made sure of that. I had no idea they were so very angry at finding me in her furs until Bek and Vaza came after me with their fists. To them, I am a betrayer.

I do not care what they think, though. Only Tee-fah-nee. But she has been silent, and when Taushen won, she smiled at him and agreed to leave with him in the morning.

My jealousy is fierce. I should have all her smiles. I should be the one taking her to the elders' cave. I should be inside even now, feeding her choice tidbits of meat to ensure that my mate is healthy. Instead, I am outside, angrily gnawing on a quilled beast leg and seething.

Why is my khui silent? Now is the time to claim her. Now is the time to declare that she belongs to me and only me. I do not trust Taushen to keep her safe. He is a good hunter, but younger than I am and easily distracted. He will have two precious females with him, and while the trail is safe, there are always risks.

I should go along with them to provide protection. It is the only wise thing to do.

Footsteps crunch behind me in the snow and I stiffen.

"Ho, friend," Aehako calls out into the darkness. "Mind if I join you?"

"Yes."

He laughs and comes to my side anyhow, gazing up at the stars. "It is a nice night."

I grunt. It was nicer when I was alone.

"Come," Aehako says and claps me on my arm. "Do not be surly like Haeden. Today was bad. Tomorrow will be better."

"She leaves tomorrow for the elders' cave," I say, voice flat with anger. "With Taushen."

"Yes, she does." Aehako is silent for a moment, and when I look over, he's gazing up at the stars. "It is hard to think, sometimes, that they are a very different people than us. Most times, my Kira is easy to predict, but then she will say something that I cannot comprehend, and I remember where they come from. The place called Urth."

I say nothing. I know all too well that Tee-fah-nee is different than a sa-khui woman. I need no reminder. I like her differences. I accept all her unique traits.

"They have different courting rituals on Urth," Aehako continues. "Strange ones. Perhaps that is why she does not speak up to declare that she wants you, when it is clear she has affection for you and not the others."

She does not speak up because she is afraid. I know this, and some of my anger burns away. Bek and Vaza used their fists on me this day. I did not care, because I am strong and can handle anything they might try. But Tee-fah-nee fears that they will become violent against her. The thought of a male striking a precious female is incomprehensible, and yet she has been hurt by others in the past. "She has her reasons."

"She must," Aehako says easily. He squeezes my shoulder, and I wince when he touches a bruised spot. "And we must respect the human rituals. That is why you cannot go after them when they go to the elders' cave."

I scowl. How did he know what I intended? I look over at Aehako and his face is grim.

"I know you are thinking it, because I would do the same for my Kira," he says. "But you must not. If you value tribe harmony, you will claim one of the hunting trails and go out for several days. Cool your head. Get your mind back to where it should be. Do not think about the female."

As if I can simply push thoughts of Tee-fah-nee from my mind. I snort at the ridiculous thought.

"I am telling you as a chief," Aehako says. "I am sending Bek and Vaza and Hassen out on hunting trails as well. It is time we stop with all the foolishness of fighting over females and return to our true task—providing enough food for the brutal season. There have been far too many distractions as of late."

He's not wrong. I have spent more time with Tee-fah-nee than hunting lately. I think of my mother and father, my younger sister, Farli. My brothers, Pashov and Dagesh, and their mates and young. They do not deserve to go hungry simply because I cannot focus.

But Tee-fah-nee is not safe with only Taushen to protect her. The humans are all too vulnerable. "I will hunt the trails," I tell Aehako. There are many familiar paths our hunters take, and along the way there are scattered caves and icy caches of frozen kills that will be useful in the brutal season. Those caches must be replenished, and hunting the trails will keep me away from the main cave for many days in a row.

It is a lie, though.

Instead of hunting, I shall follow Tee-fah-nee and ensure that she is safe.

Tiffany

"You watch dvisti?" I point at little Chompy in his pen and Farli nods at me eagerly. She spits out a stream of fluid syllables and gesticulates with her hands. I have no idea what she's saying, but she's nodding and pointing at the baby animal, so I'm sure she's agreeing to watch him. One good thing out of this trip will be the language dump. I'm ready to understand what all the sa-khui are saying. I've picked up some of the language in the last year and a half, but it's so fluid and so many of the hunters speak English to us that I'm not as good with it as I should be.

Farli looks at me, smiling. Her hand strays down to Chompy's little triangle-shaped head and the dvisti bleats and licks her fingers. He loves her, not me, because she's been the one tirelessly taking care of him while I deal with my issues.

"When I get back, you and I are going to have a long talk

about animal husbandry," I tell her. I'll give her the little animal for her own and help her raise him, but at this point? He's her pet, not mine.

"Ready to go?" Josie calls out to me, snowshoes in hand. She's bundled up in several layers of furs, and those furs are strapped down to her chest with a leather harness to keep them from flapping in the wind and catching the cold air. I'm dressed similarly, even though it's hot in the cave. It'll be cold once we get out in the elements, and my khui won't be able to keep up.

Kira's nearby, ready to see us off. She's made breakfast for us, and is now breastfeeding her baby. Her mate went off hunting earlier, so she's by herself. Other than that, the cave is rather empty.

"I'm ready," I tell Josie and give one last smile to Farli, a pat on the head to Chompy, and then head over to her side. Josie hands me a second pair of snowshoes and we head to the mouth of the cave, where Taushen is waiting for us, all eager grins.

He's clearly excited for this trip. I wish I could feel the same enthusiasm, but all I feel is the same familiar dread. I'll have to pay a lot of attention to Taushen on this trip. He won fair and square and I should at least reward him, even if the reward is just listening to him talk about his favorite subject: me.

There are a few people lingering near the mouth of the cave to see us off. Kira's nursing Kae, Haeden is watching us, and two of the elders sit by the fire. I'm surprised that Salukh is nowhere to be seen, nor are my other failed suitors. It must be intentional.

Taushen holds out our packs, both filled with extra furs, waterskins, fire-making implements, bone knives, and the spicy travel rations that the sa-khui love. "The morning grows late. Let us get started."

"We're on it," Josie says, and bends down to put on her snowshoes. I do the same.

"I don't like this," announces a hard voice. I look up in surprise to see Haeden frowning down at us. "It's not safe."

Josie shrugs. "Why do you care?"

"I don't." He spits the words at us and straightens to his full height, all imposing horns and blue muscle. "But it is foolish to go to the elders' cave now, with only one hunter to guide you. The South Cave is farther away from the elders' cave than the main cave is. You should wait until we rejoin the other cave and go with a large party, when it is safer."

"It is an easy walk of a day and a half," Taushen says, jogging up to us.

"Humans are slow," Haeden sneers, giving the younger hunter a disgusted look. "Did you consider that? Did you bring enough travel rations to accommodate for the fact that they are weak?"

"Jesus, what is your problem?" Josie glares at him and looks as if she wants to hit him with her other snowshoe. "We're going and that's final. Or are you pissy because you can't come along?"

His lip curls as he gazes down at her. "I do not wish to go."

"I don't want you to go, either!"

"But it does not change the fact that you should stay here." He points at the cave floor. "It is safe here."

"We're going to get the language laser beam and you can't stop us!" She's practically hopping in anger, not an easy feat given that one of her snowshoes is strapped on.

I just look over at Taushen. "Are we going on a dangerous path?"

He shakes his head. "It's very clear and not close to any watering holes. There are no metlak caves and very few snow-cats travel the paths we shall take because they prefer the cliffs. Ours is a straight walk so easy we send kits out on it on their first hunts alone." He's frowning at Haeden in confusion, as if he doesn't understand the man's anger at letting us go. "It is very safe."

"Taushen won this prize fair and square," Josie retorts. "If you wanted to win, maybe you should have competed, Mister Crabby Pants."

"If this is his reward, then let Tafinee and Taushen go. You stay here. You do not need to go along and slow them down."

Josie's eyes widen and she sputters. "Fuck you! I'm going! I don't know why you care anyhow—you don't like it when I'm here, and now you don't like it when I try to leave. Make up your freaking mind!"

His eyes narrow with anger at the small human defying him. "I shall speak to Aehako about this."

"Who do you think gave me the friggin' snowshoes, you idiot?" She waves one under his nose.

Haeden snarls and then turns away, stomping back to his cave, his tail lashing angrily. I watch with wide eyes as he leaves. I don't understand the dynamic between him and Josie. If he hates her so much, why does he care if she goes or not? Shouldn't he be glad she's leaving for a while, because now she won't bother him with her incessant talking and singing and needling him with comments?

"I do not understand him," Taushen says to me.

Boy, at least it's not just me, then. I turn to look at him. "Do we have everything?"

He rubs one ear. "I should get more rations . . . just in case. And another set of waterskins."

"We'll wait here," I tell him and smile. I should smile at him, right? To make him feel like he won a reward instead of just being our tour guide? I don't hate the guy. He's young and sweet, but I'm just . . . not interested in the slightest. Still, if anyone had to win other than Salukh, I'm glad it's Taushen. Spending three or four days with Bek might have broken me. His anger scares me in a way Haeden's never does. Maybe because Haeden's anger is never directed at anyone but Josie? Who knows? I watch Taushen disappear into one of the storage caves. If it couldn't be Salukh, I am glad it had to be Taushen.

Speaking of Salukh . . . I glance around the near-empty early-morning cave. "Where are all the hunters?"

Kira pulls baby Kae from her breast and starts to burp her. "Did you not hear them all leave early this morning? Aehako sent them all out on the trails. They'll be back in a few days."

I try to hide my disappointment. Out on the trails? That means no goodbye from Salukh. I wanted to see his face one more time before I set out, even though I know he's got to be stinging with disappointment right now. "Oh, okay."

Why does that hurt my feelings? I didn't stick up for him and declare that he should be my man. I let this stupid contest go on. It's my own fault. And yet . . . I was hoping he'd be around. That maybe I could somehow convince him to go with us. That I could at least say goodbye for a few days.

Guess not. Guess saying goodbye to me wasn't important to him.

As if she can sense my dismay, Kira wags a finger in my direction. "Don't stay out too long," she tells us. "It's going to be boring here in the caves with just me and Farli. Aehako will be back, but late tonight. That dvisti of yours is going to get showered with attention while you're gone, just because we're going to be so bored."

I laugh despite my disappointment. "He'll probably love that. Tell Farli thank you for me?" She knows the language.

She nods and we hug briefly. Taushen returns, and then it's time to go.

I'd be lying if I said I didn't scan the horizon for Salukh as we left.

Traveling on Not-Hoth is not fun. The snow is endless, and even when both suns are high in the sky, it's not even remotely close to warm. I imagine this is what Antarctica is like, but the light the suns give off is so faint that we don't have to worry about snow blindness. And no penguins, which is a shame. I would kind of like to see penguins.

What we do have, though, is snow. Lots and lots of snow and cold air. It snows a little as we walk, dusting our hair, but it's not enough to slow us down. Taushen is all eagerness, chatting constantly as Josie and I do our best to keep a good pace, our snowshoes dragging in the powder. As far as the sa-khui are concerned, this is fantastic travel weather. It's mostly clear, the snow isn't too thick on the ground, and for them, it's warm. Meanwhile my fingers feel like blocks of ice, my toes feel like they could snap off in my heavily padded boots, and I keep wishing for someplace to sit down and rest. I'm sweating under my thick furs, which makes them stick to my body and ice up. The khui inside me helps me stay warm, but humans are still too fragile to go running around half-naked like the sa-khui.

By the time it's midday, I'm exhausted and Josie's steps are slowing, too. Our cheery, light conversation of earlier in the day has dwindled to nothing. Now we just pant and lift our feet, one after the other. At least the terrain is relatively flat. As Taushen said, it's a baby trail by their standards.

Nevertheless, I'm thrilled when our guide jogs back up to us—jogs!!—and suggests we rest for a time in the protective shade of a nearby cliff. Josie and I gratefully collapse against the stone cliff wall, and even though the rocky base isn't the most comfortable spot and it's cold in the shade, there's no breeze.

"Wait here and I shall hunt you both something fresh to eat. I saw a quilled beast's tracks nearby." Taushen holds his spear eagerly. "Will you eat my kill if I provide?"

"Sounds great," I tell him, offering a thumbs-up.

"You're so sweet, Taushen," Josie says, beaming at him. "Thank you."

He grins at both of us and then leaps away, bounding through the snow like a big blue gazelle. He's got so much energy, and I'm so dang tired already. I can't believe we have a day and a half of walking to do. Maybe Haeden was right and we are too weak to do this. Too late now, I suppose.

I pull off one of my gloves and tuck my hand into the front of my thick jacket, pressing my cold fingers against my warm throat. "This is . . . less fun than I imagined."

"It sucks," Josie agrees cheerfully. "You're allowed to say that."

"It does suck. I'm sorry you came with me. You didn't have

to." Josie has been a great friend, but I wouldn't wish this on anyone. It reminds me all too much of the relentless cold we endured in that week of hell when we were waiting for Georgie to come back with a rescue. It also makes me realize how spoiled we are with the sa-khui to protect us and keep us warm and safe in our comfy caves. The males hunt tirelessly while we putter around in the caves. Sure, there's a lot—okay, an endless stream—of chores to do, but compared to this? I don't know how Liz does it. I can't wait to be back home around my fire and playing with my leatherwork.

"I have to admit . . . I'm not doing it just for you," Josie says, adjusting a strap on her snowshoes.

"Oh?"

She gives me a sly look. "I'm going to use the sick bay computer and have my IUD taken out, like Kira had her translator taken out."

My jaw drops a little. "You are?"

"I am." She gives a happy little sigh and sits up, hugging herself. "I'm ready for my happy ever after, you know? I want to resonate to someone. I want babies. I want a mate that will love me. I'm tired of being single and unloved."

I stare at her dreamy face, envious of her confidence. She assumes that the khui is going to fix all of her problems. That it'll match her up with the perfect man and she'll immediately be in love with the guy that puts a baby in her. It's romantic, sure, but it's also overly optimistic. What if it matches her up to one of the elders who never mated? What if it matches her to someone she hates?

What if it matches her to someone who decides to take what he wants instead of asking for permission?

I shudder at the thought. I'm envious of Josie. Her decision might be right for her, but I'm still living in fear of what might happen if I do resonate. Sure, I might be hooked up with the man of my dreams . . . but I might also be hooked up with a pure nightmare.

Right now, I'm just happy I haven't resonated to anyone. There's no one I want to mate.

Even as I think it, though, my mind goes back to Salukh. Salukh with his velvety skin, intense gaze, and the way he touches me so sweetly, never demanding. He lets me take the lead and is infinitely patient. He makes me feel like every touch is a gift that I've given to him.

I'm lying to myself when I say I wouldn't want to resonate to anyone. I'd take Salukh and I'd take him gladly. If he can help me get over my fear of sex, he can help me learn to love again. He's kind and generous and looks at me as if I'm a slice of chocolate cake he can't wait to eat up.

I just worry I messed things up, and when we get back, his hot, possessive stare will have changed to one of distaste.

Maybe I missed my chance with him. The thought is a depressing one.

CHAPTER THIRTEEN
Salukh

I watch in the distance as Taushen hurries off, leaving the two human women alone and vulnerable at the base of the cliff. Anger surges through me and I push it away.

They are not unprotected; I am here to watch them.

It's a foolish move for Taushen to make, and yet I understand it. He is eager to win over the humans with fresh game, and is torn between guarding them and providing for them. Still, it is not the choice I would have made, and it angers me to see Tee-fah-nee's small form huddled in the shadows of the rock. A snow-cat could wander in this direction. A herd of dvisti might cross the plains and trample them. A scythe-beak might decide to swoop down and investigate, and their beaks are like swords. Just because it looks safe does not mean it is.

I clutch my spear close. It is a good thing I ignored Aehako's command to go hunting and followed them instead. I am hunched low on my belly in the snow, downwind from Taushen's trail. They will not see me unless they look up, and judging from the tired posture of the humans, that is not a worry.

Tee-fah-nee's hair springs forth as she lowers her hood, and

I can see her movements as she talks to Jo-see. She looks tired, and it takes every bit of control in my body to not clamber down the side of the cliff and go to her side, to swing her over my shoulder and carry her all the way to the elders' cave.

Is this how Vektal felt when he first saw his Georgie? Then I remind myself that he and Georgie resonated, and my heart is heavy with sadness.

Why do you not claim her, my khui? You know she is the one for us.

My breast is silent, and my heart remains heavy and alone.

I stay at my watch post, unmoving, as the women relax and stretch their legs, talking. Eventually Taushen returns with a fresh kill, and I relax a little, too. The women eat, and then they put back on their snowshoes and the trio head off into the snow again. As I watch, Tee-fah-nee stumbles, and I leap to my feet, my heart racing.

They stop. Taushen and Jo-see both go back to Tee-fah-nee's side. My female picks herself up off the snow, pushes away their helpful hands, and adjusts her snowshoe. Then they begin to walk again.

She limps, though, and I fight a surge of irritation that Taushen would push her so hard that she would harm herself.

She should be pampered. She should be carried if her leg hurts her.

She should be *mine*.

Tiffany

Rolling my ankle makes an already un-fun trip even more miserable. Josie and Taushen are both worried about me, but I shrug off their concerns. I tell them that I'm fine. What option do I have otherwise? We're too far from the South Cave to go back, and we might as well continue forward. So I soldier on, ignoring the pain in my ankle as much as I can.

We stop that night in one of the small "hunter" caves and it's eye-opening to me. Taushen explains to us that these small caves are all along the tribe's hunting grounds and are used as shelters for those out on the trails. The cave we stay in is tiny, barely tall enough for either Josie or me to stand up in; Taushen has to squat. There's enough room for all three of us to lie down, but barely. Taushen ends up putting his furs by the cave opening so Josie and I can have the interior. My ankle throbs and it's cold despite the small fire we start. All in all, it's not a fun night and it makes me appreciate the tribe cave even more with its big interior and the friendly faces that are always present.

When we get up the next morning, my ankle is swollen to twice the size it was before. It's tender to the touch, and walking on it is excruciating. Josie helps me wrap it tight in the hopes that I'll be able to limp along, but I can't even close my boot, much less fasten my snowshoe on my boot.

"What do we do?" Josie asks, a worried look on her face. "Can you walk at all?"

"I'll have to," I tell her tightly. There's no other option. I can't force all three of us to remain in the cave; it's not warm enough for a long stay. Plus, there's a machine that can fix wounds and ailments at the elders' cave aka the old spaceship. "Might as well keep going. We're close to the elders' cave anyhow, right?" I look to Taushen for reassurance.

"Half a day's walk if we keep a brisk pace," he says, frowning down at my leg. "Longer if not."

"It's going to be longer," I say with a wince. "I'll keep up as best I can."

"Should you even walk?" Josie asks.

"I can carry her," Taushen volunteers. "It would be an honor." His voice is breathless with excitement, his eyes bright.

"I can walk," I snap. The last thing I want to do is spend the day draped over Taushen and feeling like I owe him. No thank you.

He stiffens and I know I've hurt his feelings. The old anxiety and tension return, and for a moment I hold my breath, worried he's going to lash out . . . or worse.

"Let us go, then. The morning grows late." Taushen's voice is wounded, his shoulders slightly hunched as if protecting himself from my anger.

I release a pent-up breath and get to my feet. My ankle throbs in response, but I ignore it. "Can I borrow your spear to use as a crutch?"

He hesitates. "What if I need to protect you?"

"Then you can come and snatch it from me?" I extend my hand outward. "I promise I won't put up a fight over that."

He doesn't look happy, but in the end hands it over. "I still would rather carry you."

"I'm sure you would," I say, and force myself to keep my voice sweet. "But I can walk." And I give a hobbling step just to prove that I can.

It's gonna be a long damn day.

Salukh

Tee-fah-nee cannot walk.

When the trio limps out of the hunter cave—and they *do* limp—I am incensed to see that my Tee-fah-nee, my *mate*, is leaning heavily on a spear. It's clear to me that her leg is worse today, not better. Taushen tries to put an arm around her and she pushes him away, and I can see the young hunter flinch backward.

Good. She is *my* mate.

I will not allow her to walk all the way to the elders' cave.

As I have followed them, I have taken great care to remain out of sight and downwind. I have covered my tracks and kept my distance. No more. No longer. My female is hurt and in pain, and I refuse to sit back and let her struggle. I jog through the snow, making my way toward the group. They are ahead of me, but they move so slowly that it takes no time to catch up.

As I come into sight, I hear Jo-see's gasp. She points in my direction. "Someone's coming."

Taushen turns, and I watch as he tenses at the sight of me. By now, he has figured out that this is no coincidence, that I followed them because I did not trust that he would keep the humans safe. Anger blossoms on his face and he stalks toward me, furious.

"What do you do here, Salukh? You are supposed to be hunting!"

"I am watching over the humans." I gesture at Tee-fah-nee, who, even now, is trying not to put weight on her leg. "She is hurt and cannot walk. I am here to help."

"You are not supposed to be here," Taushen protests again. "This is my prize!"

I glare at him. I do not care about prizes. I care about my female. He scowls at me but does not stop me as I approach Tee-fah-nee. Jo-see watches me with wide eyes, but all I see is Tee-fah-nee's face, her smooth human features lined with pain.

I touch her brown cheek with my fingertips in a gentle caress. "You should not be walking."

"What choice do I have?" Her voice is soft, pained.

"I will carry you," I state, and when she stiffens, I add, "If you will let me." I must remember her fear, always.

She hesitates, and then nods. "Taushen's going to be mad," she murmurs, even as she lifts her arms to go around my neck.

I do not care if Taushen hates me. All I care about is getting my mate out of the cold and someplace safe where she may rest her leg. I lift her into my arms and she weighs no more than a kit. Humans are so fragile, so soft, so poorly equipped to survive. It makes my chest clench with fear.

Taushen voices a protest, but I ignore him.

"You can carry me if you want to carry someone," Jo-see offers. "I'm freaking tired."

"Caring for Ti-fa-ni is to be my prize," Taushen states again, and he sounds like a petulant child. "Aehako will hear of this and he will not be pleased."

He will not be, no. But he can be angry with me later. "Let us get to the elders' cave and we can argue when the women are safe."

"I guess this means no one wants to carry me, huh?" Jo-see says, and laughs at her own joke. "Figures."

Even with Jo-see's brave attempts to keep pace with us, it takes many hours for us to get to the elders' cave. The suns are low in the sky and both humans are exhausted by the time the smooth oval mountain comes into view.

"Finally," exclaims Jo-see, and I inwardly echo her sentiment. Tee-fah-nee is shivering against my chest, and her face is tight with pain. I want to get her to safety and care for her. She needs a warm fire and blankets and warm, comforting food. She needs the healer, too, but that will have to wait.

As we enter the strange cave system that is the elders' cave, I see more of the ice has been removed from the interior, revealing strange rock walls that are too smooth and more flashing lights. Tiny spurs of rock stick out everywhere, and there are lights flashing on a flat surface set into the cave wall.

"You can set me down anywhere," Tee-fah-nee murmurs. "I'm sure I'm heavy by now."

"You are not heavy to me," I state staunchly. I would carry her across the mountains if I had to. It is no pain to hold her.

"Over there," she murmurs, and there is a strange stool with a back by the remains of what looks to be a firepit. I set her gently down on the stool and she relaxes. I begin to unwrap her leg but she pushes my hands away. "I'm fine. I can get it."

I frown but do as she asks.

"Harlow?" Jo-see calls out, disappearing into one of the side tunnels. "Harlow, are you here? Rukh? Harlow? Anyone?" She returns a few moments later, disappointment on her round face. "They're not here."

"They must be back at the main cave," Tee-fah-nee says. "They split their time between here and there."

"Well, damn!" Jo-see looks upset. "I wanted to see their kit."

Taushen steps forward. "The suns are going down soon and it will grow colder. If Tee-fah-nee's leg is hurt, we will be here for several days. We will need more food, and firewood."

Both Jo-see and Tee-fah-nee look at me.

I straighten and get to my feet. "You are right." I gesture at the females. "You stay here. Taushen and I will get supplies. We will be back soon." I don't miss the irritated look that Taushen sends in my direction. If it were me in his place, I would be mad, too. I have taken over, and the women look to me for assurance, not him.

"Oh, but if the computer's working, it can fix Tiff's leg," Jo-see says, her face eager.

My nostrils flare. I don't like the thought of a *com-pew-turr* mending my woman. It is too strange for me to understand, and I do not trust it, but I will allow it if Tee-fah-nee is in that much pain. I touch my mate's cheek. "Do not do anything until we return. I will bring back some faa-shesh root. It is good for pain."

She nods and shifts in the chair. "Be careful." Her gaze flicks to Taushen, and I realize she is thinking of the competition, where Vaza and Bek attacked me. Taushen is not like them. He is all words and little action, and he is young. He will be angry, but he will not use his fists.

I nod and head out of the elders' cave, down the strange dark ramp that has been uncovered. It only has a light layer of snow on it, which tells me Rukh and his mate with the orange mane were likely here just a day or two ago.

Taushen follows me out, and the moment we are away from the cave mouth, he shoves my back. "Salukh," he hisses. "What do you do here? She is *my* prize."

I grit my teeth and ignore his anger. Were I in the same position, I would feel the same helpless rage. "I am here because she is my mate."

He sucks in a breath. "You do not resonate."

"It does not matter, my friend." I place a hand over my heart. "I feel it here. It is simply a matter of time." Time, and convincing my silent khui that there is none for us but Tee-fah-nee and her dark curls and soft skin.

His eyes narrow as if he does not believe me. Then, a disappointed sigh escapes him. He hangs his head. "There is nothing I want more than a mate, but it is clear she does not care for me. I have tried to impress her and she does not notice. I offer to carry her and she is offended. Yet the moment you arrive, she puts her arms around your neck."

I try not to feel too triumphant in the face of his defeat. I put a hand on his shoulder and squeeze it. "There is yet another human woman, and Farli will be of age in a few seasons. You may yet have a mate."

He sighs.

I understand; it is cold comfort to think of another when the female he wants is as attractive as Tee-fah-nee. But she is mine; even Taushen can see it. "Do you wish to hunt or shall I?"

"I will hunt," he says glumly, pulling his spear from the carrying loop over his shoulder. "You collect wood and dung and the root for Ti-fa-ni. Maybe if I feed the human Jo-see, she will appreciate it." He doesn't look thrilled at the thought.

I clap his shoulder. "We had best get started, then."

Tiffany

"I can't believe it," Josie wails. She clutches a thin sheet of plastic in her hand that crinkles like foil and thrusts it toward me. "I found that on the medical bay."

"Out of order," I read aloud, smoothing out the odd "paper." "Harlow must have left the note in case anyone else stopped by."

"How is it out of order?" Josie's voice is despairing. She drops to the ground near my propped-up leg and her eyes are shiny with tears. "I need it to work. I *need* it!"

I shift in my chair, my leg throbbing. "You aren't the only one."

She looks over at me and dashes her fingers under her eyes. "Shit. Sorry. I just . . . I had my hopes up, you know?"

I do know. She's ready to start her new life. She wants a mate and babies. She's tired of being held back by the past. Boy, do I know how that feels. Her face is so sad that it makes my heart hurt. "I'm sure she'll be back soon, Jo. If it can be fixed, Harlow can fix it. We'll just stick around for a while, get the language beamed into our brains, let my leg heal, and wait for them to come back."

Josie nods, but the disappointment is still written on her face. "She probably got the stonecutter working again and went back to the main cave. That means more caverns will be opening up and everyone will be moving back."

"Mmm." I'm not looking forward to that. Moving back means travel—which I'm rather sick of at the moment—but it also means more people crammed into one cave system. Normally I wouldn't mind that, but more people means more men falling all over me to try and get my attention.

I'm pretty damn sick of that.

My thoughts stray to Salukh, and I shiver under my furs, thinking of the way he strode across the snow, all fluttering dark hair and intense, angry eyes. He'd made a beeline right for me, and I knew, somehow, that he'd been watching over us and had come out the moment he saw I was hurt. And I should be annoyed that he was following us, but I'm all warm and fluttery instead, because he's *here*. He's here and he's going to take care of things. He's going to make sure I'm safe.

For some reason, I feel instantly better at that thought. It doesn't matter that I have a bum leg or that Taushen is mad or that the machine is broken and Harlow's nowhere to be found. None of that matters, because Salukh is here and he makes me happy. Actually, seeing him cross the snow toward us like some big blue avenging devil made me feel happier than I've felt since landing on this planet.

Maybe when we get back to the South Cave, I'll invite him to share my furs on a more permanent basis.

I turn to Josie. "It's going to be a while before the men get back, I imagine. Should we go ahead and get the language beamed into our heads while they're gone and get the head-ache over with?"

"Might as well," she says, and the cheerful note is back in her voice. Not much keeps Josie down for long.

CHAPTER FOURTEEN
Tiffany

Getting the sa-khui language downloaded to my head involves standing very still while the computer shoots a laser beam into my eye. I'm not sure about the logistics of it, other than it nukes your brain momentarily and makes you wake up with a splitting headache. Josie and I take turns getting the language and then sit, waiting for the men to return.

My head throbs and aches, and my brain feels as if someone took an apple peeler to it. Not fun, but it had to be done. "I can't wait for Salukh to come back," I tell Josie, leaning my cheek against the weirdly comfortable chair that's been moved into the "main cave." It's probably more like a cargo bay, but it's open and makes the aliens less skittish. Plus the door is nearby and there's a metal section of the floor that's been set up to use as a firepit, encircled with stones. A few pieces of odd furniture have been moved into the area, and I wonder if that's Harlow's work or other visitors that have stopped by. Near me on the other side of the firepit, Josie is curled up in her cloak and seated on a stuffed pillow.

"So you can practice saying dirty things to him in sa-khui?" Josie teases, but her words are accompanied by a wince and a press of her fingers to her temples.

The idea isn't a bad one, but with the way my brain feels, I'd settle for having someone rub my head and hand me a drink of water. "Nah. Just feels like they've been gone for a while now. I hope everything's okay."

I really hope Taushen isn't being a dick to Salukh and trying to start something. I know he's not supposed to be here, but I can't help but be glad that he bent the rules and showed up anyhow.

"That's because they *have* been gone for a while," Josie says, and tugs the blankets closer around her body. She flops down on the pillow and yawns. "I'm going to try and sleep off some of this migraine. Wake me if a chocolate bar shows up and wants to cuddle."

I stifle my laugh—mostly because it hurts to laugh—and peel myself out of the chair. It's chilly away from the fire, and I rub my arms as I wander over to the doorway. The suns are setting, the endless snow outside taking on a purple tinge. They should be back soon.

A furious breeze whips at my thick hair, and I'm shocked at the strength of it. Good lord, where did that come from? I take a few more steps toward the door and lean against the entryway, peering outside. There's no snow falling, but the temperature is definitely getting colder and the wind is picking up. Gonna be a cold night. I'm glad we're inside.

I watch the snow for a bit, but when it's clear no one's on the horizon, I wander away again. It's too cold to stay near the door for too long. Instead, I move toward the computer panel at the far end of the room. There are very few buttons and the ones that are there have extremely strange writing on them and are shaped oddly. I know the button that turns things on, though, and I push it.

"System activated. How can I assist?"

"Can I get a weather reading?" I ask. "What's the temperature outside?" I'm not sure if the computer knows standard units of measurement, so I add, "Set the freezing point at zero degrees."

"The temperature outside is pleasant and slightly above normal for this time of year. Going by your guidelines, it is one degree below freezing."

Pleasant? One degree below freezing? Barf. How I wish I'd gotten stranded on Planet Florida instead of Planet Iceland. As soon as the thought crosses my mind, though, I dismiss it. Salukh wouldn't be there if I were anywhere else . . . and I'd miss him. I feel warm thinking about him and I am smiling to myself. "What about the weather tomorrow?"

"The temperature will be dropping due to a cold weather system incoming. Would you like to see an overview of the terrain?"

"A map? That'd be great."

I wait impatiently as the computer pulls up a visual on the screen. At first it's all white, but then the picture starts to fill in slowly. I touch the screen and it zooms in, but I'm not sure what I'm looking at. "Can you point out where I'm at on the map?"

A moment later, a red dot appears. "You are located here."

Glad I asked. It looks like a whole lot of nothing to my eyes. I lean closer, peering at the picture. I have no idea where the main cave and the South Cave are in relation to where I'm at. I'm not sure the computer would know the caves, either. I drag my finger over the map, making it zoom in and out, looking for landmarks of any kind. "Can you show me where the crashed ship is?"

"Query: I do not understand what 'crashedhip' is."

Well, this is as bad as talking to Siri on my old iPhone. "It's how the humans landed here. We were in a large metal ship. Can you locate that?"

The computer blips and then a blue dot shows up on the map, in the mountains to the east. "There is a deposit of metal here, according to my scanners."

"That must be it," I murmur to no one in particular. It's northeast of here, which means that the main tribal cave should be nearby somewhere. It's a half a day's journey from the main cave to the elders' cave—the old, broken-down ship I'm standing in—and it's a half a day's trek from the main cave to the South Cave. Different directions, though. "Can you zoom out? I want to see the entire area."

"Query: I do not understand what 'zoom' is."

Oy. "Make the picture bigger so I can see the entire region. I want to see all of it."

The screen changes again, and this time I can see a very large chunk of land, along with the mountains to the east and what looks like the sea—or even an ocean—over to the west.

One thing dominates the entire picture, though: an enormous white swirl situated to the southwest. "Um, what is that?" I point at it without touching the screen. It's covering over half of the map, and that's throwing me off. It's unnerving just how big the shape is, and reminds me a lot of a hurricane when it would show up on a weather radar.

"That is an incoming weather system," the computer explains calmly.

"It looks . . . big."

"Scans show that the system will be bringing high winds and a larger than normal amount of frozen precipitation to all affected areas."

Well, I'm no Not-Hoth weather girl, but that doesn't sound good to me. "Exactly how much is a larger than normal amount?"

"Expected precipitation will be somewhere within twelve to sixteen *nashae*."

My brain automatically processes the strange word and tells me that it's a unit of measurement used by the sakh people. "Compare one nashae to a human measurement of one foot."

"One nashae is roughly equal to 1.34 human feet."

Holy crap. "And this storm is going to bring twelve to sixteen feet of snow?"

"Incorrect. The weather system will bring twelve to sixteen nashae of snow. The correct measurement in human terms is 16.08 human feet to 21.44 feet of precipitation. In addition, precipitation will fall as a mix of both snow and ice, later leading to snow as temperatures continue to drop."

I can feel my eyes bugging in my head. "Does this happen often?" I mean, I've seen snow since we landed here, but not twenty feet at once.

"This storm is an outlier and unusual in size and strength. Systems such as this tend to occur over water but rarely make it far inland."

Sounds a lot like a hurricane or a typhoon to me. A snow-hurricane. Crap, crap, and double crap. "When is it going to hit us? Tell me in hours."

"Snowfall will begin in less than twelve hours. The storm's

full impact will be felt twenty-six to thirty human hours from now."

That does not leave a lot of time. Shit.

"Mmm, what's twenty-six to thirty human hours from now?" Josie asks sleepily. She pads across the room to me and looks over my shoulder, yawning.

"Trouble," I tell her. "We need to find the guys."

Taushen arrives at the same time Salukh does, and I'm relieved to see them both. I quickly explain the situation and show them the map. "We have to warn both caves," I tell them. "Anyone that's out on the trails is going to be cut off from the cave and vice versa. We need to warn everyone so no one is caught unprepared. You both need to leave and leave now. One of you go to the South Cave, and one go to the main tribal cave."

Taushen nods and grabs his spear, even as Salukh shakes his head. "And what about you and Jo-see," he says. "You will be trapped here and you will starve to death."

"We can all go back," Josie says. "Salukh can carry you—"

"We will not go fast if I carry Tee-fah-nee," he says. "That is not a solution." He looks right at me with those intense eyes. "I will stay here and take care of Tee-fah-nee."

I look over at Taushen, but he nods like this is the right thing to do. "But what about the caves? Taushen can't run to both."

"Hello, two perfectly good feet right here," Josie says, waving a hand. "I'll go."

Both men frown at her.

"Oh, come on. Liz does this sort of thing all the time! I'm not so fragile." She flexes an arm.

"You are female and must be protected," Taushen says.

"Gross. Do not even try that." Josie puts her hands on her hips. "Thing is, someone competent needs to stay behind and care for Tiff. I'm not great at hunting but I can walk like a champ, okay? So you might as well let me go to one cave, you go to the other." She points at Taushen. "Everyone's warned. Tiff and Salukh stay here until her leg gets better, and everyone's fine."

"I'm not sure." I cross my arms over my chest, concerned. "It's dangerous for you to go alone, especially for a full day."

"Then I'll go to the main cave. It's a half a day's walk from here, right?"

"For sa-khui feet, yes," Taushen says. "It is an easy walk. But human feet are—"

"Yeah, yeah, I know." She waves a hand. "Humans drool, aliens rule. I got it already. I'll just do a lot of jogging. I'll hustle." She smiles brightly at me and pats my shoulder. "Don't worry, Tiff. This is the best solution."

"The best solution would be for Salukh to run to the other cave and you guys can just leave your rations with us and—"

"I will not leave you," Salukh growls at me. "Do not even suggest it."

A little quiver of pleasure shoots through me at his indignation. "But—"

"No," Salukh says again. "I will not leave your side."

I shouldn't be so ridiculously pleased, but I am. I look over at Josie. "I just worry it's too dangerous for you."

She rolls her eyes. "Didn't everyone say this was the easiest hike in the area? That all the sa-khui kits walk here as their training wheels? Am I less competent than a kid?"

Taushen opens his mouth.

I shoot him a look.

He closes it again. "I will go to the South Cave and I will leave this evening," he says, handing his freshly hunted kill over to Salukh. He looks at Josie. "Do you know the way to the tribal cave?"

"Vaguely. But I was a Girl Scout. I can make a compass with a bit of metal, and as long as I know what direction it's in, I'll just keep heading that way. It'll be fine."

I bite my lip. It doesn't sound fine. I shoot a pleading look over to Salukh again, but he shakes his head at me. "I am not leaving your side, Tee-fah-nee."

"Then it's settled," Josie says, and claps her hands. "I'll go to the tribal cave, and Taushen will go to the South Cave. Tiff and Salukh will stay here."

Salukh

"I hope she's going to be okay," my woman murmurs as we stand in the entrance to the elders' cave. It is morning, and Jo-see's small form is retreating in the distance, bundled in her furs and Tee-fah-nee's heavy outer cloak. According to her and Tee-fah-nee's information, she will be just ahead of the storm if she keeps a good pace. We are both worried for Jo-see, but she is insistent on going. Her footsteps are quick despite the snowshoes on her small feet, and her *com-pahs* in her hand. I didn't understand why she rubbed a sliver of metal with fur and then floated it in water, but both she and Tee-fah-nee assure me it will point the way.

"She will be fine," I assure my woman. "It is an easy walk to the tribal cave."

"Yes, but she waited for daylight and already the wind is

picking up." Tee-fah-nee frowns at the skies. "The weather is going to be on her before she gets there. I feel like she should have left last night like Taushen."

"In the daylight, she is safe. At night she is prey to many beasts that hunt. She will be fine," I reassure her again. "Come away from the door." She is shivering, her clothing not thick enough for the strong wind that rushes into the elders' cave.

I help her hobble back to the seat near the firepit. When she is comfortable, I crouch near her leg and put my hand on her knee. "Will you be safe if I leave for a few hours?"

"I will be fine," she assures me, and it's strangely erotic to hear her speaking in my tongue instead of the choppy, harsh human tongue. She pulls a fur blanket into her lap. "I shall keep the fire going."

"Let it burn low," I warn her. "We must conserve our fuel if this large snow is truly going to come." The com-pew-turr says it and it knows many things, so it must be true. "I will go out and collect more and hunt what I can to last us."

She bites her plump lower lip and looks worried. "Will *you* be safe?"

I reach up and caress her cheek. "Nothing could keep me from returning to your side."

A smile curves her mouth then, and she puts her hand over mine. She leans into my palm and nuzzles it, and a bolt of lust shoots through my body. "Hurry back. We will have much to talk about, you and I."

"I shall be the swiftest of hunters."

Though I would like nothing more than to return to Tee-fah-nee's side and bask the day away, there is much to be done. I find Jo-see's footsteps and follow her for a time, picking up frozen dung chips and the occasional bit of wood for a fire. I do not let Jo-see know that I follow her, hanging back just enough to stay out of her sight. I just want to make sure that she can truly do as she says. The little human huffs along in the snow, shuffling at a brisk pace and singing to herself in a breathless voice. She has the bone knife I gave her out in one hand, and her strange *com-pahs* in the other. Every so often, she pauses, adds water to the cup she keeps the *com-pahs* in, and checks the direction. She is going the correct way, though, so I eventually break off from her trail and set to hunting.

The wind rips at my hair and clothing, and I realize that any sensible creature will already be taking shelter from the weather. I spot a bit of color at the base of a whipping tree nearby and head toward it. Jutting from the snow is one of the bones we use as a cache marker. This one is smeared with a bit of dried blood at the end of the bone and marked with three notches—Haeden's cache, then. I mentally note the location and head back to the elders' cave with my satchel of dung chips and firewood. We have Taushen's kills and we have travel rations. I will return to the cache as our supplies run low.

When I return to the cave, Tee-fah-nee is sleeping, curled up in the strange stool, her hurt leg propped up and sticking out. She looks peaceful and I do not disturb her. Instead, I set down my supplies and fill the skins with snow to melt. The meat from last night's catch is smoking on a spit, and I consider the small pile of fire-making supplies. If this will indeed be as bad a storm as Tee-fah-nee says, it will not be enough to keep her warm. We will need more.

I peer down one of the winding, dark tunnels of the elders' cave uneasily. I do not like to explore here, like the human

Har-loh and her mate. To me, this place is a reminder of the dead. I prefer to think of here and now. But my Tee-fah-nee will need much to keep her safe, and it is my job to ensure that. So I explore, and with every step I take, my unease grows. The ice has been thawed from the tunnels, revealing dark panels made of a strange, smooth rock that does not feel like rock at all. Lights flash, and as I walk, more lights beam along my footsteps, illuminating my path.

I do not like this. I do not like that there are many privacy screens that cover each doorway, and they are made of the same strange stone. I do not like that behind each one is a cave full of strange objects that remind me just how different my Tee-fah-nee's world is from mine. She knows what some of these things are. I pick up a small square made of the same strange stone and sniff it. I do not know what any of this is, nor do I know if it will burn. Unnerved, I return to Tee-fah-nee's side, unwilling to explore further.

I know my world. I know my hunting trails. I know my snow and my mountains. I know my people. I know Tee-fah-nee will be my mate.

I do not care to know of anything else. I do not care about *com-pew-turrs* or strange stone caves with flashing lights or people that come from the stars. Only she matters.

I return to her side and watch her sleep, my mind unsettled by strange thoughts.

When she awakens several hours later, she stretches slowly and gives me a smile. "Hey. Sorry I slept for so long." She rubs her eyes with delicate fingers.

"Never apologize to me." She is tired and it has been a hard journey for her fragile human flesh. "How is your leg?"

She shifts and winces. "Stiff and sore."

"Let me look at it." I move closer to her and kneel at her feet. Because she is seated higher than I am, when I kneel in front of her, it puts us at an equal height. I gaze into her bright eyes, my body full of need for her.

Now should be the moment I claim my mate. Here, when we are alone and can explore resonance to its fullest. *Wake, my khui, and claim her!*

Silence.

Biting back my sigh, I place her ankle in my lap and carefully unwrap the bindings. Under the layers of fur and leather, her tiny ankle is still swollen larger than it should be, the flesh bruised. "Can you move it?"

She gives it a small wiggle and then sucks in a breath. "It hurts."

I smooth my fingers over her lovely brown skin. Her legs are small and dainty and I want to run my hands all over her. "I will carry you wherever you need to go."

Her wry look eases my troubled heart, and I stroke her leg.

"Mmm, that feels good." She closes her eyes in pleasure. "I wouldn't mind if you did that for a while."

She wants me to touch her? I would have no greater joy. My hands stroke her leg, smoothing over muscle and skin. I caress her foot and massage her calf, careful to avoid the sore ankle. She shifts in her seat and sighs, and my cock stirs in response. Her sounds of enjoyment are making my body respond. I cannot help it—I am attuned to her pleasure. I want to give her more. I imagine taking her small, soft foot and rubbing it against my cock. Not her hurt one, but her other foot. I imagine her dragging her toes over my erection, the hot look in her eyes when—

"Do you think Josie made it?" she asks in a soft voice.

I look up and meet her gaze, and there's worry there. I tamp down on my aroused thoughts. "I followed her for a while when I went out earlier, to make sure she knew where she was going."

Her expression brightens and her eyes fill with tears. "You did?"

I still, worried at my female's reaction. "I did not do this to make you weep. I merely wanted to ensure that she would be well. That she could find it on her own. She moved swiftly and was heading in the correct direction. I am positive she will be fine." I stroke her leg again. "Please do not cry."

"I'm just happy." She swipes at the tears falling from her eyes. "You're so thoughtful. What would I do without you?"

"It does not matter, because it will not happen."

Her smile becomes even brighter. Then she shivers and hugs her furs closer to her body. "Should we shut the doors and lock everything down? It's getting colder by the minute."

I get up, gently placing her foot back down on the floor. "I will do as you ask."

She starts to get up. "I'll help—"

"No," I tell her, and put a firm hand on her shoulder. "You rest. I will close everything."

"Then it'll be just you and me," she says, voice soft. There's a gleam in her eyes.

And my cock gets hard again. For the first time in what feels like far too long, there will be no one but Tee-fah-nee and me.

I can hardly wait to go to sleep, my mind full of thoughts of caressing her naked body as she clings to me in the furs.

This storm might be the best thing that has ever happened to me.

CHAPTER FIFTEEN
Josie

Man, it is a friggin' *trek* to make it to the tribal caves. I'm relieved when a familiar valley comes into sight. I'm also ready to collapse on my feet. My throat feels dry from sucking in cold lungfuls of air, and I'm sweaty from the constant jog I've kept up for hours. It is not easy to jog in snowshoes, but the rising wind and the snow flurries are reminders that there's no time to spare. So jog I must.

By the time I make it to the cliffs and the yawning mouth of the main cave comes into view, I'm weaving on my feet. There's someone digging at the base of one of the trees, no doubt for a not-potato. The person pauses at the sight of me, and then rushes forward when I trip over my own heavy feet and splat in the snow.

"Hello?" a voice calls out. "Who's there?"

It's Claire. She used to live with us in the South Cave until she resonated to Ereven and moved back. I'd raise a hand and wave at her, but suddenly that feels like too much effort. I'm not surprised she doesn't know it's me—I'm so bundled up in furs that I probably look more like Chewbacca than Josie.

She runs up to my side and I sit up slowly. Her eyes widen at the sight of me. "Josie? What are you doing here?" She scans the horizon, looking for additional travelers. The wind tears at her cloak and she tugs it tighter against her body. "Where are the others?"

"It's just me," I pant. When she offers me a hand to get up, I take it and drag my tired body to my feet. "Big storm coming. We have to warn everyone."

"Big storm?"

I nod. "We saw the weather on the screen at the old crashed ship. I'll explain more inside."

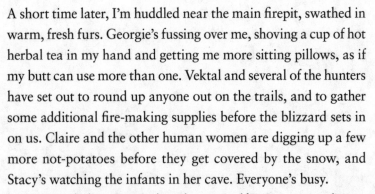

A short time later, I'm huddled near the main firepit, swathed in warm, fresh furs. Georgie's fussing over me, shoving a cup of hot herbal tea in my hand and getting me more sitting pillows, as if my butt can use more than one. Vektal and several of the hunters have set out to round up anyone out on the trails, and to gather some additional fire-making supplies before the blizzard sets in on us. Claire and the other human women are digging up a few more not-potatoes before they get covered by the snow, and Stacy's watching the infants in her cave. Everyone's busy.

"I can't believe you're here by yourself," Georgie exclaims, taking my half-drunk cup of tea and switching it out for a new one. Her fat, wriggling baby, Talie, is slung over her belly, attached to her by some sort of complicated long wrap that has been folded over and over her body again. She hands me a cake of not-potato and then settles in next to me. "I mean . . . walking all this distance by yourself? That's crazy!"

"To be fair, it was only from the elders' ship to here. That's really just a half a day." I'm being modest, of course. I'm exhausted but I'm pretty proud of myself. Humans are considered quite weak given that we can't handle the elements, and we usually don't go anywhere without an escort. Me traveling a distance alone ahead of an oncoming storm? I'm feeling downright heroic. I hum a few bars to Christina Aguilera's "Fighter," just because I can. And then a new thought occurs to me and I giggle. "Haeden's totally going to shit himself when he hears about this, isn't he?"

"You guys aren't still fighting, are you?" She gives me an exasperated look and adjusts her wrap as the baby stuck to her middle flails and waves its fists. Dang. She looks so domestic.

"Does a bear shit in the woods? Of course we're fighting. He's breathing, I'm breathing, therefore we're fighting."

"Josie, you've got to try harder." The look she gives me is practically motherly, which is weird considering we're the same age. "We're all moving back into the main cave together and we need to have harmony with this many people around. I'm not saying be best friends with him. I'm just saying . . . don't antagonize him, all right?"

"Everything I do antagonizes him," I tell her, sipping my tea. Somewhere in the distance, a baby wails, and I feel a bolt of longing. It's baby central here, with all the new births thanks to the chain reaction of resonances and mated couples that have been happening ever since we landed.

Happening to everyone but me, of course. Well, Tiffany, too, but I get the impression that she doesn't want a mate. Me? I want a mate and a family more than anything. More than all the cheeseburgers and chocolate left back on Earth.

"You needle him, too," Georgie says. The baby takes that moment to barf on her top, and I feel a little stab of envious glee at the sight. She makes a face, then whips out a towel and mops up her tunic and the baby's round little blue cheeks. "I'm just saying—"

"I know, I know," I interrupt, not wanting to hear this again. It's the same softly worded lecture that Kira gives me on a regular basis. "It's not all me, though. I could smile at the man and say 'good morning' and he'd find a way to take it wrong." There's something about him that makes me . . . tense and unsettled. Like my skin is itching or I'm about to burst. It's irritating and so is he, and it normally comes out of me in the form of bitchiness vented in his direction. "I'll try harder."

Lies. I can't stand Haeden. I don't know why everyone cares that we don't get along. It's not like we have to hold hands and sing "Kumbaya" to live together. We just have to coexist without killing each other, and we've done a great job of that for the last year and a half.

"Well, I'm glad you're here." She loosens the wrap around her middle and pulls Talie off her lap, setting her down and changing her fluff-stuffed diaper with quick movements. "It's so good to see you, and you were so brave to come and warn everyone. So Taushen went back to the South Cave?"

"Yeah, and thank God he did, because it was really hard just jogging here. I can't imagine trying to jog a full day back to the other cave." My little Girl Scout floating compass saved my butt more than once. That, and I was lucky enough to find a trail with a lot of footprints leading back to the caves. That helped, though I'll never admit it aloud.

"And Tiffany and Salukh?" She fixes Talie's clothing and picks the baby up again, smiling and nuzzling its tiny nose before looking over at me. "You said they were at the old ship with you?"

"Yupper."

"And they stayed?"

"Tiff hurt her ankle and Salukh stayed behind to help her out." I bite my lip. "I'm pretty sure they're hooking up."

Her eyes widen. "Oh. But I thought she had a bunch of other guys flirting with her? What about Hassen and Vaza?"

My tea's cooled enough that I can down the rest of it, and I finish it quickly and put my cup away before Georgie can try and refill it again. I extend my arms toward her, yearning to hold the wriggling, happy blue bundle of baby in her arms. I want a baby so bad. I want a mate even more.

Why does everyone get a family but me?

She hands the baby over and I try not to show how surprised I am at how heavy she is. She's a huge baby—Kira's little Kae is smaller, but Kira's tinier than Georgie and Kae's a lot younger. The sa-khui men are enormous, though, so it makes sense that they'd make big babies. Man, Georgie's poor vagina. I heft Talie in my arms and she reaches for my mouth, smacking at it with a fat baby hand. So cute. "Tiff's love life is kinda complicated. First it was just Hassen and then Taushen. Then Vaza, because you know that old coot's desperate for anything. Then Bek joined in and she started freaking out and getting all overwhelmed, so I helped out."

Her brows draw forward. "You helped out? How?"

I explain to her the competitions I set up, the games I made them compete in. She laughs at a few parts and shakes her head at the reactions. "Aehako was wise to step in when he did. That could have been a really volatile situation."

"Mmm." Sounds a bit like criticism to me, but Georgie always thinks like the chief's mate, so it's not unexpected. I boop Talie's tiny little nose. She's so stinking cute with her fuzzy blue skin and the mess of golden-brown curls atop her head and her witty-bitty horns. I'm so hugging the snot out of every baby in this cave before I go back. "So are Harlow and her family here? The surgery machine was broken back at the ship and I wanted to ask her about it."

Georgie nods and gestures deeper into the cave. "We've opened up three more caves and she's running scans on the walls to see if there's more to be found. She thinks the cutter has one or two more caves in it before it craps out again. The parts burn out fast."

I sure hope she's not cannibalizing from the surgery machine or I might lose my shit. If I can't get this IUD out—and believe me, I've tried the manual method—I'm going to go nuts.

"You okay?" Georgie asks, giving me a concerned look.

"Yep! Just wanted to check out a few things in the girl area."

Understanding dawns on her face as I hug Talie close to my chest again. "It'll happen, Josie. Just be patient."

I'm tired of being patient, though. Everyone says be patient when they don't have to be. But I smile at her, because moping does no good. "You're not getting this cute baby back until I leave."

She laughs. "A few hours with a babysitter? I'll take them and be glad of it. You have no idea how bad I want a nap."

Probably not as bad as I want a baby.

Tiffany

It's quiet with just me and Salukh here at the old spaceship that the sa-khui call the elders' cave.

I think we're still adjusting to the fact that no one else is around. Every time I glance over at Salukh, he's keeping his hands busy: sharpening spears, stoking the fire, checking supplies, or melting snow. I'm more or less chair-bound with my bad ankle, and I don't have any of my usual work implements. My skinning tools, my scrapers, my bone knitting needles, and my spindle—all are back at the cave. I've literally got nothing to do.

It's nice at first. I doze off and on in my chair, trying to get comfortable without bugging my leg. After a while, though, I get bored. There's a bathroom of sorts set up in one of the back rooms and I refuse to let Salukh help me walk there. I spend longer than I should and use some of the melted water to wash up, wiping down my body and cleaning up the travel grime. Once I'm done, I'm restless and don't feel like returning to my chair, so I limp over to one of the doors and order the computer to open it so I can peer outside at the weather.

The moment the doors slide open, I want to close them again. The wind is gusting so hard it nearly knocks me over, and the air that rushes in is bone-chilling cold. There's snow everywhere, and it's so gray outside I can't see a thing. I gasp at the sight of it. Josie's out there in that, if she didn't make it to the cave in time. If her compass didn't work, she could be wandering in the storm, desperately trying to find shelter . . . and no one at the main cave will know she's coming.

I quell the panic I feel and take a wobbling step back from the door. "Close, please."

The doors slide shut again slowly, and I watch as the ice forms where the landing snow melted against the warmer metal. It fills in the cracks and hardens immediately, and I shiver.

Be safe, Josie. Be safe.

"She will be fine," Salukh says, his voice gentle. He's standing next to me, and as I look over at him, he puts his hands on my shoulders. "She is smart and brave. She will make it. Likely she is already back at the cave and being fussed over."

He's probably right. "I just worry." His hands are big and warm, and comforting. It feels good to have his touch, and I lean back against him. "I'd be a bad friend if I didn't."

"You are a good friend to her," he assures me.

"Is it bad that I haven't worried a bit about Taushen?" I grimace.

He chuckles, and my skin prickles with awareness at that low sound. "It is because he is a capable hunter. He will be fine, even if he is caught in the storm. It is far more dangerous for humans than for a sa-khui hunter."

That seems to be the story of everything on this planet. I nod and start to limp back over to my chair. My ankle's throbbing fiercely, protesting the fact that I'm standing. Before I can move farther than two steps, though, he scoops me up in his arms and carries me back over by the fire.

I don't protest—what's the use? Besides, it's kind of nice to be babied when I want the attention, instead of having it foisted on me. Salukh settles me into my chair with the utmost care and I give him a smile of thanks. His long, thick hair brushes against my arm as he stands, and I can't help but run my fingers through it as it whispers out of my grip. He's so . . . sexy. I shouldn't be thinking about how sexy Salukh is when he's taking care of me, should I? But I can't help it. I watch his butt flex as he strides across the room to get another fuel chip for the fire, and I watch as he squats to tend to the flame. He moves like a dancer—a dancer the size of a basketball player mixed with a linebacker. People his size shouldn't be so lithe, but he's graceful and beautiful to watch and I just want to run my nails down that rock-hard chest. Mmm.

Of course, perving on Salukh makes me feel another stab of guilt that we're here, perfectly safe in the elders' cave with a nice fire, food to eat, and a roof over our heads. We're out of the wind and the snow while Josie and Taushen are out in the elements. I think for a moment and then look over at Salukh as a new thought occurs to me. "I'm surprised Taushen didn't put up a fight, you know."

He looks over at me, eyes gleaming in the firelight. "A fight? Over what?"

I refuse to let his confusion stab at my ego. "That he didn't protest when you told him you were staying with me. It's odd he didn't say a thing, considering how excited he was over this trip." He was the *only* one excited. Well, maybe Josie, until we got here and the surgery machine was broken. Poor Josie.

Salukh shrugs his wide shoulders. "He did not complain because he knew he had lost."

I frown. "What do you mean, he knew he'd lost?"

"I told him that you were my mate."

My jaw drops. "You what?"

The gaze he focuses on me is utterly serious, utterly heart-felt. "You are mine, Tee-fah-nee. You are my woman and my mate. I know this to be true."

I stare at him, and then I sputter for a moment when no sensible words spring to mind. Eventually, I manage a shocked, "B-b-but we didn't resonate! We can't be mates!"

"We have not resonated yet," he says. "Patience. It is only a matter of time. Our khuis must simply catch up with our hearts."

He's utterly serious. There's no question in his mind that

I'm his. It doesn't matter that the symbiont that plays match-maker hasn't kicked in. To him, I'm his just as surely as if our chests were purring in unison.

My heart aches. I'm not sure if it's aching with love for him and his confidence, or sadness that we haven't resonated and he might be wrong. I don't want to love him only to lose him.

"Oh, Salukh," I say softly. "You should have said something to me."

That sexy half smile curves his mouth. "I have always known this, my mate. I was simply waiting for you to realize it."

It dawns on me that one of the things I find so irresistible about Salukh is this: his utter confidence. He truly has no doubt in his mind that I'm his mate. That if we wish hard enough, everything else will just fall into place.

I wish I possessed the same confidence.

But I smile and extend a hand to him. He takes it and presses my fingers to his mouth. I feel such love for him, but I'm terrified of it, also. I'm terrified of everything.

"It is all right." He moves to my side and caresses my cheek. "I see the worry in your eyes."

I shake my head and slide out of the chair, moving into his arms. "Then make me think of something other than worry."

A playful smile of arousal curves his mouth. He gazes at me, and then leans in so his nose can rub against mine. "Do you think to distract me, Tee-fah-nee?"

Absolutely. It's not just to distract him, though; it's for me, too. I want to forget about everything but him for the moment. I want the world to go away for a while. I want nothing to exist except us for a while.

I slide my hand down his chest and then lower, caressing

the erect bulge in his leggings. "Looks to me like you are quite willing to be distracted."

"I am a simple man," he murmurs, then nips at my lower lip with a sexy little bite. "If my woman wishes to play, who am I to say no?"

His woman. The title feels unsettling. I do want to be his, but I'm . . . afraid. I smile brightly at him to hide my worry and rub his cock through his leggings. He's hard as rock already, and my mouth waters at the thought of a new round of teasing pleasure. Salukh is so wonderful; I want to do more for him than just teasing kisses and petting. And I know just what I can do to blow his mind.

I kiss him hard, my mouth on his, our tongues twining. Then, I give him a gentle push on the shoulder, indicating he should lean back. He does, his eyes gleaming with interest as I crawl over him. I'm going to seduce this big, beautiful man, and suck his cock until he cries out.

Just the thought gets me wet with excitement, and I straddle him, my hips over his. In this position, I feel small against him. His entire body is much bigger than mine, but I still feel safe. Salukh would never hurt me, never lose his temper. He would never take me against my will or try to punish me by forcing me to do things I don't want to. Which is why I want to do this for him. I want to lick him all over and drag my mouth over the ridges of his cock. I want to tongue his spur. I want to see the look on his face when I blow his mind as I blow his cock. I want to give him this, because he's given me so much. He's loved me and never doubted me, not once.

The thought is humbling. I slide forward to kiss his mouth again. I want him to feel all the love and affection and sweetness in my heart for him. I want him to realize what he means to me, even if we never resonate. I want him to feel half as cherished as I do whenever he's around.

I move a hand down his chest. His vest is open and I push the fabric aside, exposing suede-soft skin and muscle. "God, you're pretty to look at. I'm a lucky girl."

"It is I who am lucky." His voice is rasping, and I can feel his erection seemingly growing even larger under my bottom. It gives me another little thrill.

I move lower, sliding down to his legs. When I'm sitting on his knees, I reach forward and start to undo the laces of his leggings that hold the waist together.

"What is it you do?"

I look up at him, my smile sultry. "Something we human girls are very good at." Then I pull his leggings open and tug them down, exposing his cock. It thrusts up into the air, proud and gorgeous, and I can't resist. I lean down and take him in my hand, then drag my tongue along the length of his root.

The breath hisses out of him. "You . . . will use your mouth on me?"

"All over you," I purr. "I'm going to put my mouth everywhere." To back up my words, I start pressing soft, open-mouth kisses along the ridges of his cock. "Then, when I'm done tasting you, I'm going to take you deep in my mouth and suck you until you come."

He gives a full-body shudder and I see pre-cum bead on the head of his cock. I immediately move my mouth there and lap up the salty drops. More follow, and I take several minutes to just lick and explore the crown of his cock with the tip of my tongue. His skin is soft here, not velvety like the rest of his body. It gives way to ridges and texture down the length of his cock, and I drag my fingers over it, my pussy clenching in response.

"Let me take you this time." Salukh reaches up and caresses my hair as I drag my mouth over his cock again, rubbing my lips over his hot flesh. "Let me sink inside you and claim you as my mate."

"Hush," I tell him softly. My hand slides to his spur and I give it a teasing stroke, and he groans, falling back onto the floor and closing his eyes.

Am I being fair? Probably not. I'm giving him oral because I want him, but . . . it doesn't feel right to take his virginity. He said he wanted to save it for his mate when we first started playing. He thinks I'm his mate . . . but what if he's wrong? I don't want to rob him of that first pleasure with the woman that will be his forever. So I take the head of his cock in my mouth and suck hard.

He makes an *unh* sound in the back of his throat and his hand strays to my hair again, tangling in my curls. Encouraged, I take him deeper, rubbing the length of my tongue against him as I pull him into my mouth. I can't take him very far, so I wrap my hand tight along his length and pump it as I use my mouth. His hips rise along with my movements, and the taste of him fills my senses.

"My mate," he growls. "You tease me so sweetly."

"Mmmm," I hum, because I know he'll be able to feel it all along his cock.

His hand tightens in my hair, and he starts to guide my mouth, his hips moving in time with my head. He's fucking my mouth now, and it's gloriously filthy and wonderful all at once. I keep a finger over the tip of his spur so he doesn't bonk me in the nose with it, but the truth is—he's got such a big dick that I'd have to take him a lot deeper to be in danger of that.

Not that I'm complaining about his size.

I pull back and tongue the head of his cock again, and my hand goes to his sac, teasing the sensitive flesh there. His balls are enormous, and it's a little odd to me that he's entirely hairless here when he's suede everywhere else, but I kind of like it. There's no messy pubes to get in the way of a girl's business. I lick down the length of his cock and grip him in one hand as I move lips and tongue over his sac. He groans again, and I feel his body tremble against mine. I love touching him.

I'm eager to make him come, though, and I move back to his cock and take the head of him in my mouth again and begin to pump him with my hand, faster than ever. I remember how he worked the head of his cock with a flick of his wrist and so I try to mimic that with my mouth, giving a little tug with my lips every time I pull back.

He hisses and his hand pushes me away gently. "Tee-fah-nee, I . . . I am close—"

"I know," I tell him. "I want you to come in my mouth."

He makes another pained groan, and then he's dragging my head back to his cock. My giggle at his enthusiasm is stifled as I take him back into my mouth and begin my ministrations again. *Suck, pump, flick.* His hips work faster, and I can feel the tension in his body under me.

Then, hot warmth spills into my mouth. I look up at him and see he's watching me, so I open my lips and let his spend slide down my lips and chin, because it's the most obscenely sexy thing I can think of. And he comes even harder, gritting my name out between clenched teeth and covering my mouth in endless amounts of his come.

He falls back to the floor a moment later, taking a huge breath, and I use the back of my hand to wipe my chin clean.

"I am undone, my mate. You have unraveled me like a knot." His hand reaches up to caress my cheek, even as I use the hem of my tunic to clean myself up.

"I'm glad you liked it," I tell him with a smile. I kiss his palm and hold his hand to my face.

Just because we're not mated for real doesn't mean we can't enjoy each other.

CHAPTER SIXTEEN
Tiffany

The orange, scaly hand moves along the bars of my cage.
There's no escape. Even in here, we're so cramped we can
barely move, and another girl's stinking flesh is pressed against
mine, her body cold with fear-sweat. The alien guard stares at
us with those weirdly lidded eyes, and then his hand rises.
He's pointing.

He's pointing and I should move, because if he points at
me, I'll be chosen.

I try to move away, but there are arms and legs everywhere, and that finger keeps pointing closer and closer to
where I am. I can't let it land on me, though. Not me. Not me.

I belly-crawl on the floor, not caring about the filth that
cakes my clothing as I do. There's a space behind one of the
other girls and I worm my way toward it. I don't care that I'm
pushing someone else in front of me, I just . . . I can't be
chosen.

Not me.

Her, the creature says, and there's screaming and gasps of

horror. The girl in front of me, the girl I've burrowed behind, is grabbed and dragged away. I sit up, shocked, as a familiar round face contorts in horror.

It's Josie.

I've traded my safety for hers.

"Wait," I cry out. "Not her! I didn't mean to push her in front of me!"

No one's listening. Josie kicks and screams, but they're still taking her away. I try to get up, but it's like my legs are full of cement.

"Wait," I cry out again.

A hand touches my arm, startling me. I open my eyes, not really seeing Salukh's face near mine. I'm still lost in thoughts of the cave, of Josie.

But I can move now. I can move, and the need to escape is overpowering. Everywhere I look, I see metal and spaceship, and it's just like when I was stuck in the hold when the aliens first grabbed me. I can't take it.

I have to get out.

I bolt up from the warm bed of furs I'm sharing with Salukh and race toward the closed doors of the old ship. "Open up," I scream. I need out. I need sunlight.

There's a sound like ice cracking, and then the doors slowly slide open to reveal . . .

More white.

There's nothing but white snow piled on top of white snow. There's no sky to be seen. We're completely buried.

"Tee-fah-nee?" Salukh walks up behind me and gently touches my arm. "What is it?"

I shrug his touch off and start to claw at the snow. It's wet and cold, and falls forward in massive clumps, chilling my body. I keep clawing, desperate to see sunlight, to dig a tunnel so I can see the sky above. So I can know I'm on a planet and not back in space.

"Tee-fah-nee?"

"I have to get out!"

"Why? Why do you do this?" He pulls me away, and my fingers feel like ice cubes, wet with slush. He holds them in his big warm hand. "You will harm yourself if you continue—"

"I have to save Josie," I tell him, hot tears starting to spring to my eyes. My nightmare flashes through my head. The dream is calling me out for being a coward, because I sacrificed Josie's safety so I could stay here with Salukh and play house. And now there's God knows how many feet of snow on the ground and she could be out there, turning into a human snow cone—

"Jo-see is likely back at the main cave now, drinking warm tea and sitting around the fire." He rubs my arm and then steps in front of the snowy mess I've been making. "Why all the panic over Jo-see?"

I bite my lip and fight the sob threatening to escape. "She traded her safety for me! She's not *safe*!"

He leans down and cups my face, staring into my eyes. "Tee-fah-nee, life is not *safe*. Life is full of danger. There are sweet parts and there are terrible parts. The not-knowing is what makes it worth living."

I tremble, my body caught by his intense stare. "I'm afraid." God, I'm afraid of so many things.

"It is normal to feel fear." His thumbs brush away my tears. "But you cannot let it control you, Tee-fah-nee. You must accept that there will be things in life that are not good, but they are outweighed by the good things. If there were no bad, we would not appreciate the wonders that life has to offer. There will be fear, but you must not let it win." He smiles down at me, so wonderful and so understanding. "Jo-see is fearless. She knew it was dangerous to go, and she was afraid, but she did not let it control her. She made her choice."

I breathe in and out slowly, taking in his scent and his touch. He's right.

I'm so tired of being controlled by my fears, of endless worry and being afraid to say the wrong thing and upsetting someone. I cling to his hands, tears rolling down my face. I think I've lived in a state of constant panic ever since we arrived here on the ice planet. That's why I'm so determined to stay busy—because if I'm productive and I work hard, no one will fault me. No one will notice that I'm causing trouble or that I won't pick a man if I do other things. No one will see just how scared I am, or how broken inside.

He's so right—Josie is fearless. She doesn't let the past destroy her. She makes her choices and looks forward to every day. If she's not fine, it's because she chose to do something with her life. Me? I'm the one that stays behind and huddles, afraid.

I'm so tired of being that girl. I can't keep living this way or I'm going to lose everything.

I look into Salukh's eyes. He's been so understanding all through my head games. I didn't choose him when I should have spoken up and put an end to the games, and still he loves me. I've pushed him aside, and when he's asked for sex, I've given him alternatives because I wanted him to save himself for someone else, even though he says I'm his mate.

It's time for me to stop pushing him away. It's time for me to live, too.

I have to make my own choices, like Josie. I can't wait for life to come and decide things for me. I have to grab at what happiness I can find.

"You're right," I say softly. "I can't be afraid anymore. I'm going to do better, I promise."

He nods at me, and straightens his big body. He pulls me against him in a warm embrace and I go into his arms easily. He's been there for me every step of the way, and I close my eyes and press my cheek to his chest, enjoying the feel of his big body against mine.

I'm always going to have the nightmares. Maybe they won't ever completely go away, because my past won't ever go away. But it doesn't mean I have to let it rule my life. It doesn't mean I have to let one bad moment destroy any sweetness and love I can find for myself. I need to trust.

More than that, I need to take a chance.

"I love you, Salukh," I tell him. I look up into his shining eyes. "You're my mate. No matter what happens, you're mine."

"Of course I am."

He doesn't understand what I'm trying to say here. That I've chosen, really chosen. That I'm leaping forward. But it's okay. I can show him just as easily. "From now on," I tell him, "I'm going to live my life. And if anyone doesn't like it, they can suck it."

"Suck . . . it?" He frowns, clearly puzzled by my words. "What would they suck and why?"

"Aren't you cute?" I grin up at him. "It's a human expression, and one that doesn't need to be described. Just go with the flow."

He tilts his head, adorably confused. "Flow?"

"Never mind." I take his hand in mine and drag him away

from the door and the flood of snow now melting there. "Let's go back to bed, shall we?"

"Are you yet tired?" The look on his face changes to one of concern.

"Nope."

"Are you hungry? I can feed you—"

He's going into protect mode. Sweet man. I continue to pull him toward the furs, taking care not to put much weight on my bad ankle. I'm not hungry, not thirsty, not anything other than filled with the need to fling him down in the furs and claim him as my own. To take charge of my life. To love him and have no regrets.

I feel good now that I've decided it, like the last puzzle piece has slid into place. I feel calm and settled. This feels right. His hand in mine feels right. And when his body is over mine, that's going to feel right, too, I just know it.

"Are you sure you wish to sleep after your bad dream?" He seems skeptical. "I will stay awake and keep you company if you like—"

"No one said anything about sleeping," I tell him, and step into the furs. Then, I turn and give him a sultry look and begin to peel my clothing off my body.

His eyes gleam with understanding. "Back to the furs, but not for sleep."

"Bingo." I undo the laces at my neck. I'm wearing several layers of warm clothing, and they're not sexy, but it doesn't matter. I feel sexy around him, regardless of what I have on.

"I shall not even ask what that word means," he murmurs, and when my laces are loosened, he helps me pull the heavy outer tunic over my head. I have a second layer on underneath, and it comes off just as quickly, leaving me in my leggings and the wrap I use as a bra.

"It means you're about to get lucky," I tell him.

He snorts. "I already am lucky. Am I not here with you?"

He always knows just what to say to flatter a girl. "Then get naked so I can enjoy that fine body of yours, too."

Salukh doesn't need much convincing. He strips off his vest and the blades he wears strapped to his body within moments, and then starts to remove his pants. I pause to admire him—because how can I not? The most gorgeous man on the planet is stripping for me.

My mouth goes dry as he drops his leggings to his ankles and straightens. His cock is already growing erect, and it seemingly lengthens as I gaze at him. Damn. "I'm such a lucky woman."

"I thought it was I who was to get the luck?" He finishes pulling his pants off with ease and tosses them aside. "My mate is beautiful, and smart, and eager to play in the furs. Surely I am the one with all the luck this day."

I giggle, because he's bastardizing the saying and it's so darn adorable. I'm practically giddy with happiness. Is this all it took to feel whole? Acknowledging that I can't let the past rule my life?

Wish I'd done it sooner.

No, I correct myself. I'm glad things happened as they did. If they hadn't, I wouldn't be here now with Salukh, alone and about to have what will surely be awesome sex. The only worry I have is Josie, and like Salukh said—she made her choice. She wanted to go. She assured me she could do the journey, and she was excited to test herself. I can't keep second-guessing that, so I just won't think about it any longer.

Time to get naked, instead. I undo the waistband of my pants, but pulling them down is a bit trickier. With my injured ankle, my balance is crap and I wobble and pitch forward trying to remove my clothes, only to be caught by Salukh before I smack into the ground.

"Careful," he tells me. "I do not want my mate to hurt herself undressing when I have two hands. Shall I undress you? It would be my pleasure."

How can I resist that? I sit, perched in his lap as he gently pulls my tangled clothing from my limbs. He smooths a big hand down my newly bare legs, and I shiver at the feel of his touch. Even though the khui keeps me warm, his body still feels that much warmer than mine. It's like snuggling with a heated blanket, and given that we landed on a planet of eternal winter? It's addictive. I can't stop running my hands all over that velvety skin, and he touches me everywhere he can in response.

Then he tugs at the band I have around my breasts. "Take this off."

I undo the knot at the front and let the leather slide to the ground, and then I'm naked on his lap. He leans in and nuzzles my neck, licking and kissing at my skin. "My beautiful mate," he murmurs. "Lovely in every way."

In his arms, I do feel lovely. I feel cherished and whole. He's been so good to me every step of the way, endlessly patient with my hang-ups and my worries. No woman is as lucky as me to have someone like him. "I love you," I whisper again. "Thank you for never doubting me."

He pulls back and gives me a surprised look. "Doubt you? You are mine. What is there to doubt? I know it here." He points at his head. "Even if this part of me does not realize it yet." He taps his chest. "It will come in time."

I nod. Even if it doesn't, I don't care. I have him and that's all that I want. I can be happy, just like this, forever in his arms. I turn until we're facing each other, and press my chest to his. My nipples scrape against his pectorals, and I moan when he puts a hand to my back and pulls me closer, capturing my mouth with his. This is not the lover that asks for permission before touching me—this is a man who wants to kiss and lick and caress and isn't worried if his caresses are accepted.

I love it. And I love it because it's him. With Salukh, everything is all right. Everything is acceptable, because I trust him. If he grabs me, I know I'm still fine because he would never harm me. So I kiss him back with equal intensity. Our mouths link and his tongue grazes mine. I give a small sigh of pleasure at the taste of him—he's wild and masculine and yet utterly delicious to me. The flick of his ridged tongue sends ripples of pleasure through my body, along with naughty suggestions. Ridges all over—it's like someone took a page out of my naughty-dream journal or something. I rub my nipples against his chest as we kiss, feeling the need to move against him.

His hands skim over my body and then slide down to cup my ass. He groans against my mouth as his fingers move over the cleft of my bottom. "I will never get used to the fact that you have no tail."

"Don't like it?" I ask, burying my fingers in his thick, gorgeous hair. It's a little coarse but smooth and thick and lovely. Makes me think about what our children would look like—his strands and my curls? That would be the most magnificent head of hair ever.

"I find it . . . fascinating." His fingers play against my bottom, as if he's trying to figure out where the tail would have gone. It's an arousing feeling, and I wiggle against his touch.

"There's lots of me that's fascinating," I tease him. I flick my tongue against his lower lip and then catch it between my teeth. I love his sexy little groan of response, too.

"Then I shall explore all of it," he murmurs, and his fingers trail lightly up my spine. "I will find all of your soft spots and touch them. I will learn all of you with my fingers, and then with my tongue."

A ripple of pleasure moves through me at his words. Damn. That sounds like an amazing promise. "You're on."

He shifts, looking around curiously. "What am I on?"

I giggle. I'm loading him up with all the Earth-slang when I get horny, apparently. I grab him by the horns and pull his face back toward mine for another scorching kiss.

He falls backward, his lips still locked to mine, and then we're on the floor, me straddling his body as we continue to kiss. His hands move to my breasts and he cups them, teasing and rolling the nipples with his fingers. I gasp and rock my hips against his belly.

"Sit up," he tells me. "I would see all of you."

I do, rocking my pussy against his belly. I can feel his cock brushing against my butt, and it makes me rock my hips in a little circular motion just so I can rub up against him. His hands immediately return to my breasts and he plucks at my nipples, teasing them as I put my hands down on his chest and continue to rock against him. He's got ridges down his abdomen where a happy trail should be, and they feel . . . oddly amazing against my sensitive pussy.

"You are so beautiful," he breathes, and the intense look

in his eyes makes me feel like I'm a goddess. I'm this man's goddess, and that's all I need.

I grind and rock my way a little farther down on his abs, and his cock bumps up against my bottom. "You like it when your mate rides you?"

His eyes gleam and he pulls me back down against him. "I want to taste you."

"Then taste me." I lean in for a kiss.

He nuzzles my nose again. "No, I want to taste you like you did to me last night."

Oh. He wants to go down on me. I moan at the thought of his wonderful mouth on me. "If you want to."

"I want to more than anything."

I scratch my nails on his chest. "Should I lie back? Or should I sit on your face?"

Salukh groans deeply and he buries his face against my neck, horn brushing against my cheek. "You . . . you would do that?"

"If you wanted me to. Some men don't like it because—"

He puts his hand to my mouth, silencing me. "There is no one else before now. Nothing else matters."

I can't stop smiling. "Then yes, I would do that."

He kisses me again, all over my neck and then my face, his hands going to my hair. I'm dazzled by his caresses—for a man that's a virgin, he's damn good at foreplay and at distracting me. I could do nothing but kiss and cuddle all day long. But at the same time, I'm hungry for more.

I'm also a little nervous as he lies back on the floor again, his expression hungry. I've had sex—both willingly and unwillingly. I've done a lot in the sack, but I've honestly never done what I suggested. I'm a face-sitting virgin. And this is

Salukh's first time to go down on a girl. What if it's too much? What if he hates it and then I've ruined oral for, like, forever? I bite my lip, thinking. Maybe we should start slower, ease into the kinkier stuff—

"You think too much, my mate," he murmurs, reaching out to caress one of my breasts as I straddle his stomach, my head full of worries.

"I just . . . if you don't like it, we'll try something else, okay?"

"Not like it?" He looks at me as if I'm crazy. When he sees the worry in my face, though, he nods. "If I am not happy, I will let you know."

"Okay." I take a steeling breath, and then lean forward, lifting my hips. The movement presses my breasts almost into his face, but I'm not exactly sure how to, well, how to mount. "How do we want to do this?"

"Take my horns."

I do.

"Hold on, my mate," he murmurs in a husky voice, and that's the only warning I get before his hands go to my thighs and then he's lifting me straight up onto his face.

I gasp, because he's stronger than any human guy I know, and wow, there's no time to adjust before my pussy is right over his damn mouth. I cling to his horns. My knees make it to the floor and then I'm braced on them and his horns, and it's a bit like riding a horse, except . . . his mouth is the saddle.

Salukh groans and I tense.

"The scent of you is overwhelming like this," he says thickly.

"Is . . . is that good?" Shit, I hope it's good.

"It is . . . beyond words." And then he nuzzles at my folds, his tongue dragging over my sensitive flesh.

Oh, sweet baby Jesus, that felt incredible. I shudder, because I just felt every single ridge on his tongue go over my pussy. I'm getting wetter by the minute, and it doesn't matter how open and vulnerable this position is, because I want that to happen *again*.

Like, yesterday.

I get my wish. He pushes my folds apart with his seeking lips, and then his tongue drags all the way down my pussy, from core to clit. "Tastes so good," he breathes, and I have to cling to his horns as he starts to lick me slowly up and down, over and over. A soft whimper escapes my throat, because this is the most delicious kind of torture. His hands caress my booty as he licks me, exploring my folds with his tongue. And did I think his tongue felt good in my mouth? It's nothing compared to how it feels on my pussy.

"I think I shall demand to taste your sweet cunt daily, my mate," he tells me between licks. "I shall wake you every morning with my face between your thighs and my tongue deep inside you."

I shudder against him, crying out because he punctuates that thought by dragging his tongue against my core, and then dipping the tip of it inside me.

"So good," he murmurs. "All the other hunters shall be jealous of the noises my mate makes as I pleasure her. They will wonder why I am so silent, and do you know why it will be so?"

Oh God, oh God. "W-why?" My hands clench his horns tight, and I'm doing my best not to jerk my hips or move in any way, because I want him to keep doing those magic things with his mouth.

"It is because my mouth will be full of you. My tongue will be inside your cunt, fucking you, and my hands will be full of your thighs and your sweet bottom. And I will not stop until I have tasted every drop of your sweet cream."

Then he pushes his tongue deep inside me again and I moan, my body shuddering. It feels incredible. I'm so close to coming, to grinding my pussy down on his face, but I need more. "My clit," I pant. "Please."

"You are so wet," he says, and I can feel the words against my folds. I hold on to his horns tight as he nuzzles his way up my folds and finds my clit, then begins to tease it with his tongue. "I love your taste."

I love his mouth there, so that makes both of us very happy. My fingers curl tighter around his horns—and really, they're in the perfect spot for me to hold on to, and my hips move, just a little, as he sucks on my clit. "Oh, right there," I breathe. That's the ticket.

He does it again and another whimper escapes my throat. He continues to work my clit, his fingers digging into my bottom, holding me against him. I can't help but move with him, until I'm grinding down against his tongue, forcing those ridges to drag hard against my flesh. I'm so close to coming—

And then I'm there, and stars explode behind my eyes. I cry out, and I feel my pussy clench in response, feel him lapping up the new wetness that coats my folds, and he's murmuring something that I'm too dazed and lust-drugged to understand. I collapse forward, then roll off of him onto the floor, utterly spent.

Lord have mercy, but that was incredible.

He's there a moment later, moving to my side and pulling me against him. I moan as his big warm body moves against mine, because even though I just came, everything feels ultra-sensitive. My pulse is pounding hard in my veins and I'm at the in-between stage of feeling loose and good and wanting more. It seems I'm always, always wanting more of this man.

His mouth moves to my shoulder and he kisses it softly. He begins to kiss every inch of skin he can reach, going to my neck, down to my breasts, and then kissing my stomach. I feel caressed and loved, and utterly beautiful in his arms.

I gently tug on him, pulling his body over mine. When he moves over me, I hook one leg around his hip, spreading my legs underneath him. He pushes his body down against mine until our hips are joined, and his cock rests against my pussy. The weight of him over me is enormous, but he's bracing himself with one muscled arm and I love the feel of his body over mine. It makes me feel tiny and fragile, and utterly possessed by him.

He leans in to kiss me, his mouth moving lightly against mine. "If you want to stop now, we can."

I smile up at him. "There's no chance of that happening. I'm claiming you as my mate. I want you inside me."

Salukh gives me an intense kiss in response, his teeth lightly scoring my lower lip. He lifts his head and closes his eyes for a moment, as if steeling himself, and then looks at me. "Shall I . . . claim you now?"

I bite my lip and nod up at him. I want this. I want him. I touch his cheek, full of love for this tender but possessive man. He's so perfect for me. I spread my legs wider as he reaches down between us and settles his cock at the entrance to my body. My blood is pounding in my veins and I'm filled with a wild sort of eagerness that surprises me. It feels like . . . like something big is about to happen. Like I'm about to orgasm again.

Which is silly, because he hasn't even penetrated me. I'm just excited that we're finally going to be together, I decide. I stroke his gorgeous, thick hair and move my hands over his muscles, just pleased with being able to touch him and play with this big, glorious body of his.

I feel him fit the head of his cock against me, and then give a gentle push. The moment he does, my heart starts to pound a little harder. And harder still, even as I gasp at the feeling of him entering me. He's going slow, but that doesn't disguise the fact that he's not equipped like a human guy, and everything about him is enormous. I feel stretched full, my body tight as he inches into me, and the blood is pounding so hard in my veins that I feel like I'm going to explode.

Then his eyes meet mine, and I realize . . . I'm not the only one with a pounding heart. I can hear his. It's pounding so loud and so quickly that—

It's not pounding. He's purring. I'm purring, too.

We're *resonating*.

I gasp and put a hand to his chest, over his heart. "Salukh!"

"I feel it," he grits out. "I knew. I have *always* known you were mine, Tee-fah-nee."

A happy sob escapes my throat, and I fling my arms around his neck. "You did! You did, and I should have listened. Oh, I love you so much."

His lips brush over mine. "This changes nothing. You were mine before resonance, and you are yet mine."

"I am," I choke out, tears sliding down my cheeks. "I'm all yours." I arch my back. "Take what is yours."

In response, my mate's body stiffens over mine.

"What? What is it?"

His forehead presses against mine and he closes his eyes. "I need a moment. The resonance . . ."

I understand. The resonance—while amazing and totally welcome—is making it hard for him to keep control. He *is* a virgin, after all, and this is his first time. The fact that the resonance is ratcheting things up? No wonder he's struggling for control. I smooth a hand down his side, touching him because I can't seem to help myself. I'd probably die if I stopped touching him in this moment. I can wait.

Right here, right now, I feel complete. My mate is buried deep inside me, my breast is resonating to him, and the world feels full of wonder and opportunity.

Salukh thrusts into me shallowly, then freezes again. "I do not know," he begins, and then groans. "You . . . but—"

"You're fine," I murmur, stroking a hand over his cheek, his brow, down his hair. God, I just want to keep touching him everywhere. "We can go fast. We have all the time in the world for more."

Even as I say the words, it strikes me with wonder. We *do* have all the time in the world. We absolutely, positively belong to each other now. Our khuis have paired us and there's no chance that another person can ever come between us. I could laugh for the sheer joy of it.

"I do not wish to frighten you, Tee-fah-nee," Salukh grits out. "But if I move, I do not believe I can move slow." His brow is dotted with sweat, and strain shows in his face. The cords of his neck stand out, as if it's taking everything he has not to just go buck wild on me.

But I'm down for buck wild.

"Salukh?" I whisper. "Lean in for me?"

He does.

I knot my hand in his hair and bite at his jaw, then run my tongue along the mark.

He growls low in his throat, the sound nearly lost with the steady thrum of our resonance. A moment later, he bares his teeth in a snarl, the look in his eyes wild.

And he pounds into me with a quick, brutal stroke.

I gasp. A million sensations rocket through me—the ridges of his cock dragging against my inner walls, the push of his spur against my clit, the feeling of his penetration—it's all incredible. I still know I'm safe, and it's a little shocking—and exciting—to see my self-contained Salukh lose his cool. I put my hands on his hips and dig my nails in. "That's it, baby. Lose control for me."

He snarls again, and begins a rapid, rough rhythm of thrusts. He's moving so quickly that I can't lift my hips fast enough to match his movements. His spur teases my clit constantly as he hammers into me, and he's pumping so hard that the furs are bunching up under us. Not that it matters one bit to me—the way he's moving against me feels incredible. My mouth hangs open in a permanent whimper, and I'm unable to form a coherent thought. There's too much pleasure in my body, and it is only moments before I cry out and my pussy clenches around his cock, my body tightening with my orgasm.

"Mine," he grits out between his teeth. "My woman. My mate." His thrusts become rougher, harder, and I moan as another orgasm sweeps through me. "*Mine.*"

Then I feel it—a hot, liquid splash inside me, and I know he's coming. His body shudders over mine even as he pumps into me. I cling to him as he comes, my body still surging wildly with my own orgasm. When he collapses on top of me, I moan with relief. If he'd kept pumping, I have no doubt I'd have kept coming, over and over and over.

Sweaty, suede-like blue skin sticks to mine, and his long hair is tangled in my face. I could care less, though. I close my eyes and lose myself in the sensation of his chest purring against mine. It feels so . . . intimate. Even more than sex. It's like our khuis are declaring their love for one another.

Salukh lifts his head and gazes down at me, then begins to press hot little kisses to my face. "I am glad," he murmurs.

"Glad?" I ask, gazing up into his wonderful face. "About what?"

"Glad that my khui has finally listened to my entreaties." He gives me a wry grin. "I have been pleading with it for many moons now to claim you as my mate. It has been silent until now."

I smile shyly up at him. Has he been in love with me for that long? "I think I had to come to terms with things first." The moment I say it, I realize I'm right. I don't have an IUD like Josie, and I wasn't on the pill like Megan, who resonated to her mate a few months after we landed. There was no reason physically for me to not immediately mate to someone.

It was all mental. Maybe my khui knew that, and knew I needed time to come to terms with life here. That I needed to be okay with a man touching me before I could ever move forward.

Maybe it knew that I needed Salukh.

Smart khui, I tell it. *You're the best.*

CHAPTER SEVENTEEN
Tiffany

For the next four days, we barely leave our furs. We eat, we hydrate, we wash the sweat off our bodies with a few handfuls of snow, and then we crawl back into bed and make out like teenagers. Really, really dirty teenagers.

I love it. I love every moment I have with Salukh. He's insatiable in bed and adventurous to boot. There's nothing too kinky or weird for him, and we try out all the positions I can think of and one or two that he comes up with. Also? The man loves to eat pussy. I've woken up several times to find him between my legs, determined to bring me to orgasm to start the day.

How could I possibly complain about that?

Resonance is a big part of why we're insatiable—the purring between our bodies is nonstop, and I suspect we'll be horny as fools until he plants a baby inside me. I can already tell a few differences in sex—the moment I hear him purring, I get wet. Doesn't matter if we just had sex, it's an instant panty-dampener. Well, if I had panties. As for Salukh? He's no longer shooting blanks. Now when he comes, it's milky and thick instead of more fluid like before. I can only guess that it's full of a lot of swimmers doing their best to make their way to my end zone. I'm fine with that. I've started to dream about babies that have Salukh's horns and my wild, kinky curls. It'd be the cutest darn baby ever.

Even after the initial resonance craziness wears off and we no longer feel the intense need to bone each other's brains out, we don't do much exploring. I'm not interested in a lot of what the ship holds; to me, it's all sad, broken stuff. I'm not like Harlow, constantly trying to think of inventions. I'm more of a crafts girl. And it's clear to me that Salukh doesn't trust any of the old ship stuff, so we stick to our main fire.

After a week or so, the fuel for the firepit runs low, and so does the food. We snuggle for a day or two under the covers with no fire before Salukh decides that it's time to venture out into the snow and do a little hunting. I offer to go with him, but he refuses. My ankle's doing better now, no longer as swollen, but he wants me to stay off of it for a little longer. So I pass a lonely day pouting by the cold firepit, swathed in blankets, and do some napping. The day is long and really damn lonely without my mate at my side.

When Salukh returns with a frozen dvisti carcass and a bag full of fire fuel, I shower him with kisses and groping until he forgets all about food or fire and makes love to me. After we eat and build a fire, we snuggle in the furs, naked. My fingers are interlaced with his larger ones, and he keeps kissing my shoulder, no doubt ready for another round in the sack.

He surprises me with his words, though. "Do you miss home? Your home before here?"

I look over at him. "Why do you ask?"

He presses another kiss to my shoulder and then lightly licks my skin. "Because I imagine you in a place like this." He gestures at the old ship. "And it makes me wonder how you can ever be happy living in a cave."

I smile and pull his hand to my breast so he can play with my nipple. "My home wasn't like this."

"No?"

"Nope. I grew up on a farm. We had chickens and cows and even had a little garden. It was a lot of work."

"Did you have a mate? A family?"

"I had an aunt. My mother's older sister," I explain, because I realize there's no word in their language for "aunt." "Both of my parents were soldiers and they died overseas. My father died in a transport accident, and my mother from friendly fire." I used to think I was the unluckiest kid ever to lose both parents in the same war. "My aunt was older than my mother by about fifteen years, but I didn't have anywhere else to go, so she took me in. If I wanted to earn my keep, I had to work, she said, so I did. I woke up every morning and fed the chickens, collected eggs, then I went to the barn and baled hay, fed the cattle, milked, let them out to the pasture, and then I went to school. Came home and did more chores, cleaned up around the house, and went to bed. When I graduated high school, I went to cosmetology classes for a bit, but I had to drop them because they were expensive." My aunt wasn't giving me money to help, and between my farm chores and the classes, I barely had time to hold down a job. "It was . . . tough sometimes."

"And that is why you are always working? Because you feel you must?"

I blink at the fire, surprised by his words. "I've never

thought of it that way, but I guess you're right. My parents loved me, but my aunt didn't know what to do with me. She made it clear that I needed to earn my place if I wanted to stay." I'd never felt loved by my aunt, just felt like a frustrating sort of obligation or maybe even more like a farmhand that she couldn't get rid of. Add to the fact that I'd had diabetes pre-khui and I felt like a never-ending problem for her. I never felt like family. I'd carried that feeling over onto the ice planet, where I kept myself busy with tanning and farming and trying to come up with ways to show that I could pull my weight. Some of it was the fact that I just couldn't sit around idle, and some of it was insecurity.

Huh.

He nibbles on my shoulder and then kisses his way up my neck. "And now? Now you will become fat and lazy and have your mate bring you foods?"

I laugh. "I doubt that. More like I'll still work my tail off, and then when you come home, I'll work your tail off in the furs."

He gives my butt a sad pat. "You have already worked your tail off, my mate."

My giggles fill the elders' cave.

Salukh

I rub at my teeth with a small stick to clean them and watch as my mate sits curled up near the fire, sewing. It is daylight outside and has not snowed for two days, which means I should get out and gather more fuel for the fire, and look for hunting. I am strangely reluctant to leave, though. My chest rumbles contentedly as I gaze at my mate, my khui humming a happy song.

My mate. She is breathtaking to look at and know that she is mine. I watch as Tee-fah-nee bends her head closer to the fire and pushes the bone awl through the furs, then tugs the cord through with long, delicate fingers. Her brown skin is flecked with orange in the firelight, and her wild halo of hair gleams. She catches me staring at her and a small smile curves her mouth.

"What is it?"

I shake my head. "Just admiring my beautiful mate and her busy fingers."

Her smile broadens. "Your mate wouldn't have to stay so busy if you'd be more careful with the furs at night."

I grin, thinking of last night. In my eagerness to put my mouth on my mate, I might have ripped the furs . . . twice. "Your male is hungry for his female."

"My male is not just hungry, he's insatiable," she teases. Her words are sharp, but the look she gives me tells me that she's thinking about sex, too. Her breasts are rising and falling more rapidly and I can hear the hum of her khui as her arousal begins. Ah, being a resonance mate is the finest pleasure I have ever known.

I toss the tooth-cleaning stick into the fire. I'll go hunting later. For now, there's a very enticing female who is just begging to have her cunt licked—

"Hell-oooo," calls out a high, female voice in the distance. "Anyone there?"

Tee-fah-nee's head snaps up. "Ohmigohd! Jo-see!" She scrambles to her feet.

All thoughts of fur-play are forgotten, and I follow my

212 • RUBY DIXON

mate as she dashes toward the entrance to the elders' cave. I
dug a tunnel through the snow out to the open a few days ago,
and it has not yet filled in. Footsteps crunch and my mate does
a happy bounce, clapping her hands, as fur-bundled figures
waddle in through the entryway, their snowshoes tracking
snow inside.

"Jo-see!" Tee-fah-nee flings her arms around the first figure, giving her a long, happy hug. "You're safe! I'm so glad!"
Then she turns to the next one and her happy squeal gets
louder. "Leezh! And Har-loh! You're all here! Where are your
bay-bees?"

The one called Leezh pulls off her hood, shaking out bright
yellow hair. "Back at the cave. Stacy's playing day care while
we have a girls' night out. Or day out. Or whatever." She looks
over at me and smirks. "Sorry to interrupt the *hon-ee-mewn*."

My Tee-fah-nee shoots me a look and her face is ruddy
with color. "Oh, stop."

Curious. I hang back and let the females catch up with my
mate. They are all chatting excitedly, shedding their furs as
Tee-fah-nee takes them in hand and brings them to the fire to
dry out. She has no more limp—it has been two weeks and her
delicate ankle is healed. She's radiant with happiness right
now, reaching out to touch Jo-see's arm over and over again,
her relief at the sight of her friend evident. The women all
move toward the fire, talking about the *sur-jree ma-cheen* and
how Har-loh wants to look at it again and Leezh's kit is starting to crawl and Jo-see has been at the main cave for the last
two weeks and the new caverns have been opened and how
wonderful and spacious they are and how Tee-fah-nee should
see them!

After two weeks of relative quiet, it feels odd to have so

many voices talking again. I feel a pang of regret that my time here with Tee-fah-nee will come to an end, but we will go back to the cave and start our own fire together. The thought is more than appealing, and I press a kiss to my mate's head as I pass the fire to get more fuel.

It grows silent.

"Well, that's new." Leezh's voice is coy. "Someone's been knocking boots."

The words do not make sense to me, but Tee-fah-nee's giggle does. My khui starts purring at the sound, and I hear hers join in. At once, the women gasp.

"No effing way," Jo-see shrieks. "For real?"

"For real," Tee-fah-nee says, and beams at her. "Salukh and I resonated." She reaches a hand out to me and I put my palm in hers. There is such beauty and contentment in my mate's face, I resonate even louder, the song in my breast one of pure happiness.

Leezh and Har-loh both exclaim happiness, patting my mate and pulling her forward to hug.

Jo-see bites her lip and the smile on her face fades a little. "I'm happy for you, but sad for me. Now I'm the only one left."

Tee-fah-nee's face grows sad and she extends her other hand to her friend. "Give it time. It'll happen."

"We'll see." Her expression looks like she doesn't believe Tee-fah-nee.

"If the ma-cheen," Tee-fah-nee begins. Then, she stops.

All of the females look at me.

I am not a fool. I can tell when a male is not wanted. I kiss my lovely mate's brow again and then gesture at the fire. "Remain here. I will hunt something to feed all of you."

I hunt for several hours to give the females time to talk amongst themselves. As I walk, I pick up fallen branches and dung chips, adding them to the satchel I carry over my shoulder for fuel. The snow is thick and crusty, and my legs sink up to the shin with every step, but the game is plentiful. I spend most of the afternoon checking traps and then bringing the fresh kills back to the cache I have been using to feed my mate. I add new game to it for the next hunter, and then bring home a fat scythe-beak for my mate.

When I return, the women are not in the main room. I find them all in one of the back rooms, with Har-loh halfway in the wall, pulling on what looks like a lot of colorful sinews. Nearby, Jo-see stands with her hands clasped, a hopeful expression on her face as my mate talks quietly to Leezh. Tee-fah-nee's face brightens at the sight of me, and my khui immediately starts to purr the moment our eyes make contact.

"Oh, that is so damn cute," Leezh proclaims. "I'd tell you two to get a room but you have a whole ship already."

"Are you hungry?" I ask, glancing uneasily at Har-loh as she pulls out the guts of the wall. I did not even know the wall had guts.

"We should eat," Tee-fah-nee declares. "You, too, Harlow. Josie."

"I'm not hungry," Jo-see says.

Har-loh sets down the wall's guts and wipes black smears off her hands. "This is going to take a while, Josie. I don't know how many days, but it's going to be a process of finding the burned-out component and then seeing if there's a similar one anywhere else on the ship. It might be weeks. You'll probably be back in the main cave by the time it's up and running. If that's the case, I can send a runner to come and get you."

Jo-see nods slowly and the women emerge from the room to come and eat near the fire. It's clear whatever Har-loh has told her is not the answer she wants to hear. Poor Jo-see. She seems sad. I rebuild the fire as the females talk amongst themselves, skinning my kill and then putting half of the meat on for charring, the way humans like it, and leaving half raw. As the food cooks, Tee-fah-nee settles in next to me and I put my hand on her leg, pleased at the simple action of being able to touch her. I will never get enough of that.

When everyone has eaten enough, Leezh looks over at us. "So what's the plan?"

"Plan?" I look to Tee-fah-nee.

She puts her hand over mine and gives it a squeeze. "I guess I'm ready to go back to the South Cave whenever it's safe to travel. My leg is better."

"I'll go with you," Jo-see says. "Might as well get my things."

Leezh nods. "There's no reason to split the caves anymore. With the new cave system opened up, there's plenty of room for everyone, even newly mated couples." One of her eyes closes in an exaggerated motion.

At her side, Har-loh groans. Leezh does it again.

"Is something wrong with your eye?" I ask Leezh.

All four women break into laughter. Tee-fah-nee just pats my knee and murmurs something about me being sweet.

I don't understand what I missed, but my mate's touch reminds me of what is important. "If Tee-fah-nee does not want to go back just yet, we will stay here."

"It's fine," she tells me in a calm voice. Her fingers stroke mine. "It's not like the others can still try to pursue me as their mate. I've been thoroughly claimed."

And her expression becomes embarrassed as the other women titter.

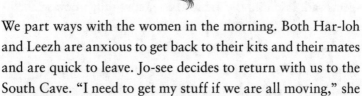

We part ways with the women in the morning. Both Har-loh and Leezh are anxious to get back to their kits and their mates and are quick to leave. Jo-see decides to return with us to the South Cave. "I need to get my stuff if we are all moving," she says. The smile is back in her eyes and her expression is bright once more.

The snow is thick on the ground and both Jo-see and Tee-fah-nee exclaim over the changed landscape. They are slow to walk the paths, thanks to the snowshoes on their feet, and I make sure they have plenty of time to safely cross the sloping ground. I will not rush them as Taushen did. We make camp in one of the hunter caves overnight, and I build a fire for both Tee-fah-nee and Jo-see to stay warm while they sleep. I guard the entrance, ever on alert. My mate is the dearest thing in the world to me and I will not let my guard down for a moment if it would mean her injury.

In the morning, we clean up the small cave and then head on toward home. Both women are in good spirits, Tee-fah-nee smiling instead of her normal pensive look, and Jo-see chatting and singing along the way. I am watchful, but I cannot resist staring at my mate constantly. I could gaze at her fine features for hours on end and never be bored. Truly, I am the luckiest of sa-khui to have won the most attractive, smartest mate. To add to my blessings, we will soon have a kit. My heart is full.

"Look," Tee-fah-nee calls out as we near the South Cave. "My plants are growing!" She tromps forward in her snow-shoes, toward the fragile pink stalks that jut from the snow. "It worked!" She digs her furry mittens into the snow as Jo-see moves to her side.

"The plants use the same fuel as the fire?" I ask, remember-ing her task of dropping a dung cake into each hole dug for seeds.

"I guess it nourishes the seed itself. I just remembered a story about Native Americans and the first Thanksgiving and the Indians putting fish in with the seeds to make them grow, so I thought manure might do the same." She claps her mittens and beams up at me. "This is so great! This means we can plant our own food and have lots of not-potatoes for the next brutal season."

She is clever, my mate. I smile my pride down at her. "You are wise as well as beautiful."

"Oh barf, get a room, you two," Jo-see says and stomps on ahead.

Tee-fah-nee giggles and gets to her feet, smiling at me. "Se-riously, this is so great. I'm stoked."

I'm not sure what *stoked* means, but it is clear to me she is pleased at her own cleverness. I am, too. "It is a shame we will have to leave them behind if we are all moving back to the main tribal caves."

"I can plant them there, too. I've been saving seeds. I'd like an entire snow garden, if I can swing it."

"I shall dig all the holes you need," I tell her.

"I was counting on that."

We arrive back at the South Cave a few moments after Jo-see and it's clear there is much celebrating. The human women hug and Aehako gives me a friendly clap on the shoulder. "We will talk later about your disobeying my orders," he murmurs.

"If I did not, the women would have been in danger and the hunters would have been caught out in the storm un-awares."

He grins. "Which is why we will talk later instead of me booting your tail right now."

I know then that things are fine. He is smiling and not angry, and everyone in the cave is safe. The hunters are all there. Taushen is by the fire with the others, and Haeden has a strange look on his face as he gazes from the back of the cave at Jo-see. I can't tell if it's relief or anger.

My sister, Farli, comes running out to hug me, and the tiny dvisti scampers at her feet. She flings her arms around my neck and I embrace her, laughing. "We have been gone but a few weeks and already it follows you?"

"He does! He thinks I am his mother," Farli says with a giddy laugh, and then looks over at Tee-fah-nee, uncertain.

"It's all right," Tee-fah-nee says, smiling. "You've been taking care of him more than I have and he should be yours."

Farli gasps. "Oh, it is so strange to hear you speak our language! Strange and wonderful!"

"That is not all," I tell my sister proudly, and move closer to Tee-fah-nee. As I do, our khuis begin to purr in unison, and the sound fills the cavern. Around us, eyes widen in surprise and then delight.

Aehako whoops with laughter and the smack on the back he gives me turns into a hug. "No wonder you fought so hard for her! Your brain knew before your khui did!" He slaps one of my horns.

I smile proudly. "She is mine and I am hers."

"Then we should celebrate! Who has the *sah-sah*?"

Both Tee-fah-nee and I are hugged over and over again, everyone in the tribe wishing us well as two skins of fermented sah-sah are found and a celebration begins. There are not many left in the South Cave, so it feels like a more intimate gathering, but it is still enjoyable. One by one, my recent rivals approach me and wish me well. There are no hard feelings, though it is evident that they are disappointed. How can anyone compete with resonance? It decides no matter what we choose, and it did not choose them. I see a few eyeing Jo-see with mild interest, but she seems lost in thought, chatting with Farli and petting the little dvisti. My sister has covered the creature with braids and colorful streamers woven into its thick mane. Since he runs around loose now, it is to ensure that no one hunts him by accident, she tells me between sips of sah-sah.

A freshly hunted snow-cat is spitted over the fire and we eat strips of bloody, raw meat while the humans wait for their bits to be cooked. Tasty seeds are passed around, and everyone laughs and has a great time. Jo-see sings a song called "Geeli-gans Eye-land," which causes no end of amusement to the human women. The last of the sah-sah is brought out and Farli pulls out her paints, drawing colorful designs on the skin of anyone who will let her.

I do not drink much. Tomorrow will be a busy day. We will pack up the South Cave and begin the trek back to the main tribal caves. There, we will start anew. Tee-fah-nee and I will have our own cave, private and away from the others. Our life together starts now.

She looks over at me as Farli draws a yellow swirl on her brown cheek, her eyes shining with happiness. My khui sings at the sight of her, luminous in the firelight. Mine, it says, singing a rhythm in time with hers. All mine.

My mate.

My cock swells in response as her gaze moves up and down my body and there's a sultry look in her eyes. Though the fever of initial resonance has died down, I am still aroused when my chest hums along with hers. She murmurs something to Farli and gets to her feet, moving to my side.

"Shall we leave the party early?" she asks me, her hand sliding into mine.

"Are you tired?" I ask.

"Exhausted," she murmurs, but the look in her gaze is not one of sleep. It is one of promise.

I grin. "Then shall we go and find our furs?"

"Sounds like a wonderful idea to me." She glances around as if to see if anyone is watching. Then she gives a small shrug of her shoulders and pulls me toward the cave she shares with Jo-see. Someone hoots in response and I laugh, because this cave has no secrets. This time, though, it does not matter if they know. We are mated. Nothing changes that.

Let them know I will take my mate to my furs and lick every bit of her flesh. Let them hear her cries of pleasure. It will let them know that she is mine. My mate, my resonance.

My everything.

CHAPTER EIGHTEEN
Josie

I sigh as I watch Tiff and Salukh not-so-furtively sneak into the cave for some nookie. I'm happy they're happy, but being with them the last few days is trying my last damn nerve. They resonated. Great. I'm stoked for them. Jealous, too, but mostly stoked. What's hard is that I keep worrying about me. I'm the last single woman, the last lonely human. Am I going to have a cave by myself? Am I going to be stuck in someone else's cave like a reject? Am I going to have to listen to everyone else make out and know that I'm never going to have a mate because Harlow can't fix the stupid surgery machine?

I stare glumly at the fire. Even all the terrible sa-khui singing (and man, they are *terrible* at it) and the alcohol can't get me happy. It wasn't so bad when I wasn't the last human alone. I didn't feel like a total reject then.

Now? Now I feel like a total reject.

It's a feeling I'm kind of used to, after being dumped from a half dozen foster homes growing up. Here, though, I felt like I was part of a family, at least for a while. Then one by one, the family paired off with mates. Not just any mate, fated mates. And now they're all popping out babies and here I am, still sitting on the bench, waiting my turn.

A small movement catches my eye and I look up from the fire to see Haeden scowling in my direction from his vantage point in the shadows. He looks pissier than usual, which is kind of a feat for him. Our eyes lock and he crosses his arms over his chest, as if daring me to confront him. Whatever. I make a face at him. I don't know why he's got a hate-boner for me but I'm tired of it. I'm a little pleased—and weirdly disappointed—when he stalks away.

I nudge Farli, who's settling in next to me with her paint pots. "So what's with Haeden lately?"

"Hmm?" She dabs a brush in red and then paints a dot on my arm.

"He looks more angry than usual," I tell her, and obediently turn my arm so she can paint an accompanying blue dot next to the red one.

"Oh. He was very . . . sour . . . when he found out you went to the main tribal cave alone. He yelled at Taushen for many hours."

My eyebrows go up. "Why? He hates me."

She shrugs and holds my arm, painting a ticklish circle on it. "He is protective of females. He thinks it is foolish to risk them."

Oh barf. So he's a chauvinist. "I was perfectly fine." Sure, it was a little scary, but I handled it.

"Yes, but humans are weak. He says that risking your life means risking more than just one life. It is potentially robbing another male of his mate and kits."

"Good thing I'm only worth my vagina to him," I say blandly. Joke's on him: my girl parts have a permanent no-vacancy sign on them, alas.

"What is *va-shy-nuh*?" Farli asks. "I do not know this word."

"Never mind." I probably shouldn't be teaching Farli dirty human words. She can't be more than fourteen or so. "He's just a jerk. Always has been and always will be."

"What is *yerk*?" She draws another circle on my arm, this time a sickly green. "You're fun to paint on, Jo-see. You are white like Chahm-pee's belly. The colors show up nicely."

Greeeaaaat. "A *jerk* is a man who thinks with his male parts."

She giggles.

So much for my vow not to teach her bad human words. Oh well.

The murmur of voices dies for a moment, and as it does, I hear a throaty moan coming from my cave. Ah, crap. Tiff's definitely getting it on with Salukh, and it sounds like they don't know—or don't care—how loud they are. Farli seems unfazed by the noise, though Taushen gets up and leaves the fire. Yeah, I know how he feels, but at least he doesn't have to room with the happy couple. I do.

Well, at least for tonight. Tomorrow, who knows. I'll probably be rooming with the baskets tomorrow. Or the dvisti. Great. Me and the dvisti—the only creatures no one wants to hang with.

I'm not that chatty, so Farli eventually moves on to someone else, and I stay by the fire, moping. I can't go back to my cave, not with those two getting it on. Maybe I'll go borrow a blanket from Kira and hide in one of the now-empty caves. I get to my feet, and as I do, a soft clink at my feet catches my attention.

I look down, and there's something gleaming in the firelight on the tip of my boot. I pick it up, frowning. It fell out of my leggings. What in the heck? It looks like a plastic little Y of sorts, which is weird. Did it get stuck in my boot from when we were at the elders' spaceship? But if so, how . . .

I gasp as I realize what I'm looking at. It's not from the elders' ship.

It's my IUD.

Somehow, my body has forced it out. My khui must have been silently working on pushing it out of my system. I clutch it in my hand, my heart hammering with excitement.

This changes *everything*!

Now, I can get pregnant.

Now, I can resonate. I can have a mate!

I can have a family, a happy ever after. I can have everything I always dreamed of. I don't have to wait for Harlow to fix the surgery machine, because my body fixed itself. *Thank you, khui! Thank you! I take back all the awful things I said about you.*

I look around eagerly at the people by the fire. Who's going to be my mate? There're several males in the tribe that are attractive. Vaza returns my gaze with an assessing look of his own, and to my relief, my khui remains silent. Good. It's not desperate. Vaza's older and nice, but he's also tried hitting on every single unmated woman. He's seated next to Bek, and I'm glad that my khui isn't making a sound for him, either.

Hassen is probably my number one draft pick at the moment, because he's sexy, but he's nowhere to be found. Taushen, either. There are two elders talking off to one side but I'm pretty sure one had a mate back in the day and the other could be my grandpa. Just to make sure, though, I stroll past them.

Nothing. Whew.

No problem, cootie. We still have lots of man-meat in this cavern before we run out. "Anyone seen Hassen?" I ask.

"He's in his cave, packing," Vaza says.

"Super." I jump to my feet and head in that direction. Even if I don't resonate to Hassen, there's a few guys back at the other cave that might not be bad picks. Rokan, for one, is kinda studly and he's always been nice to me. I'd be down with that.

I head for the cave that many of the single hunters live in, and the privacy screen isn't up. "Yoo-hoo," I call out, my voice sweet. Tonight's the night, I can feel it.

Tonight, I get my mate and my happy ever after. I'm so excited I could cry tears of joy. Tonight, my life starts. Tonight, I get my family. Tonight, I'm no longer a reject.

Hassen pops out of his cave, a confused look on his face. "Yes? What is it?"

I smile at him, but . . . nothing happens. "Just . . . thought I'd say hi? Have you seen Taushen?"

He narrows his eyes at me. "He is here."

"Can I say hi to him, too?"

"Is this a human custom?"

I keep smiling, because even his puzzled look is not going to get me down. Not tonight. "Yes, yes it is."

He grunts and heads back into the cave. I admire his ass for a moment, because, darn, it *is* a rather nice ass. Not my ass, though. Oh well. I'm sure mine will be awesome. Taushen's got a tight little bod himself, and—

—And he pops out of the cave a moment later, giving me an eager look. "Ho, Jo-see. What is it you need?"

Nada. Dammit.

I make my excuses, citing a sudden need to find a potty, and hurry away. Who's left? There's Vadren talking to Harrec, and while both are older than me, I could learn to love me some May-December relationship action. I sidle up to them, pretending to listen to their conversation. Nothing.

Is . . . my cootie on vacation?

I put a hand to my heart, worried. I've approached every guy in the cave that's single. Maybe my mate's back at the other tribal cave? That's disappointing, but I guess I can wait another day or so. I start to head back to the fire when . . . my chest feels funny.

I automatically look down and my small boobs are vibrating. I gasp, clutching my tunic tighter to my body so no one sees that. My chest continues to vibrate, and as it does, the noise grows louder. I'm resonating.

I'm motherfucking *resonating*!

I want to scream with joy. I look around with excitement, trying to see who it is that set my cootie off. Who did I forget? Or did someone trigger me on a second chance? Or—

I turn around and Haeden's standing right behind me, frozen in place.

My eyes widen and I clutch my vibrating boobs.

No.

Hell to the no.

"It's not you," I whisper.

He looks down at his chest, and then at me.

Then, I hear it. A matching thrum, a low purr.

And it's coming from my worst enemy. As I watch, his

nostrils flare and there's a look of such anger and agony on his face.

It has to be echoed on mine. Has to be. This is my worst nightmare. All I've ever wanted is a family. Someone that loves me. A happy ever after.

Resonating to Haeden?

My dream is completely destroyed.

EPILOGUE
Tiffany

A menacing orange hand moves along the bars of the cell.

I'm shoved in here, sandwiched between several other human girls, and I'm unable to move. I'm trapped here as that hand drags over the bars ominously. In a moment, it's going to pick someone. In a moment, that girl will be taken away and unspeakable things will be done to her.

I squeeze my eyes shut, trying to ignore the stink of bodies around me. Not me, I beg. Not me.

The whimpers in the cell die away. The smells die away. Around me, a low, steady purr begins. The hand disappears.

The cage fades away to black.

I'm safe.

The body against mine purrs and thrums, matching its song to the one in my breast. As it does, I know things will be fine. I'm safe.

And I sleep.

ICE PLANET
HONEYMOON

SALUKH & TIFFANY

Tiffany

"He looks utterly ridiculous," I tell Farli as Chompy prances in the snow nearby.

I'm supposed to be gathering roots for leather dye. Hemalo tells me there's a certain kind that if you boil them long enough, they turn a dark, deep shade of green, and I want to see if I can make a tunic that color for Josie. She's been so stressed ever since resonating to Haeden. I want to give her something to look forward to, and perhaps seeing a new, special tunic come together will help. It's small, but it's an idea. The problem is that I haven't found a single root, because Farli and tiny Chompy followed me to keep me company. Now, every time I kneel down in the snow to dig, Chompy thinks we're playing a game. He makes this weird, excited bleat, prances to my side, and shoves his nose into the hole I'm digging.

It's such an amusing situation that I'm not getting anything done. If his actions weren't bad enough, the fact that he's trussed up like a Not-Hoth show pony cinches it. Farli has him covered in strands of dyed leather that flutter like ribbons around him. His thick, fluffy mane has been worked into several fat braids that stick out, and she's worked the colorful skin-paints into each one. Farli tells me it's so no one mistakes Chompy for a wild dvisti and shoots him. I secretly think Farli just likes dressing him up. She's always the first one to the paint pots during a celebration, and Chompy is a willing canvas.

A willing, silly canvas. True to form, the moment I bend down to dig again, he charges, bounding through the snow like a goat, bleating. Farli peals with laughter as I straighten, grinning. "I'm tempted to throw my stick aside and call it a day. I'm not sure how you get anything done with this little clown shadowing you."

Farli giggles. "He is smart! I've taught him how to hunt with me already. Watch!" She claps her hands twice, the sound soft. The change in Chompy is immediate. He flattens himself to the snow, right onto his belly, and gives Farli an expectant look.

I've seen cattle dogs that weren't trained half so well, and my brows go up. "That's impressive. How'd you manage that?"

"Snacks," Farli says proudly. She taps her leg once, and Chompy jumps to his feet again, prancing over to her. The moment he does, she pulls a bit of dry not-potato out of a pouch and gives him a cube. "Leezh told me that her father had hunting animals that he trained to bring down birds. I do not know if Chompy would be much use against a scythe-beak, but I figure I can teach him to be quiet." She scratches his ears, then gives me a thoughtful look. "Unless you want him back . . ."

"Farli," I say in a warning tone. It's clear my new "little sister" carries a load of guilt when it comes to Chompy. Sure, he was supposed to be mine, but she absolutely adores him and he loves her. Add in the fact that Chompy follows her around like a shadow, and that clinches it for me. He's adorable, but I've got enough to do without a baby animal at my heels.

And I still need those darn roots.

"I know," Farli chirps happily. She moves to Chompy's side and picks him up, squeezing him by the middle. Even though he's growing by the day, she doesn't care. She nuzzles his furry head and laughs when Chompy licks her. "It's just that . . . he's so wonderful."

He is. He's also a baby animal and needs lots of attention, and I've got so much going on in my life right now that, as much as I adore him, I'm glad he's hers and not mine.

Sometimes all the changes in my life in the last few weeks feel a bit overwhelming. I haven't told Salukh this, because I tend to shut down when I stress or worry. I curl inside myself, in a way. Always have, ever since both my parents passed in accidents overseas and I was shipped off to Oklahoma to my aunt's farm. My aunt was a wonderful lady, but she didn't have time for nonsense. She taught me how to be self-sufficient and how to run a farm. How to help a cow birth a calf. How to garden and can your vegetables for the lean times. Wasn't much of a hugger, though, and we never spoke of the family we lost.

Maybe that's why I struggle now. Because Salukh is wonderful. Of course he is. He continues to be everything I ever wanted in a partner, and every day I'm more and more thankful for him. I'm now pregnant, with resonance's insistence wearing off a bit and leaving nothing but mellow affection and constant attraction. I no longer feel as if we have to have sex or I won't be able to function. Instead, I see Salukh flex an arm, or the way the light hits his face, and it fills me with a pleasant heat that makes me want to touch him. I liked resonance, but I like the aftermath so much more.

The thing with Salukh, though, is that he has a huge family. Farli, Zennek, and Pashov are his siblings. His parents are

Kemli and Borran, and all of them are now back together. In addition, both Zennek and Pashov have families now, which means more people. And they all want to do stuff together, or help one another out. It seems every time I turn around, there is a helpful sibling or parent wanting to give us furs or herbs, or wanting to help—like right now—with gathering.

After growing up with just my aunt, it feels overwhelming at times. I can't say anything to Salukh, though, because they're his family and he loves them. They depend upon him— the brothers hunt for their parents, and the parents make meals and clothing for the brothers. Theoretically not too much in my life has changed—everyone has always been around. The caves have always been busy and crowded.

But now I'm suddenly *related*. Everything is different in subtle ways, and even though I don't want it to bother me, sometimes it does. I wish I could be like Marlene, who seems completely unbothered by everything. She's utterly blithe, even with a fussy infant to take care of. Stacy, Pashov's mate, loves being part of the big family, and I see her with Kemli all the time. It makes me feel like I'm the wrong person in this equation, that I'm missing some key component.

It just takes time, I tell myself. Everything takes time. This is the new normal, and things are changing again. We spent the last year at the South Cave, and now we're back at the main cave. It shouldn't feel more crowded. It should feel like a homecoming.

And yet when I lean down to dig at another root and Chompy bleats and attacks my digging stick again, I find myself wishing for five minutes alone. Just five minutes.

I'm not even mad at Farli. How can you be mad at someone so effortlessly happy? I just want a breather.

Salukh

I watch as my mate returns from her gathering excursion with my young sister, the dvisti colt at their heels. Tee-fah-nee laughs with Farli, but there is something reserved in her manner that is not there when she is with me. I study my mate, absorbing her every reaction.

This reticence is something I have noticed growing over the last few days, and it troubles me. I do not think she is unhappy with our resonance, but I am attuned to her moods. I want to know her thoughts, her emotions, so I can be the best mate that I can for her.

It is what I do. I observe, and I strategize, and then I stalk my prey.

And while my mate is not *prey*, I yet feel the need to chase after her. To observe her every smile, to take apart the reasons behind every frown. When I am not out in the wild, I obsess over observing my mate. No male could blame me. How could they?

It is true that I am the luckiest of males when it comes to

mates. Tee-fah-nee is full of beauty and spirit. She is clever and brave. But I also know that she is a perfectionist who does not like things when they do not meet her standards. I have seen her rip all the stitches out of a sleeve because she did not like the way it lay against my arm when I wore the tunic she had crafted. I have seen her plant and replant her seeds because she needed the row she created to be straight. I have seen her discard a pot of dye because it was not the right shade she wished for. These are not bad things. They are just bits of information, tiny details that make up the whole that is my complex mate.

So I observe, because she is my favorite thing to watch. She fascinates me. I could be mated to her until I am as old as Drenol and I would still find new things about her to please and delight me.

As my sister and Tee-fah-nee approach, I move to the entrance of the main cave, leaning against the rocky wall. I can see the exact moment that my mate notices me. Her eyes light up and her smile becomes broader, full of delight. I love that moment, that first glimpse that she has of her waiting male. I love that the sight of me pleases her as much as the sight of her pleases me.

I will have to pry the reason for her reticence out of her later. I can be patient. The best prey is one that leads a hunter on a difficult yet rewarding chase.

"Hi there," Tee-fah-nee says to me when they approach, breathless. Just the sound of her voice sends a low, pleasant thrum through my body, and my khui purrs at her nearness. "I hope you haven't been waiting on us long."

"Not long at all," I say, reaching out to brush a few flakes of snow from my mate's collar. I want to tell her that I can wait forever, that I will always wait for her, that watching out for her is a joy and not a chore, but Farli will just giggle and ruin the moment. So I only touch my mate's chin and lean in over her.

"What are you doing?" Tee-fah-nee asks.

"Smelling you," I murmur, my voice low enough so only she can hear it. "It has been too long since I drank in your scent. I missed it." I let my nose brush against the line of her jaw and then straighten, sliding a hand over her shoulder. "How did the hunt for roots go this day?"

"Terrible!" my little sister, Farli, announces, grinning. "Chompy attacked the digging stick every time Tee-fah-nee brought it out! We got nothing!" She sounds pleased, as if she had a thrilling day, and when her young dvisti scampers into the cave and darts toward my mother's den, Farli giggles and chases after him.

A day of root hunting and no roots to be found? Farli might be pleased, but I suspect Tee-fah-nee will be less so. She wished to start on her friend's tunic soon. I know an unplanned delay will nag at her. She gives me a smile, but it is a little tight. "Chompy made things tricky. Couldn't be helped."

"Do you want me to go back out with you? We can find a few before the suns descend. Or if you are tired, I shall go."

She gives me a funny look. "They're just roots, Salukh. They can wait." Her eyes brighten as she slides an arm around my waist, leaning in against me. "Did you catch anything hunting today?"

I wrap my arms around her, loving the feel of her slight form against mine. All right, the roots are not the issue that bothers her. I make a mental note of this and will continue to observe. "I set traps today," I tell her. "I did not hunt."

I do not tell her that I accompanied Aehako because I wished to talk with him of mates and things. I could have spoken with Zennek or Pashov, my brothers, but they would tell my parents and Farli, and this is a private matter. I spoke to Aehako instead, as I know his mate can be somber at times, though she smiles quite a bit more with him. If anyone knows how to lighten a mate's spirits, it will be him.

And Aehako was full of suggestions.

"Gifts," he'd told me immediately. "Have you given her a courting gift?"

I had stared at him as if he were crazed. "Like your carving? Was that not a joke? A prank that Leezh teased you with?"

"It was," Aehako had told me, amused. "But it has its uses. I bring it out sometimes when I want to see my Kira blush, but she never blushes for long." He grinned at me. "It starts a conversation, and it makes them smile. It is fun to use to see your female squirm. I do not see the downside to such a gift. Just . . . do not tell others if you give her one." He leaned in. "Kira gets very shy when it is mentioned."

I think about his words even now. Tee-fah-nee has pushed away most gifts, because they were from suitors and she had no interest in such things. But now that we are mated, things are different. And perhaps Aehako is right, and a carving will strike up a good conversation for the two of us.

I am just not very talented at carving. Not like Aehako. It is not something I want to ask him to make, though. It is personal, and only for my mate's eyes, so I must give it my best effort.

"No fresh meat this day, I am afraid," I say to Tee-fah-nee. "But my mother has made a hearty stew and we can eat with her."

The smile she gives me does not reach her eyes. "Great," she says, her words enthusiastic even if her eyes are not. "I'm starving."

"You are not," I reassure her, aghast. "That is simply your belly rumbling. True starvation is very unpleasant and I will not let it happen while I can feed you."

She blinks and then shakes her head, burying her face against my tunic. "Oh, Salukh. You really are the best."

So it is my family that bothers her in some way.

I ponder this through the evening meal. It is a delicious one, and I sit next to Tee-fah-nee as my father and my mate discuss leather-making and the dyeing of quills for decoration. She laughs when my father jokes about the quilled loincloth he made when he was a young hunter, and how he had spent many moons working on it, only for the final creation to be so stiff he could not walk with it on. She smiles at Farli's eager questions, and eats a second helping of my mother's food. I watch all of this, and I observe.

If something is troubling her about my family, it is my duty as her mate to correct it, if I can. This strange remoteness in her eyes was not there when we left the South Cave. It has only appeared now that we have returned here. Has someone said something that hurt her feelings?

My shoulders stiffen when my mother tsks, her gaze on the main area of the cavern. "Still no mating between those two."

Jo-see and Haeden. It is the talk of the entire cave—they claim to hate each other and yet they have resonated. Or at least, their khuis are singing. True resonance happens when both mates give in and make a kit. They have not, yet, and seem determined to hold out for as long as possible. I glance over at my mate to see her reaction. She stirs her bowl but does not say anything. Tee-fah-nee is a great defender of her small, chatty friend, and I wonder if this is what troubles her. Has my family said something to offend her?

But Tee-fah-nee only shrugs. "Josie's struggling. She wanted resonance very badly, but not with him. It is taking her some time to adjust. I can't imagine how hard it must be for her, and I can't blame her for her unhappiness. Give her time."

My mother nods, a worried look on her face. "I just do not want another Vaashan and another Daya."

"They will not be Vaashan and Daya," I reassure my mother. It is a worry many have put forward recently when it became obvious that Jo-see was not happy with her khui choosing Haeden. But Haeden is no Vaashan, ready to destroy his family rather than let them leave him. I never understood the stories of Raahosh's (and Rukh's) father and his crazed determination to keep his mate at his side.

But now that I am with Tee-fah-nee? I fear I understand it all too well. My suns rise and set upon her smile. I put a possessive hand on Tee-fah-nee's thigh, as if reassuring myself that she is mine.

"It'll be fine," my mate says, her hand covering mine. "Give them time."

We return to our cave a while later, after tea and some admiring of my father's newest sewing project, a cape for Farli and a matching one for Chahm-pee. Tee-fah-nee does not look upset, but she also seems relieved when we are alone, the two of us. The moment I pull the privacy screen over the door, she sighs and dramatically flops down upon our furs.

"Tired?" I ask, amused at this very Jo-see-like display.

"Been a long day," she tells me, sitting up and giving me a wry smile. "I'm ready to put on my bonnet and go to sleep."

"Can I help?"

Tee-fah-nee arches one small brow at me. "The last time you helped me get ready for bed, you ended up distracting me and we had sex. Twice."

"And I intend the same tonight," I agree, grinning. "But if you are tired, we will only mate once. And I will make you come quickly."

"Well, when you put it that way," she teases, and holds her foot up in the air.

I pull off her boot, watching her signals. If there is any sign of tension in her, any hint of stress in her eyes, I will stop. I know my mate has trouble trusting, and the fact that she trusts me is a gift I will not abuse. But I do not see shadows in her eyes, only a languid pleasure as she lifts her other foot.

Even now, my cock gets hard. Just knowing that I have a mate to look after, to tend to and see to all her needs? It is enough to keep me erect constantly. Tee-fah-nee and her smiles, her laughter, her scent . . . nothing is better. "Have I told you this day that you have my heart?"

"Not today." She pulls at the ties on her leggings and obediently lifts her hips when I pull on them, sliding them off her form. Then she is in nothing but her tunic. She watches me with expectant eyes, and when I kiss the inside of her ankle, she lets out a small sigh.

"Then let me tell you again. You have my heart, and I never want it back."

"I have no intention of giving it back, so that's good." She smiles up at me and pulls her legs from my grasp, then raises her arms in the air.

I pull her tunic over her head and then sink to my knees. As she leans back, I cup her teats and bury my face between them. It is my favorite spot to rest my head now, I think. Well . . . second favorite. My first is between her thighs, and I did promise to make her come quickly. Last night she fell asleep after we mated, and so I crawl away from her inviting body and move to the hook beside the bed. "First, your bonnet."

She sits up on her elbows, watching me. "You sure you want me to wear that when we make love?"

"Does it matter?" I shrug and hold it out to her. "As long as I get to taste your cunt and feast upon your teats, you can wear all kinds of furs upon your head." I watch, rapt, as she pulls her thick, curly mane up and then tugs the strange hood on. She crafted it for herself, with the delicate hopper fur on the inside to cradle her curls. She says it helps them remain undamaged while she sleeps. Once her mane is pulled up into the hood, she tugs on the drawstring and then looks at me expectantly. "Beautiful," I tell her. "Mine."

"You're pretty good at this mate thing," she tells me with a chuckle.

Am I? She makes it easy.

I move back over her again, cupping her teats in my hands. I am so big against her I practically swallow her torso, and my thumbs look enormous next to her nipples as I tease them. She moans, arching against me, her hips lifting. "That feels good," she breathes. "I think I need you to do that all night long."

Does she want that? Then that is what I will do.

I nuzzle her skin, pressing kisses to the bare spots. I slide lower, between her thighs, and find her juicy and wet for her mate. Tee-fah-nee sighs happily and slips her legs farther apart, and when I encourage one over my shoulder, she places it there, pressing against my horn. Keeping one hand on a teat as promised, I lap at her cunt, teasing the delicate third nipple—the clit, she calls it—between her legs. She sucks in a breath, her hands on my horns as I tease her with my mouth, edging her toward her climax. Her cunt grows wetter by the moment, and her movements frantic, but I keep the slow, tapping rhythm of my tongue steady on the underside of her clit. She whimpers, tugging on my horns, and when her body trembles under me and her folds flood with her release, I am the proudest hunter who ever lived, all because I have pleased my mate. I continue to lick her sweetness, my cock throbbing and hard under me, and I wait for a signal from her that she wants more. My Tee-fah-nee will lead me in the furs, because if she is not comfortable and happy, I am not happy.

As I continue to tease her cunt with my tongue, she shifts on the furs underneath me. Her hips move in small circles, and she covers the hand I have upon her teat. "Salukh," she breathes. "Oh, my mate."

Just that soft, breathless sigh of my name is enough to make my cock twitch. I groan, licking her with renewed intensity. *Tell me to claim you*, I silently beg. *Tell me to push into you and mate you. Tell me you want my cock.*

"Need you," she whispers, tugging on my horns.

That is all I have to hear. I lift my head, kissing my way back up her front. I pause to tease one beautiful, soft teat with my tongue and teeth, and then I move up to kiss her lovely mouth. Her lips cling to mine, and she makes low noises of pleasure in her throat as I tease her nipple even as I nip at her mouth. "Tonight," I murmur, "I will hold you against me and play with your teats while I drive into you. Yes?"

She moans, shuddering. "Yes. Let's do that."

My mate moves onto her side, showing me the curve of her hip and the rounded swell of her buttocks. This is a position she suggested a few days ago and I am fascinated with it. I fit myself against her backside, rubbing my cock between her thighs and along her folds. She arches back against me, resting one leg on the outside of my knee, and I slowly press my cock into her from behind. She has no tail, and the knowledge that there is nothing to impede me from sinking into her like this drives me wild. I push in as deep as I can, until my spur is pressing up against the pucker between her buttocks. Then, I reach forward and tease her teat with my fingers as I stroke into her.

Tee-fah-nee rocks her hips with mine, making small, urgent noises as my thrusts go from easy to desperate. I wrap one arm around her from underneath, pinning her against me even as I pinch her nipple. We come together harder, faster, until my sac is so tight it feels as if it will rise all the way into my body. I curl over her, my tail wrapped around her ankle, as I drive into my mate. I cannot come. Not until I feel her shudder around me again—

Ah.

The moment Tee-fah-nee's cunt clenches around me, I am lost. I release, spurting seed deep inside her even as I grind against her backside. By the ancestors, mating with her gets better every time. I press my face against the bonnet she has covering her mane and stifle my groan as I pulse into her, over and over again.

My mate.

She stays on my mind even after we clean up and curl around each other once more, this time for sleep. Tee-fah-nee sleeps easily, buried under a mountain of furs, but my mind is busy with other things. I think of my mate and the reluctance I sometimes see in her eyes, and I turn this over in my mind again and again, trying to examine the problem from new angles. Is she tired? Is there too much for her to keep up with? Something with the kit?

It is difficult to tell with my Tee-fah-nee. She keeps her hurts buried, determined to hide her problems. It makes me all the more determined to figure them out. I contemplate this, even as I extricate myself from the furs and dress.

It is a moonlit night, and I know exactly where to find the roots she was hunting for. Perhaps I can have a couple for her by the time she wakes.

Perhaps I can work on a carving for a bit, too.

Tiffany

It's a quiet morning. I snuggle into the furs, feeling lazy and warm. I'm going to enjoy this while I can, I decide. I have a few weeks before morning sickness starts to hammer me like it has the other women, and until then, I'm going to just bask in my newlywed state.

Newlywed . . . I reach over in the furs and there's no mate there. Hmm. Maybe I slept a bit too late and he went to find breakfast. I'm a little disappointed, as I like the idea of waking up curled up next to Salukh and maybe waking up specific parts of him. I don't know if it's resonance or Salukh—or both—but I'm finding myself really loving sex lately. More than that, just being touched. Being caressed. Being *loved* and cared for. I'm drinking it in like a flower in the desert drinks rain.

Thinking of plants makes me wistful for the saplings I had growing outside of the South Cave. I hate that I had to abandon them. I was hoping to nurture them from seedlings all the way to fruition, but I suppose that's selfish of me. It just makes sense for us to return to the main tribal cave with everyone else. The baths here are warm, and there are so many more people available to help one another out.

Even so, I hate starting a project and abandoning it. It bothers me at a bone-deep level. Maybe I'll ask Salukh to go and check on them sometime for me . . . but then he'd be gone overnight, and I don't like the thought of that, either.

I dress in my leathers and pull off my sleep bonnet, finger-combing and working a bit of oil into my dry curls. When there's still no sign of Salukh, I figure either he's eating at his mother's fire or he's out hunting already, and I emerge from our cave to see which one it is.

"There you are," Kemli calls out as I enter the main part of the tribal cave. Her eyes brighten and she immediately moves to my side. "I have been waiting for you to awaken."

"Oh, um, is Salukh around?"

"Off checking traps," his mother says with a wave of her hand. "Come with me. I saved you a meal and I need to take your measurements."

"My measurements?" I echo, letting her lead me by the hand toward her cave. "What for?"

"I am making you a tunic," Kemli announces, beaming at me. "Are you hungry? I have a big bowl of seeds and roots, and I kept some of the hraku to mix in with it. When I was carrying Salukh, I wanted so many seeds and tubers." She chuckles. "You will probably be the same."

Oh. I know the hraku seeds and the sweet, sticky substance they make when cooked are quite the delicacy right now. They are one of the few sweets on the planet, and no one turns them down when offered, especially not me. It's so thoughtful of Kemli to save me a meal, and even as I'm grateful, a little part of me retreats in fear. "You don't have to make me anything," I reassure her. "I have tunics."

"I am making tunics for all three of my new daughters," she continues. "Ones that gather at the waist so you will have plenty of room for your belly. I am making Farli one, too. You will all match!" Kemli looks thrilled at this. "Everyone that sees you will know we are family."

Everyone knows that already, considering it's a small tribe. I keep smiling, but the urge to flee rushes through me like a freight train. I don't want to wear matching tunics with Marlene and Stacy. I don't want to be one of Kemli's many daughters. I want . . . I want . . .

I want to run away.

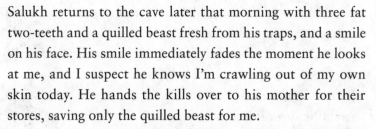

Salukh returns to the cave later that morning with three fat two-teeth and a quilled beast fresh from his traps, and a smile on his face. His smile immediately fades the moment he looks at me, and I suspect he knows I'm crawling out of my own skin today. He hands the kills over to his mother for their stores, saving only the quilled beast for me.

"A present," he says in a loud, cheerful voice, though his gaze is searching mine. "So you can practice dyeing quills. Just do not make me a loincloth."

I manage a chuckle. "Thank you, I think?"

"Come," he says brightly. "I will help you take the quills off." Putting a hand on my shoulder, he steers me toward our cave. Once we're inside, he sets the quilled beast down and pulls the privacy screen over the entrance. Then he takes my hand and steers me toward the fire, sitting next to me. "Now you will tell me what troubles you, my heart."

My lower lip trembles. I feel like such an awful person. How can I tell him that his family is doing their best to invite me into their lives and all it's doing is making me want to run away? I lost my parents and I thought the grief would destroy me. I'd gone from loved and doted-upon daughter to silent, lonely worker at my aunt's farm. My aunt was good to me—of course she was—but it wasn't the same as being with my parents. Kemli is wonderful. Borran is wonderful. Farli is all I could ask for in a little sister.

And I'm terrified.

Because this world is harsh. People die from khui-sickness or hunting accidents or a variety of other things. What if I let myself love a family again and I lose them a second time? Being part of a family is different from what I have with Salukh. He's my other half. If I lose him, it's game over. But family is tricky. The more I want to pull back and guard myself from feeling too much, the more they seem to invite me in.

Salukh won't understand, either. He's the devoted son, the responsible one. He makes sure his parents want for nothing. He won't know what I mean when I say I can't get close to them. It'll hurt his feelings, and I can't lose him.

He knows something is bothering me, though. I can't hide anything from Salukh. I study my mate's comforting, focused gaze. I know if I tell him I have a problem, he'll want to fix it. He can't fix this one, though. So I make something up. "I keep thinking about my plants," I blurt out. "Back at the South Cave."

Salukh doesn't laugh at how ridiculous I sound. He simply nods, expression thoughtful. "The ones we left behind. This troubles you?"

"It does," I exclaim, leaning into this problem. It's true that abandoning my garden bothers me. "They're food, and it's something I know I can handle. I can grow them to full size and then we can harvest them in time for the brutal season. It'll be a help, I know it will. I want to go and bring them back. I can dig them up and replant them here, if they're alive. Will you . . . will you take me?"

"My mate." Salukh squeezes my hands. "Of course I will. You know you have but to ask."

"It's such a silly, small thing—"

"It is not silly. It is important to you. And I know you well enough to know that leaving such a task incomplete will continue to trouble you. Of course we can return to the South Cave and dig up your plants, if that is what you wish to do."

"We'll need a sled," I tell him. I've thought about this in the past and dismissed the idea as silly and selfish, but if he's on board . . . "And a few days to dig everything up and repack them so we can bring them back here. You're sure you don't mind?"

He rubs my knuckles. "My Tee-fah-nee, if this will bring you joy, then it will be done. You are sure nothing else troubles you?"

"Nothing at all," I lie. "Just that."

Tiffany

The next day dawns bright and clear, as if announcing to me that, yes, a honeymoon is in fact a terrific idea. I'm in high spirits as we pack bags and Salukh goes to tell Vektal that we've decided to take a brief honeymoon to visit the South Cave and retrieve my plants. As I wait near the entrance, one of the tall hunters approaches. This one has long, flowing hair and a quiet, somber mien. Warrek. He brings a sled with him and sets it on the ground just outside the cave entrance.

"For you," is all he says.

"Oh, that's really not necessary," I say, flustered. Gifts make me suspicious, especially gifts from men. But I'm mated now, and things should be different, right? Even so, I don't like to depend on others. "I'm sure we can craft one as we go."

Warrek watches me with thoughtful eyes. "Why?"

"Why what?"

"Why craft one when you can borrow ours?" He tilts his head. "Do you doubt my father's workmanship?"

Oh, is it his father's? Old Eklan is as kind as can be, though he looks so very ancient that a strong breeze could blow him away. "No, of course not. Thank you."

He nods and leaves the sled with me, and I feel like a bit of a jerk for assuming he was trying to shower me with gifts even though I am mated.

"There you are," Kemli says, rushing over. Farli is on her mother's heels, a miserable look on her teenage face. "I heard Salukh talking to the chief. You are going on a moon quest?"

"Honeymoon," I tell her. "It's a trip people take after they're married so they can spend time alone and get to know each other."

"What is there to know? You resonated." She chuckles and shakes her head. "It sounds like an excuse to be noisy in the furs, but who am I to say?" She pushes a leather bag toward me. "Take this. I know when Borran and I first resonated, we did not wish to leave the furs for hunting. There is a good deal of jerky in there and some kah that will last you for weeks if you should take longer."

I'm touched, and chagrined that here I am trying to race away from Salukh's family and they're being so very thoughtful. Again. It makes me feel like the bad guy. "It's really not necessary—"

"Shh, shh," Kemli says, placing the bag in my hands anyhow. "It is just food. Take it. If you do not eat it all, leave it for the next hunter."

"Okay." I clutch the bag, feeling like a jerk. She beams at me, then hugs me close, patting my shoulder. Her scent is that of herbs and leather, nothing like my mother's remembered scent of vanilla and oranges, but the comparison hits me hard and fills me with terror. I try to shake the feeling off as Kemli leaves, but it lingers.

"Are you really staying away for that long?" Farli asks, woebegone. She lingers after her mother's departure, looking like a kid whose best friend is moving away. "A full turn of the moon?"

"What?" I focus on my young little friend. "Oh, no, not a full turn of the moon. Just a few days. Maybe a week—two hands of days."

"Then why call it a honey-moon? Why not a honey-day?" She wrinkles her nose. "And 'honey' is the sticky stuff you make from hraku, yes?"

"Sort of, and I don't know why it's called a honeymoon," I admit. "It just is."

"When you come back, do you want to go hunting together again?" she asks, her eyes beseeching. "Or gathering? My other sisters do not."

Right, because Stacy would rather stay in camp and cook for everyone, and Marlene has made it clear that she'll only go hunting if Zennek goes with her . . . and then they usually come back with no kills and Zennek just blushes for the rest of the day. Which leaves me to take up the slack with Farli.

The burden of that suddenly feels heavy and makes me feel panicky once more. Why is Farli so desperate to be close to me?

A warm hand touches my back, and then I'm enveloped by Salukh's comforting scent. "Are you ready to go?"

I lean back against him, hugging the bag from his mother, and give Farli an apologetic smile. "We'll do something when I get back, I promise."

She looks disappointed, but hugs her brother and then me, and then races back after her mother.

Salukh rubs my back, and it takes me a moment to realize

that he's watching me with that gentle, almost too-knowing look. "Is everything all right?" he asks softly. "Can I do anything?"

"It's fine," I tell him. "Great, actually. Warrek brought us a sled. And your mother is feeding an army." I hold up the bag of rations with a wry grin. "Hope you're hungry."

"I am always hungry," he admits. "We can get going, and then you can tell me what a harm-ee is."

As we walk, I get the impression that Salukh is studying me, like a puzzle he intends to piece together. We chat as we travel, and conversation is easy between us, but sometimes his questions seem more purposeful than idle conversation. When we see a dvisti herd on the horizon, he pauses in his pulling of the sled to regard me. "Should we stop and get you another colt?"

"What? No! Of course not." I laugh at the idea, but Salukh doesn't laugh with me. "Why do you think I want another colt?"

"Because Farli has yours, and if you need one, I would get it for you."

His expression is so intensely earnest that my heart skips a beat. "I don't need one. I really don't. But thank you. I appreciate you thinking of me."

"You are all I think of," he admits, and his tail flicks toward my leg, then strokes up the outside of my thigh.

I automatically snag it, brushing my fingers over the tufted tip, and his eyes flare with interest that has nothing to do with dvisti and everything to do with sex. I know that touching a sa-khui's tail is playing with fire, but I can't seem to stop myself. Since we've paused in our walking, I circle my fingers around his tail and lightly stroke it.

"Are you tired?" Salukh asks, breathless. "Should we stop and take a rest?"

A rest, huh? "Are you asking if I want to have sex?"

"Yes."

Do I? It's the middle of the day, but Salukh is looking at me as if he wants to devour me. "Yes," I blurt out. "I do."

He groans, striding over to my side and sweeping me up into his arms. He looks quickly around the landscape, then heads for a nearby craggy boulder that juts out of the snow. Salukh moves toward it with single-minded determination, and then when we're upon it, he sets me down gently in the snow.

And then all but rips my pants off. The braided belt that holds them to my waist stretches, and then the leather slides out from underneath, and I'm bare-assed in the snow, my pants pooling around my legs. My mate growls at the sight, his hands skimming over my buttocks and rubbing them. The feel of his hot hands against my cold skin is intense and I moan, turning and placing my gloved hands on the face of the rock.

Salukh nudges my feet apart, as far as they will go while trapped in my pooled leggings, and then steps up behind me. I worry for a moment that he's going to push in without making me ready, but he grabs my hips and tilts them backward, until my butt is practically pushed out, and then he slides a hand between my thighs, stroking my clit.

"My Tee-fah-nee," he breathes, his big body pressing over mine. For some reason, sex with Salukh never scares me. Never takes me back to frightening memories. Even though he's big and powerful, I feel safe with him. I trust him, and that trust is everything.

I moan as his fingers press deep into my core, and he begins to pump in and out, working me with his hand. I grind down against him frantically, my breath sobbing from my throat with want. "Please. Oh please. Come inside me now."

He does, and I swear it's the best thing I've ever felt, that hard, stretching press of his cock as he pushes into me, the drag of the ridges on his shaft as he works in and out, the nudge of his spur against my back door. It's heaven, and when I start to whimper, he puts his hand between my thighs again, this time rubbing my clit until I come. It's hard and fast and brutal, and I love every moment of it.

Salukh takes a moment longer, slowly dragging his cock in and out as he rubs my clit, as if making sure that I've gotten my pleasure before he takes his own. I squeeze my inner muscles around him, covering the hand between my thighs with my gloved one, and rock back against him. "My mate," I tell him, knowing he loves hearing the words. "Filling me with his cock and giving me his seed. Feels so good."

He groans, and then he pounds into me from behind, the tease of his spur against my backside making me wriggle even as he grips the back of my neck as he comes, flooding me with his seed. I breathe a happy sigh as he rocks against me, his movements slower. "By the ancestors," he manages. "How is it you make me lose control so quickly?"

"Uh, that's the plan, isn't it?" I tease. "Or were you intending on making that last until sundown?"

Salukh leans his big body over mine, nuzzling at my shoulder. "What a day that would be, eh?" He presses a kiss to my neck, brushing aside my curls with his face. "Let me get some snow and I will clean you off."

I shift my weight as he slides out of me, and there's definitely a mess on the insides of my thighs. I like it, though. I like that it's his, and I like that he strokes my pussy gently as he cleans me off with snow, as if it belongs to him and he needs to take great care with it.

Then we dress again, and I tighten my belt, pulling the leather top of my leggings through it and settling my tunic over them. As I do, I give Salukh a curious look. He's gazing at the ground in a thoughtful way. "Something wrong?"

"The roots you were hunting the other day. The ones for the dye? They grow here. Do you need more?"

Ever since I didn't get any that day with Farli, I swear Salukh is showering me with the green-dye roots every time I turn around. If I have any more of them, I'm going to have enough green dye to clothe all of Ireland. "I have plenty, thank you."

"Are you sure? I could get them for you."

I chuckle. "Yes, I'm positive. Is there something behind all these gifts you're pushing on me, love?"

That intense expression crosses his face again.

"Uh-oh. What?" I ask immediately. "What is it?"

"I have one more gift for you," Salukh confesses. "I was going to give it to you at the South Cave, but perhaps I should give it now."

Another gift? I'm both touched and puzzled. I love that he's giving me something, but at the same time, I wonder what's bringing this on. I don't really need anything. The tribe provides everything we lack, and in return, we share our skins and our meat with others. It's a community that looks out for one another, and as a result, they don't have a lot of excess. Everything has its place and everything is used. But how can I turn down a gift from my mate? It's clear he's been thinking about this a lot, because his body language is a mixture of anticipation and stress, as if he's afraid I'll hate it. "Thank you?"

A smile flashes over his face, and then he jogs over to the sled we've abandoned. I follow him, adjusting my pants as I do, trying to figure out just what sort of gift he's brought for me. More food of some kind? Perhaps a tunic?

What he holds out is . . . not what I expected.

It's the ugliest . . . well, I *think* it's a digging stick. It's awfully thick, though, and too short to be of much use. But it's clear that he's been working on carving this for me, because it's made from bone, with a few awkward strikes here and there. I'm touched that he'd work so hard to make it for me, but as digging sticks go, it's not going to get me very far. Talking about the nearby roots must have reminded him to give it to me.

I take it from him, hefting it in my hand, and then give a quick smile. "Cool. Thanks."

The look on Salukh's face is all eagerness, though. "You . . . do you like it? Do you think you will use it?"

Oof. That's a tough one. As digging sticks go, it's terrible. But he made it for me, and so I war between sugarcoating the truth and telling him how I really feel. "Love . . . it's just that it's a bit short."

I'm not prepared for the offended look that crosses his face. "It is not."

"Maybe not," I backtrack quickly. I don't want to hurt his feelings. "I love the thought, though. It's appreciated."

He still looks wounded, though. "Do you truly think it is too short?"

I gaze down at the thick monstrosity in my hands. "I mean . . . I'm not going to get much use out of it. That's all." I try to deflect his hurt with a smile. "Remember that my arms are shorter than yours."

"I could use it on you," he offers, and he's almost shy about it. His tail thrashes behind him and he rubs the base of one horn, and for a moment he looks just like his brother Zennek when he gets caught fooling around with Marlene.

Use it *on* me? I stare down at the ugly tool in my hands in confusion. "I . . . this isn't a digging stick?"

Salukh is taken aback. "It is a carving of my cock."

It *is*? I eye the thing in surprise. Are those striations that I thought were slips of the knife actually supposed to be ridges? Is that why the damned thing is so thick? "You . . . you're giving me a courting gift?" I sputter. "Forgive me, love, but what the fuck?"

He continues to rub at the base of one of his horns. "Now that you mention it, it does resemble a digging stick a little. So you do not think my cock is too short, then?"

No wonder he was offended. "Salukh, if your cock was any longer, it'd rearrange my organs. Trust me when I say there's nothing wrong with the size of you." I flip the stick—the *dick*—over in my hands. I'll be damned. "Why are you giving me a replica of your cock?"

"Aehako says he uses his on his mate all the time and she likes it." His eyes gleam. "I thought it might be fun. And I thought it might make you smile."

I'm torn between cracking up and wanting to smack Aehako in the mouth. Poor Kira must never know that Aehako is giving my Salukh suggestions. "You want to use this on me," I state, my lips twitching with amusement. "Instead of your dick."

He lights up. "Or we could do both at once." He points at his mouth and then between his thighs.

"Why does this sound less like a present for me and more like a present for you?" I mutter, moving toward him. "Salukh. I love you. I adore you. You're the best person I've ever met, alien or otherwise. You don't have to give me gifts."

That watchful look returns to his face. He gazes down at me, then strokes my cheek. "It is worth many sleepless nights of carving to see you smile. I would do it over and over if it pleases you." He pauses, and then adds, "As long as you do not think it is too short."

I snort with laughter. "Now that I know it's not a digging stick? It's huge. Enormous. Disturbingly large."

Salukh's mouth eases into a smile. "That is more like it."

Salukh

After we chuckle over my gift, the shadows return to Tee-fah-nee's eyes. Whatever troubles her, it is not a lack of courting gifts. Yet something about her responses soothes me. It is a reassurance that the problem is not our relationship—or our resonance—that brings her worry. It is something else entirely, and I will continue to narrow down what it could be. I am reminded of my family, and her hesitation. I think of Farli and Tee-fah-nee this morning, when Farli was talking to my mate, and the edge of panic was back in Tee-fah-nee's eyes.

Something about my family worries her. But what? I compare my mate's reactions to that of my brothers' mates. Stay-see is a sweet, gentle sort who loves to take care of people. And Mar-lenn loves to tease Zennek, but she is a good mate for my shy brother. Does she compare herself in some way and feel lacking? It is the only thing I can think of, and yet it does not feel like Tee-fah-nee. She is good at so many things that surely she would not feel lacking in comparison to the others?

I continue to watch her as we travel. Perhaps the rescue of her plants will provide the clues I am missing. Perhaps the weight of them is upon her shoulders more heavily than I anticipated. We arrive at the South Cave and immediately stop to examine my mate's plants.

"They look good," she tells me, kneeling in front of one and touching the fragile needles that barely peep out of the snow. "I think we'll be able to transplant most of them."

"Do you want to rest before you get started?"

She gets to her feet, dusting the snow and dirt off her gloves, and looks around. "Sure, though it might be strange to be in the cave with no one else around."

The smile she gives me is a cheery one, and I take her hand and we head inside. I cannot help but notice that Tee-fah-nee's response to seeing her plants was relaxed, not the overwhelming relief I expected if they were truly troubling her so much.

It is proof that she is concealing her troubles from me, and it makes me feel as if I am failing her as a mate. Did I not promise to protect her from everything?

"It really is quiet in here," Tee-fah-nee exclaims as we step inside. Her gaze skims the empty maze of rooms, pausing only on the storage baskets clustered near one wall. "It feels so different and empty. Like it's dead."

"I think of it as simply waiting," I say. "Waiting for our return. No good cave is ever truly empty. Hunters will stop here to rest between days on the trail. Others will come here for their moon quest with their new mates. It will not stay empty forever. Instead of being someplace we go to every day, visiting here will be a treat, a delightful excursion."

Her eyes shine as she looks up at me, and she squeezes my

hand. "You have such a great way of looking at things, Sa-lukh. You're incredible, you know that?"

If I am, it is because my mate smiles up at me with such affection.

"I don't even mind if we call it a moon quest," she tells me, amused. "It makes just as much sense as ha-nee-moon does."

It is a pleasant evening. With the twin suns going down, I do not want to start uprooting her plants. It can wait for the morning, and we have already spent most of the day traveling. Tonight is for relaxing and enjoying our time together as our moon quest. We are agreed in which cave to stay in—since the others yet feel as if they belong to our tribemates, we decide to sleep in the main part of the cave. I set down the furs I brought, and pull out some of the stored ones to make a thick, fluffy bed for my mate. Perhaps after an evening of leisure, she will confess to me what bothers her.

We eat a bit of the food my mother sent along, and sip on hot tea after our meal, and I watch my mate with expectant eyes.

"What?" she asks, eyeing me.

"What what?"

"You're looking at me."

"I am not allowed to look at my beautiful mate?"

"Of course you can. But you need to tell me why you've got that particular look on your face."

"And which look is that?"

"The one that makes me think you're waiting for something." She arches a brow at me. "Spill it."

I look at my tea in my cup, and then tilt it—

She grabs my wrist before I can indeed "spill it." "It's a euphemism, love. I mean I need you to tell me what's on your mind."

Ah. That makes more sense than spilling a perfectly good drink. "I am just happy to be here with you on our moon quest. What do most couples do on such an occasion?"

"Well, they travel," she tells me, smiling.

"Which we have done."

"And they have a lot of sex."

"Now, this part, I like," I tease. "Tell me more."

Tee-fah-nee rolls her eyes, but her lips remain curved in a smile. "As if we didn't have sex a few hours ago."

"But that was then. I am always open to having more. Shall I seduce you? Is that done on a moon quest?"

"It can be." She lifts one foot in the air. "I can be swayed with a good foot rub."

"Say no more." I take her foot in my hands and tug off her boot, revealing her wiggly little toes. They are chilly despite the pleasant weather, and I press the bottom of her foot to my chest to warm it. "Tell me what else I can do to please my mate, and it shall be done."

Tee-fah-nee flutters her lashes at me. "I had no idea I was getting such a sweet deal when I asked if we could dig up my plants." She slides her hands down the front of her tunic suggestively. "I would have worn my sexiest furs." Then she winks at me. "Wait, these *are* my sexiest furs."

I grin, loving her playfulness. "You are just as enticing out of them."

"Are you trying to get me to undress?" She puts a hand to her chest and fake-gasps. "Why, Salukh. You flirt, you."

"The only female I flirt with is my mate," I tell her. "She has my heart and my spirit. She has all of me in her small hand."

Just as I begin to rub Tee-fah-nee's foot, she pulls it out of my grasp and sits up. Her hand goes between my thighs and she cups me through the loincloth. "That's not true. You're too big and thick for your mate's hand."

The breath wheezes from my lungs. I love when she is confident and prowls toward me with mating on her mind. I cannot look away from her. I nudge my hips forward, thrusting my cock against her grip. "In my mate's hand is my favorite place."

"Your favorite, huh?" She tilts her head, her dark curls sliding over her shoulders. "What about in your mate's . . . mouth?"

"New favorite place," I rasp. "I pick that one."

All thoughts of teasing my mate into confessing her secrets fly out of my head as she strokes her hand over the bulge in my loincloth, her expression fascinated. "I love being able to touch you," she whispers, as if confessing a secret. "I love being able to touch you and enjoying it. I thought I'd never be able to appreciate something like that again." Her gaze slides up to my face. "Thank you for waiting for me."

She is thanking me? As if I would not remake the world just to please her? "My sweet mate. You know there is nothing I would not do for you."

"I know. And now I want to touch you." She licks her lips and gazes up at me, her eyes shining. "All right with you if I do it here?"

"Did . . . did you want to do it somewhere else?" It is hard to concentrate with her hands all over me. I remain utterly still, fascinated, as her hungry hands move to the ties of my loincloth and she loosens them, tossing it aside. Then she gets to work on my tall boots, unwinding the ties that keep them above my knees. As she does, she moves forward, her curly mane falling over her shoulders, her hands skimming over my thighs as she undresses me.

Tee-fah-nee's nails scrape up the fronts of my thighs as she moves forward toward my now-jutting cock. Her hands creep upward . . . and upward . . . and she gives me a sultry look. "I wasn't sure if you were going to be shy if I tasted you right here out in the middle of the main cave."

And she flicks her tongue over the tip of my cock.

My entire body jolts. I grunt, unable to keep the sound at bay, and my tail flicks back and forth with excitement. "All I want is for you to continue."

"Not shy?" she asks, giving me another teasing lick, her gaze focused on my face.

I have never seen anything as fascinating as the tip of my cock dancing over her wet tongue. I am mesmerized at the sight, at the way her lips feel when I push between them, at the hot squeeze when she takes the tip into her mouth and sucks hard. One of her hands cups my sac, the other going to my shaft, and then she slowly feeds my length into her mouth.

It is *exquisite*.

I groan, unable to take my gaze off my mate as she closes her eyes and mates my cock with her mouth. Her movements are soft and sensual, and when she pauses in her sucking, it is to rub my shaft against her face, leaving wet trails of pre-cum on her cheeks. Part of me wants to wipe it away and feed it to her . . . and a darker part of me wants to cover her entire face with my seed, to see the look on her face as she wears my spend. I am completely and utterly taken by the thought, and I put a hand on the base of my cock, feeding it against her full mouth just so I can watch the tip skim over her lips. "Tee-fah-nee," I pant. "By the ancestors, you make me crazed with longing. Sometimes I think we yet resonate because I cannot think of anything but you. Of touching you. Of giving you kisses and waking up with you in my arms. I think my khui must be broken, because I am told things will calm down, that the hunger will fade, but I only want you more each day."

She moans, making a circle with her lips and then popping the head of my cock into her mouth again. This time, I leave a wet strand on her lower lip, and I watch in fascination as she licks it away and gazes up at me.

"You like that?" she asks, voice soft and husky and achingly sweet. "Like it when I put my mouth on you?"

"You have to ask?" As if I am not harder than stone right now. As if I do not stand in the midst of the South Cave, my tail dancing almost in the fire because I cannot move away from her and her wet, hungry mouth. But then I pause, because a new thought occurs to me. "Do you like it when you put your mouth on me?"

"I do," she whispers. "I like watching you come undone."

"I want you to come undone, too. At the same time." The wild, obscene thought I had earlier flicks through my mind again. "Will you ride my carving while you mate my cock with your mouth?"

She moans, her eyes fluttering as she looks up at me. "You want that?"

I nod.

Tee-fah-nee gets to her feet and stretches, her hands moving through her mane and making it cascade. I am fascinated at the sight of her, and my hand automatically goes to my cock, gripping it and working the shaft as she touches herself.

With a teasing twirl, she tugs the tunic she wears over her head, revealing the band she wears to prevent her large teats from bouncing. She removes it next, undoing the knot on the front of her chest, and then casts it aside. I groan, stroking my shaft harder at the sight of her teats bouncing, the dark nipples tight with arousal. "Keep going," I demand. "Show your mate everything."

"I'm getting there," Tee-fah-nee tells me, her voice a throaty tease. She cups her teats and squeezes them, toying with the nipples and pinching them as I work myself. I cannot look away from the sight of her pleasuring herself. The only thing better than this is perhaps me with my mouth upon her, but then I would not be able to look my fill.

I salivate, squeezing and dragging my hand up my cock as she turns and shakes her backside, swaying as she moves her leggings down her thighs. "Tease," I rasp, loving this. "Such a tease. *My* tease."

"All yours," she agrees, kicking off her boots and then pulling off the pooled leggings. She runs her hands down her glorious body once more, then shivers. "It's a little chilly without my mate to warm me up."

Visions of me covering her body with mine flood my head, and I step forward. "I will warm you—"

"Nope." She puts a hand on my chest. "Later. I'm still playing." And she slides that hand down to my cock and squeezes it tightly, her gaze on me. "You're not going to come before me, are you?"

"*Never.*"

"Good." My mate smiles and then slinks away again.

I watch her go, fascinated. Every day, my Tee-fah-nee grows bolder and more sure of herself, and every day I am struck anew at how lucky I am that she trusted me with her secrets, with her body.

And I vow to myself that I will never, never let her down. So I slide my hand from my cock, even though I want nothing more than to rub myself to completion, and wait for her.

She picks up the carving and brings it to her lips, her gaze on me. Then, she slowly feeds it into her mouth.

I cannot stop staring. It is the most fascinating thing I have ever seen, watching her fit it into her mouth, her lips stretching around the girth like they do when she takes my cock into her mouth.

A moment later, she releases it and then licks up and down the length, wetting it with her tongue. Then she holds it out to me. "Will you put it inside me?"

"I would be honored," I rasp, cock aching fiercely at the glorious sight of her.

Tee-fah-nee smiles at me and approaches. Just before she gets to me, she reaches out and strokes my cock with her free hand, then offers me the carving. She turns around and presents me with her backside, bending at the waist and pushing it up.

The sight is fascinating. She parts her thighs, presenting me with her slick folds as she stretches forward, the cleft of her backside parting and showing me everything. Biting back a groan, I rub the crude tip against her cunt, watching in fascination as it teases through her folds, then dips inside.

She gasps, and I watch her body clench around it.

"How does it feel?" I cannot stop myself from asking, even as I push it deeper into her, watching her swallow it into her body.

Tee-fah-nee pants, her legs trembling as she remains bent over. "Feels . . . big. And hard."

For some reason, this pleases me. "So, very much like my cock, then."

She chuckles, and then the chuckle turns into a moan as I work the carving inside her. "Oh, fuck. Salukh . . ."

"I am here. I have you." I slowly drag the carving out of her pretty cunt, almost to the head of it, and then feed it back into her, just as slow. As I do, I stroke my cock with my other hand, unable to help myself.

My mate sinks down to her knees, moaning. Her backside remains in the air and she clenches around the carving again. I am fascinated at the sight, and when she sits up, she gives a little shiver and then turns to me, a wild look on her face. She prowls toward me on hands and knees, and I stare as she places her hands on my thighs and then lovingly rubs my cock against her cheek. "Oh, Salukh," she breathes. "This is . . ." She rocks her hips, then takes my cock in her hand and moans, rubbing her face against my shaft. "This is a really good gift."

"You like it? It feels good?"

She moans again, and this time she hungrily feeds my length into her mouth, desperate for me. The breath escapes my lungs, and I put my hand in her thick mane, guiding her head as she takes me in and sucks hard, as if she wants to drain me right now.

"Tee-fah-nee," I growl, breath hitching as she continues to work me with her mouth, frantic and eager. "I need you to come first, my mate. I want to see your pleasure."

My mate makes a whimpering sound in her throat and moves one hand from my cock and slides it between her legs. She teases her clit with quick movements, working it faster and faster as I hold her in place, pumping into her mouth. It occurs to me that we are in the midst of the South Cave, and that anyone in the area could walk in and see my mate with my cock in her hungry mouth, her cunt stuffed with a carving of my cock.

The thought is so exciting that my sac tightens, and I know I am on the edge. "Wait—"

But then my mate whimpers again, and her eyes flutter. I can feel her body tremble, and as she shudders, I realize she is coming, her mouth stuttering around my cock.

It is enough. I pull free from the sucking, perfect heat of her mouth and take myself in hand. With three quick strokes, I come, spurting my seed all over her pretty teats and her chin, painting my release on her skin.

If this is what a moon quest is about, I am all for it. No wonder humans are so excited to have such a trip.

She collapses in front of me with a sigh, going to her back. Her fingers trace patterns into the seed I have left on her skin, and she looks up at me with a satisfied smile, as if very pleased with herself.

The sight of her is so enticing that I growl and fall over her, kissing her soft mouth, not caring that my seed is getting on my skin as well. I reach for the carving still deep between her thighs, and work it in her wet cunt until she is clinging to me and crying out with her second release.

"No more," she pants after that, exhausted. "No more for now." Her fingers skim over my face, swiping away wetness as she gazes up at me.

"We will do that again while we are here," I tell her. "Perhaps every night we are here. It will be our moon quest tradition."

The moan Tee-fah-nee lets out ends with laughter. "You're gonna exhaust me so much that I'm going to forget all about my plants."

"Is that so?" I tease back, skimming my fingers over one of her perfect teats. I cannot help but touch her constantly. "You are the one who continues to distract me from my focus."

"Focus on what?" She tilts her head, gazing up at me.

Do I tell her now? Or do I continue to watch her closely in order to figure it out on my own? I consider this for a moment, but in the end, I decide to share with my mate. "I know something with my family troubles you. That you have been hiding some unhappiness lately. I was hoping we could discuss such a thing while we are gone. I wish to understand."

She sits up and then gets to her feet. Moving to one of the baskets, she finds a rag of flawed leather and moves back to me. She wipes my seed off my skin, and then her own, and as she does, she is quiet. She says nothing for long moments, but I can tell she is contemplating her thoughts, and so I do not interrupt. If she is not yet ready to share with me, I will not push her.

My mate thinks for a moment, and then tosses the dirty rag aside. "I don't know if it helps, but it's not you; it's me."

It is a strange thing to say. "Of course it is you, my mate. I have no concerns over my family." I pause, confused. "Did I misspeak? Was I unclear in my words—"

Tee-fah-nee chuckles and presses her fingertips to my lips. "Just shush and let me speak."

I take her into my arms, hugging her to my chest and stroking her back as she props up on one elbow in the furs and thinks through her words. "Family is tricky for me," she finally says. "You remember what I told you about mine?"

I do. "You lost your parents in accidents when they were soldiers."

She nods. "Both around the same time. One day they were just . . . gone. I went to live with my aunt in Oklahoma because she was the next of kin, but it's not the same as the cave here. There weren't a million helping hands ready to assist. There was just my aunt, and she'd never had kids of her own, so she wasn't the most nurturing. I think she cared for me in her way, but she also expected me to do my share on the farm. She wasn't much of a hugger, either. It was like going from day to night. I went from being spoiled and adored to just . . . alone. And it was really, really hard. So hard that sometimes just the thought of that empty hollowness scares me."

I rub her back, not interrupting.

"So I always worked hard. I wanted to make sure my aunt knew I was grateful to be with her, but work was also a distraction for grieving. I worked, and I tried to be the very best at things so no one could find fault with me. I never gave my aunt room to complain." She manages a tremulous smile and brushes her fingers down my chest. "And I managed, you know? I never thought of myself as unhappy, but seeing you here with your family and how close you are, it makes me realize everything I missed out on. More than that, it terrifies me for the future."

"In what way?"

She is quiet for a long moment. "What if I fall in love with them the way I fell in love with you?" Tee-fah-nee chuckles. "Well, not exactly the way I fell in love with you. But you know what I mean. What if I grow to love your family and depend on them, and then I lose them, too?"

"That is always a risk, my mate. When you give your heart to another's hands, you are risking that it will be dropped."

She takes my hands in hers, laces her fingers with mine. "It's strange, because I'm not scared of losing you. Not in the same way. I've never really been in love before, so this is new to me. And I can't bear the thought of ever losing you, so it's like my brain can't wrap around it." Her fingers tighten around mine. "But I've lost a family before."

"I understand your fears," I tell her softly, studying her lovely face. "Tell me what you feel the answer should be. Will you close off your heart to everyone but me to protect yourself? I fear that will make you just as sad."

Her head hangs. "I know. I just . . . I guess seeing your family and how close you are reminds me of how it felt to lose mine. I worry about going back to that dark place. I felt so alone. So unnecessary. Like I was a burden to the world. And with that on top of grieving my family . . . it was bad."

"That was a long time ago and you were very young," I reassure her. "You are stronger now. You have survived the loss of everything you know—"

"Twice now," she adds wryly.

I chuckle, because it is true. Once when she lost her family, and again when she came to this world. "They are terrible things, these losses, but they make you stronger. If you have a fine piece of leather that wears through with a tiny hole, do you discard the whole thing? Or do you stitch it and repair the hole, and make it stronger with the changes?"

"Depends on how beat up the leather is," she replies, her words tart. "Even well-mended leather breaks down."

"After a good, long life, yes." I lift our joined hands to my mouth and kiss her knuckles. "But I can tell you are not comforted. You would rather live in fear?"

"No, of course not."

"Good, because you are the bravest female I know."

That makes her smile. "You don't know that many females."

"I know all of them on this planet."

That makes her laugh. She shakes her head, but her eyes are lit up with amusement. "Very funny. Excellent point, but very funny."

"I am a very wise male," I agree, and give our joined hands a little shake. "So heed the words of your wise male. It is understandable to be afraid. But like the other fears you have seen in your time, you will conquer it. You will not let it rule you. We will walk past these fears together. We will replant your plants at the new cave and watch them thrive, just as you will thrive."

"Oooh, good way to bring it full circle," Tee-fah-nee teases me, a smile on her face. "Bringing in the plants. Me as the plants is a good parallel."

"I know you well," I say. "It is my duty as your mate." I squeeze her fingers. "And it is my *pleasure*."

She nods, her full mouth curving into a tiny smile as she gazes down at our joined hands. "I also worry they'll be disappointed in me."

"Now I know this is fear speaking," I tell her boldly. "No one could ever be disappointed in you. Look at my sister. Farli adores you."

"For no reason," she emphasizes, widening her eyes. "What, because of Chompy? That was you more than me."

I shake my head. "There is plenty of reason for Farli to love you, and you are choosing not to see it. Think about it. Stay-see is close to my mother. Mar-lenn has her friend Air-ee-yon-uh and they are very close. But you do things with Farli. You invite her to go gathering with you. You sit and talk with her at feasts. You pay attention to her. You are a true sister to her and she has always wanted one."

"And what if I let her down?"

I snort. "The only way you can let Farli down is to push her away."

Tee-fah-nee sighs, her head bowed. "You mean like I have been doing. Man, change is hard."

"It is hard on your plants, too, but you are determined to move them."

She pulls her hands from mine and wags a finger at me. "Again with the plants."

I grin. "As I said, I know you well. I know what will make you pay attention."

Her smile curves to match mine, growing broader. She thinks for a moment, and then settles in, leaning against me once more. "If we're going with the plants analogy, they're going to be shocked when we uproot them and move them, but I'll have to baby them and make sure they get extra attention for a while so they come through without too much damage. I guess I can do the same thing with your family—give them a little extra attention to make up for the fact that I've been pulling away. Maybe by the time we're all comfortable and settled—setting out new roots, in plant-speak—it won't feel so terrifying."

"I think that is an excellent idea."

She considers for a moment longer, and then her face brightens. "You know, your mother was going to make me, Stacy, and Marlene and Farli matching tunics. Maybe I should make a special pair just for me and Farli. Make her feel special."

"I know she would love that."

"And maybe a matching collar for Chompy." Her eyes are full of excitement, and the hesitation is gone. "I have tons of root dye now, after all."

There is nothing my mate loves more than a challenging project. "And you have quills you could dye for decoration." I wrap a finger in one of her thick curls. "Just no loincloths."

She chuckles. "Does that mean you don't want me to make you anything?"

"The only thing I want from you is your smile," I tell her. And when she smiles even more broadly, I add, "And perhaps for you to use the carving again."

Tee-fah-nee gives a wicked laugh. She leans in toward me, brushing her lips over mine. "Well, we *do* have the entire week alone together . . ."

And what a glorious week it shall be.

AUTHOR'S NOTE

Hello there!

I'm so happy to see Tiffany and Salukh's story in a Berkley special edition! This edition is one I particularly wanted to see in print, because it would mean I got to write a honeymoon story for the two of them. I think Berkley has done an amazing job with the packaging, and I couldn't be more thrilled that we continue to get lovely special edition after special edition. Thank you to everyone on the Berkley team for continuing to impress me.

In a sense, it's funny. When I first anticipated the series, I thought there was no way it'd be popular enough for me to write Tiffany's story. I thought maybe I'd get to do the first three books and then move on to something else. Turns out, not so much! Likewise, I thought perhaps we'd do special editions for the first three books and then I'd have to say goodbye. So seeing Tiffany on the cover has me totally stoked.

I'm writing this in September of 2022, which means there have been seven years of Ice Planet Barbarians stories. That is absolutely wild to me. I'm actually gearing up to write a new spin-off, and as long as people want barbarians, I'll keep writing them!

In every author's note, I talk about the inspiration for the characters, why I picked the story I did, and motivations for the characters. For me, this was absolutely Tiffany's story from top to bottom. She was the one who needed to grow and change, and for that to happen, she had to have security and safety, and that's why Salukh is the same character throughout the whole story (other than him getting to fulfill his dream of having a mate). Her growth didn't work for me if he was busy changing, too. He needed to be steadfast and patient the entire time because it was what she required to flourish.

Tiffany's story introduces a slightly darker element into the story line—one of past trauma and rape at the hands of the alien kidnappers. I'd discussed it in prior books but hadn't really had a main character deal with it. Once I knew the series would continue, I decided to explore this particular aspect and how it affected the women.

In a way, Tiffany and Josie (the heroine of the next book in the series) are two sides of the same coin. Both Tiffany and Josie went through the same sort of situation on the ship—they were raped by the aliens. How they process it is unique to each character. Josie prefers to focus on the future and avoids thinking of the past. Tiffany, however, handles her trauma differently. She can't move past it because she can't let go of the terrible things that have happened to her. We all process our response to events in different ways, and that's one thing I like showcasing in this series—all of the women are survivors but approach everything in a completely unique fashion. I guess I like to present to the world that there's no one way to be a victim, just like there's no one way to recover. Everyone has their own path to wellness and happiness.

I loved writing the competition and displaying some of the different aspects of the heroes and the lengths they'd go to in order to get a prized mate. Someday, poor Vaza, your ship will come in.

Thank you so much, as always, for continuing to read and love these books.

RUBY

THE PEOPLE OF
BARBARIAN'S PRIZE

The Main Cave

THE CHIEF AND HIS FAMILY

VEKTAL (Vehk-tall)—Chief of the sa-khui tribe. Son of Hektar, the prior chief, who died of khui-sickness. He is a dedicated hunter and leader, and carries a sword and a bola for weapons. He is the one who finds Georgie, and resonance between them is so strong that he resonates prior to her receiving her khui.

GEORGIE—Unofficial leader of the human women. Originally from Orlando, Florida, she has long golden-brown curls and a determined attitude.

TALIE—Their infant daughter.

FAMILIES

RAAHOSH (Rah-hosh)—A quiet but surly hunter. One of his horns is broken off and his face scarred. Older son of Vaashan and Daya (both deceased). Vektal's close friend. Impatient and rash, he steals Liz the moment she receives her khui. They resonate, and he is exiled for stealing her. Brother to Rukh.

LIZ—A loudmouth huntress from Oklahoma who loves Star Wars and giving her opinion. Raahosh kidnaps her the moment she receives her lifesaving khui. She was a champion archer as a teenager. Resonates to Raahosh and voluntarily chooses exile with him.

RAASHEL—Their infant daughter.

HARLOW—One of the women kept in the stasis tubes. She has red hair and freckles, and is mechanically minded and excellent at problem-solving. Stolen by Rukh when she resonated to him. Now mother to their child, Rukhar.

RUKH—The long-lost son of Vaashan and Daya; brother to Raahosh. His full name is Maarukh. He grew up alone and wild, convinced by his father that the tribe was full of "bad ones," and has recently been brought back by Harlow.

RUKHAR—Their infant son.

ARIANA—One of the women kept in the stasis tubes. Hails from New Jersey and was an anthropology student. She tended to cry a lot when first rescued. Has a delicate frame and dark brown hair. Resonates to Zolaya. Still cries a lot.

ZOLAYA (Zoh-lay-uh)—A skilled hunter. Steady and patient, he resonates to Ariana and seems to be the only one not bothered by her weepiness.

MARLENE (Mar-lenn)—One of the women kept in the stasis tubes. French speaking. Quiet and confident, and exudes sexuality. Resonates to Zennek.

ZENNEK (Zehn-eck)—A quiet and shy hunter. Brother to Pashov, Salukh, and Farli. He is the son of Borran and Kemli. Resonates to Marlene.

ZALENE—Their infant daughter.

NORA—One of the women kept in the stasis tubes. A nurturing sort who was rather angry she was dumped on an ice planet. Quickly resonates to Dagesh. No longer quite so angry.

DAGESH (Dah-zzhesh; the *g* sound is swallowed)—A calm, hardworking, and responsible hunter. Resonates to Nora.

STACY—One of the women kept in the stasis tubes. She was weepy when she first awakened. Loves to cook and worked in a bakery prior to abduction. Resonates to Pashov and seems quite happy.

PASHOV (Pah-showv)—The son of Kemli and Borran; brother to Farli, Salukh, and Zennek. A hunter described as "quiet." Resonates to Stacy.

PACY—Their infant son.

MAYLAK (May-lack)—One of the few female sa-khui. She is the tribe healer and Vektal's former pleasure mate. She resonated to Kashrem, ending her relationship with Vektal. Sister to Bek.

KASHREM (Cash-rehm)—A gentle tribal tanner. Mated to Maylak.

ESHA (Esh-uh)—Their young female kit.

SEVVAH (Sev-uh)—A tribe elder and one of the few sa-khui females. She is mother to Aehako, Rokan, and Sessah, and acts like a mom to the others in the cave. Her entire family was spared when khui-sickness hit fifteen years ago.

OSHEN (Aw-shen)—A tribe elder and Sevvah's mate. Brewer.

SESSAH (Ses-uh)—Their youngest child, a juvenile male.

MEGAN—Megan was early in a pregnancy when she was captured, but the aliens terminated it. She tends toward a sunny disposition when not abducted by aliens. Resonates to Cashol. Pregnant.

CASHOL (Cash-awl)—A distractible and slightly goofy-natured hunter. Cousin to Vektal. Resonates to Megan.

CLAIRE—A quiet, slender woman who arrived on the planet with a blonde pixie cut and now has shoulder-length brown hair. She had a failed pleasure-mating with Bek and resonated to Ereven. Her story is told in the novella "Ice Planet Holiday."

EREVEN (Air-uh-ven)—A quiet, easygoing hunter who won Claire over with his understanding, protective nature. Resonated to Claire.

THE UNMATED HUNTERS

ROKAN (Row-can)—The son of Sevvah and Oshen; brother to Aehako and young Sessah. A hunter known for his strange predictions that come true all too often.

WARREK (War-eck)—The son of Elder Eklan. He is a very quiet and mild hunter, with long, sleek black hair. Warrek teaches the young kits how to hunt.

ELDERS

ELDER EKLAN—A calm, kind elder. Father to Warrek, he also helped raise Harrec.

THE SOUTH CAVE

FAMILIES

AEHAKO (Eye-ha-koh)—A laughing, flirty hunter. The son of Sevvah and Oshen; brother to Rokan and young Sessah. He seems to be in a permanent good mood. Close friends with Haeden. Resonated to Kira and is acting leader of the South Cave.

KIRA—The first of the human women to be kidnapped, Kira had a large metallic translator attached to her ear by the aliens. She is quiet and serious, with somber eyes. Her translator has been removed, and she recently gave birth to Kae.

KAE (rhymes with "fly")—Their infant daughter.

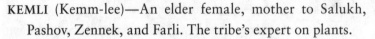

KEMLI (Kemm-lee)—An elder female, mother to Salukh, Pashov, Zennek, and Farli. The tribe's expert on plants.

BORRAN (Bore-awn)—Kemli's much younger mate and an elder.

FARLI (Far-lee)—A preteen female sa-khui. Her brothers are Salukh, Pashov, and Zennek. New pet parent to the dvisti colt Chompy.

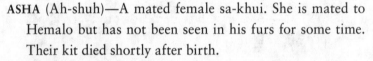

ASHA (Ah-shuh)—A mated female sa-khui. She is mated to Hemalo but has not been seen in his furs for some time. Their kit died shortly after birth.

HEMALO (Hee-mah-lo)—A tanner and a quiet sort. He is mated (unhappily) to Asha.

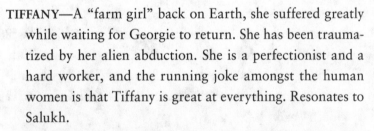

TIFFANY—A "farm girl" back on Earth, she suffered greatly while waiting for Georgie to return. She has been traumatized by her alien abduction. She is a perfectionist and a hard worker, and the running joke amongst the human women is that Tiffany is great at everything. Resonates to Salukh.

SALUKH (Sah-luke)—The brawny son of Kemli and Borran; brother to Farli, Pashov, and Zennek. Strong and intense. Very patient and helps Tiffany work through her trauma.

THE UNMATED HUMAN FEMALES

JOSIE—One of the original kidnapped women, she broke her leg in the ship crash. Short and adorable, Josie is an excessive talker, a gossip, and a bit of a dreamer. Likes to sing.

THE UNMATED HUNTERS

BEK (Behk)—A hunter generally thought of as short-tempered and unpleasant. Brother to Maylak.

HAEDEN (Hi-den)—A grim and unsmiling hunter with "dead" eyes, Haeden formerly resonated but his female died of khui-sickness before they could mate. His current khui is new. He is very private.

HARREC (Hair-ek)—A hunter who has no family and finds his place in the tribe by constantly joking and teasing. A bit accident-prone.

HASSEN (Hass-en)—A passionate and brave hunter, Hassen is impulsive and tends to act before he thinks.

TAUSHEN (Tow—rhymes with "cow"—shen)—A teenage hunter, newly into adulthood. Eager to prove himself.

ELDERS

ELDER DRAYAN—A smiling elder who uses a cane to help him walk.

ELDER DRENOL—A grumpy, antisocial elder.

ELDER VADREN (Vaw-dren)—An elder.

ELDER VAZA (Vaw-zhuh)—A lonely widower and hunter. He tries to be as helpful as possible. He is very interested in the new females.

The Dead

DOMINIQUE—A redheaded human female. Her mind was broken when she was abused by the aliens on the ship. When she arrived on Not-Hoth, she ran out into the snow and deliberately froze.

KRISSY—A human female, dead in the crash.

PEG—A human female, dead in the crash.

ABOUT THE AUTHOR

RUBY DIXON is an author of all things science fiction romance. She is a Sagittarius and a Reylo shipper, and loves farming sims (but not actual housework). She lives in the South with her husband and a couple of geriatric cats, and can't think of anything else to put in her biography. Truly, she is boring.

CONNECT ONLINE

RubyDixon.com
 RubyDixonBooks
 Author.Ruby.Dixon